UNFORTUNATE SON

BIKER

7

MIKE BARON

WOLFPACK
PUBLISHING
— EST 2013 —

WOLFPACK
PUBLISHING
— EST 2013 —

Published in the United States by Wolfpack Publishing, Las Vegas

Wolfpack Publishing
6032 Wheat Penny Avenue
Las Vegas, NV 89122

wolfpackpublishing.com

Paperback ISBN 978-1-64119-986-5
eBook ISBN 978-1-64119-985-8

UNFORTUNATE SON

CHAPTER
1

SURPRISE!

Josh looked at his father Duane, sitting on his sofa with Josh's dog Fig in his lap. The same Duane who'd abandoned Josh at a truck stop when Josh was fifteen, from whom he had not heard in two decades.

"What you doing here, Duane?"

Duane looked up with a con man's grin, deep parenthesis framing his mouth, several day's stubble clinging to his chin, lank gray hair unkempt. "Is that any way to greet your own father?"

Duane eased Fig off his lap, stood, and walked to Josh with his arms open. "C'mere, boy. How the hell you doin'?"

Josh endured the awkward embrace until Duane stepped back. Duane smelled of graphite, body odor, cigarettes. He'd found an old ashtray in the kitchen, set it on the coffee table in the living room and smoked several butts. He wore dirty blue jeans and a Dolphin's Tee with the sleeves cut off to show his ropy, muscular, tatted arms.

"What are you doing here, Duane?"

Duane went into the kitchen, Fig at his heels, opened the refrigerator, took out two cans of Capital Lager and tossed one to Josh, who caught it one-handed.

"Been hearin' a lot about you. I'm proud of you, boy. Proud the way you turned out. You're a man now. Solvin' crimes, killin' bad guys."

"You had nothing to do with it. You're as sentimental as a catfish. What do you want?"

Duane popped the can and guzzled, his Adam's apple bobbing up and down. "Why would you think that? Maybe I just wanted to see how you're doin'."

Josh snapped his fingers. Fig trotted over and sat next to him, looking up. "Because you're a con man. You haven't worked a real job in your life. The whole time I was with you, all you did was scam people. The old dropped wallet trick. Shoplifting. All those women you took advantage of."

Duane looked pained. "Maybe I've changed, you ever think of that? You changed. You were a rake hell. They called you Chainsaw because of that one thing, and now you're a born-again Christian, ain't that right? You're on a mission from God."

"What do you want, Duane?"

Duane flopped onto the sofa and put his feet on the coffee table. "I just want to stay here for a few days. I love your dog. I won't be any trouble."

"How'd you get in?"

"Climbed the fence and used the doggy door."

The anxiety Josh had experienced when he saw the Camaro in his front yard blossomed into a full-bore suck hole in the middle of his chest, summoning unwanted childhood memories. Walking in on Duane fucking some girl. Watching Duane dip into her purse while she slept. Fleeing in the middle of the night because Duane had committed some felony. The road rage. Duane waving his gun and trying to run another car off the road.

One night in November he did run another car off the road. It was a station wagon full of kids who'd dared to pass while flipping them the bird. Duane floored his 350 cubic inch Camaro and gave chase. The car's body was shot anyway. He couldn't afford a shiny new car, or even a shiny car, but he always found a way to get that Camaro with the big engine. Josh remembered the car was pale yellow with rust spots, the hood was brown, and the driver's door was primer gray.

"YO MOTHERFUCKER!" Duane bellowed into the wind, which whipped his words away. Those kids couldn't hear shit, the way they were blasting Beastie Boys. They never saw Duane coming. He cut the lights, zoomed up on their left, slammed the wheel to the right and stuck with it, big, fifteen-inch wheels and tires, ramming the wagon into the ditch where it rolled over once before coming to a stop.

Josh watched the whole thing through his window, mouth open, hanging on to the grip with both hands. Heart in mouth. What the fuck. He was ten years old.

"That'll teach 'em," Duane said, heading on down the highway.

They crashed in seedy apartments, trailers and tract houses with Duane's friends, all the same creepy crowd, grifters, drifters, penny ante thieves, prostitutes, drug dealers, too smart to work. Everyone had an angle and a rap. Everyone had a way to beat the system. Most had food stamps and disability. Some had pit bulls. Josh always wondered, why the pit bulls?

Josh slept on a lumpy sofa in the living room, or in a closet if Duane and his buddies got too loud snorting coke and drinking Fleischmann's vodka. They'd toss back valium to ease the descent.

Josh remembered waiting in a '69 Camaro with the engine running while Duane ran into a pharmacy "to get some cold medicine". Minutes later, Duane erupted from the front door clutching a paper bag, slid behind the wheel and floored it. They fishtailed out of town. Josh saw the butt of a pistol protruding from Duane's pants.

Josh popped his beer and sat in a chair facing Duane. "Who's after you?"

Duane drained his can and belched, putting his whole torso into it. Duane was proud of his belch. "What makes you say that?"

"'Cuz I know you, Duane. You're only in it for number one. You never cared about anything in your life except getting yourself over. I still don't know who my mother is."

"I think her name was Karen Pratt. Haven't seen her

since she dumped your little bundle of joy on my doorstep."

"I'm surprised you didn't put me up for adoption. Or dump me in the woods like you did that dog. Remember McKeesport? I wanted to go to school but you couldn't get your shit together? So I went down and registered myself and they asked me for my birthday. I didn't know what my birthday was. It was April first, so that's my birthday now."

Again, that pained look. "Son, you gotta give me a chance. I'm not the same person I was."

Josh stared. Duane looked away. He leaned forward to scratch Fig's ears. "Your dog likes me. They say dogs are excellent judges of character."

"Not that dog."

"Hey, I could eat a baby's butt through a park bench. Whatcha got to eat around here?"

Josh seethed. He didn't want this. He'd trained himself not to think about his father.

"Come on. We'll go get a burger."

Duane clapped. "Now you're talkin'."

Outside, Josh eyed the '97 Camaro. It was faded dark blue with rust spots and twin tailpipes.

"That there's an SS with the 330 HP LT4 small block engine from the Corvette. That there's special."

"Anyone lookin' for you?"

"Well let's get some grub and I'll tell you about that."

"Do me a favor. Lose the pistol."

Duane drew the pistol, looked at it, leaned into the Camaro and stuck it deep in the seat cushions.

They got in Josh's 300 and headed east toward Madison. Duane pulled a pack of Marlboros from his pants. "Mind if I smoke?"

Josh lowered all the windows. What was the point? Duane was going to do what Duane was going to do. He'd always been that way. They drove to the Laurel Tavern on Monroe Street, a family-friendly pub that had been there for forty years. The interior was dark and boisterous with families catching an early dinner before heading home to Netflix and video games, or couples just starting the night. They took a booth. The twenty-something waitress had long purple hair on one side of her skull, nothing on the other, and a unicorn tat on her arm. Duane stared like a hungry dog. They ordered burgers. Josh got a beer; Duane went for two shots of Canadian Club and a Miller chaser.

"You should try some of the local brews," Josh said looking around. "You don't have to drink Miller."

"By the time I get to that beer, I won't give a shit. Ja see that cooze? You got a girlfriend?"

"Had one, but she died."

"No shit. That happened to me. A couple times." He pulled out a cig and lit it one-handed with a kitchen match. A stout man with wife and two kids at an adjacent table looked over.

"No smoking in here."

Duane did a double take, stabbed the cig out on the bottom of his shoe and dropped the butt.

"Who's after you, Duane?"

Duane looked around. Con-wise, just like his son. Josh, a licensed private investigator, had never looked at Duane's record. He didn't want to know.

"Y'know who Ryan Gehrke is?"

"Sure. The Miami wide receiver who took a knee."

Duane stabbed a nicotine-stained finger at Josh. "You know why he took a knee?"

"Racism or some shit."

Duane showed yellow teeth. "He was protesting systemic racism in the justice, and in the cops. I gotta tell ya, I think he's right on the money with the cops. They're all rotten. Some of 'em are killers. That cop in Cinci. They were in a Wal-Mart when that seventeen-year-old kid picked up an air rifle in the gun department. Two cops run in screaming and shot 'em. They didn't tell him to drop the gun or put up his hands. None of that shit. Bang bang. Very sorry. They both walked. Pigs said they had reasonable concern for their safety."

"Did Ryan shoot them?"

Duane shook his head like he was talking to a dummy. "Noooo, it's just one of the issues we discussed."

"You and Ryan?"

The waitress came, plopping down drinks and burgers. Josh put ketchup on his burger. Duane tossed down the shot. He tossed down the next shot and looked around for the waitress.

Josh gripped his burger. "Whoa there, pardner. You don't want to go blotto just yet."

Duane finished his burger in six bites. He had coyote jaws. He chugged the Miller. He belched long and loud, causing heads to turn. Distaste. Disgust. Duane.

"So where were you talking to Ryan?" Josh said.

Duane pushed the dishes aside and leaned on his elbows. "At his crib in Miami. Man, you should see it. He's got this fuckin' estate in the same neighborhood as Desmond Pow, right on the beach. Pool, cabana, hot and cold running babes, the best champagne, all the cocaine you can snort, celebrities, you know who I saw?"

"What the fuck were you doing there?"

Duane spread his hands, nonplussed. "Where do you think he got his cocaine?"

CHAPTER 2

THE KINGSMAN

"Can we just cut to the chase? Why's he after you?"

Duane looked around for the waitress, caught her eye.

"Hey there, beautiful. Can I get another shot?"

"You sure can."

"And write your telephone number on the napkin."

The waitress laughed and walked away. Josh tapped Duane on the wrist.

"Focus. Why's Ryan after you?"

"He owed me six grand for the blow. Every time I brought it up, he laughed at me."

"So what were you doing at his party?"

Duane opened his mouth and stared. "I brought the blow! Dude calls me up, tells me he's throwin' a party and there will be plenty of cooze, so of course I show. Then he stiffs me."

"And?"

"So I took this painting. Dumb coon thinks I'm one of his butt boys."

"What painting?"

"Painting he had on a wall in his den. Some Mayan goddess or some shit. I could tell it was valuable because it had a gilt frame and a certificate of authenticity on the back from some big auction house."

Josh rubbed his temples. Like all good liars, Duane mixed in a little bit of truth.

"Where's the painting now?"

"I pawned it. Got six hundred bucks, which is gone. Can I hit you up for a loan?"

A marble of pain appeared behind Josh's right eye. "How do you know he's after you?"

Duane looked around, leaned forward, spoke softly, gutturally. "I got friends. You know about the Aces of Spade?"

Josh blinked.

"They're a black nationalist motorcycle gang outta Miami. Ryan's a member. I hear he's sicced 'em on me. They might be comin' here."

Josh stared until Duane looked away. The waitress set his drink down. "Anything else, boys?"

Josh held up a finger. "Just the check please."

Duane tossed it back. His face reflected years of bad living. Lines, cracks, fissures, rosacea. Stubble.

"Why the fuck would they come here?"

"You know how proud I am of you, son? I saved every article. I read about you online. A dad's gotta boast a little."

"So they might be coming here."

"Ahuh."

The waitress brought the check. Josh laid money on the table and stood, not waiting for Duane. At eight p.m. it was still light out and the swells of Madison cruised by in their Priuses, Leafs, Volts, Volvos, bicycles and boards. A BMW 740 blasted Eminem.

Duane caught up with him. "Hey, wait for your old man."

They got in the car. Josh turned on WORT. Erroll Garner swung from eight speakers.

"So, I was thinkin' I'd hang out for a day and then maybe you could spot your old man some seed money, and I'll go to Vegas to see my baby."

"Bank's open at nine. I'll give you five thou and you take off."

Duane lowered his window and leered at a coed on a bicycle. She grimaced as he sang, "Hi, sweetie!"

"I said I'll give you five gees and then you're outta here. Do you understand me?"

Duane pulled out a Marlboro, lit it, inhaled deeply.

"Mind if I smoke?" Butter wouldn't melt in his mouth.

"I said you're outta here. I don't want to know you, I don't want to see you, I don't want to hear from you. Understand?"

"Oh, come on, son. Don't be that way."

Josh stopped at a red light. "Don't call me son."

"I'm your fuckin' father! I'll call you whatever I damn

well please!"

Josh turned dead eyes on him. Duane looked away. The light changed. Garner gave way to Phineas Newborn Jr. Duane didn't talk until they crossed under the Beltline.

"I heard you found Christ in prison."

Josh kept his eyes on the road.

"Is it too much to ask if you're a Christian or not?"

"So I'm a fuckin' Christian. So what?"

"Well it ain't Christian for a man to just kick out his own father!"

Josh barked mirthlessly.

"You know what? I don't even want you in the house tonight. Christ knows what you'll take from me. We'll go back to the house, get your shit together, and you can go to a motel. I got two Cs for you and tomorrow I'll get you the rest."

"You don't want me in the house?"

"That's right."

"Shit! What kind of son are you?" Duane puffed furiously.

"Don't call me son."

"Well I can't drive the Camaro. They're looking for that."

They drove the rest of the way in silence, pulling into Josh's driveway and his modest ranch-style house. The house dated from 1959. In the nineties the neighborhood had exploded, woods giving way to ¾ acre parcels, five thousand square foot houses, three car garages. Josh, who'd lived there long before gentrification, was now an eyesore dragging down property values. A neighborhood consortium repeatedly tried to buy him out. The latest offer was seven-fifty. He told them he'd think it over when in fact he had no intention of moving. He didn't need the money. *His* property taxes were low.

Josh liked the neighborhood, the abundance of trees. Without trees, you had no neighborhood.

They went in the house. Fig effusively greeted Josh, then Duane, while Duane sullenly gathered a suitcase of clothes.

"When can I pick up my car?"

"When Ryan stops looking."

Duane opened the refrigerator and took out a canned IPA, popped it, guzzled. "Yeah. Right," he muttered.

"You ready?"

Duane looked at him with sad eyes. "You got any reefer or 'ludes? Anything to take the edge off?"

"You're fuckin' drunk. You don't need any 'ludes. I got a little reefer. Don't fuckin' get caught. Smoke it outside. I know the cops around here, Duane. If you get busted, it won't do you any good to rat me out."

"I would never do that."

Josh went into his bedroom, found a slim packet of reefer and a pack of Zig-Zags in his side table, handed them to Duane. He pulled out his wallet and peeled off two Franklins.

"Thankee, bro." Duane looked at the Zig-Zags. "Did you know Jesus was a head?"

Josh picked up Duane's suitcase and went out the front

door. "Let's go."

They got in the car and headed back toward the Beltline. Duane held up the Zig-Zags and turned on the overhead light. "See! Proof that Jesus smoked dope."

Josh glanced at the tiny logo showing a bearded man with a doobie, switched off the light and turned on the radio, punching the search button until he came across some bluesy rock.

"Hold it right there, hoss!" Duane said. "That's my jam."

Josh looked at the screen. The Doughboys, "Second Street". They sounded like the Rolling Stones. Josh drove counter-clockwise on the Beltline, took the Whitney Way exit and pulled around to the front of the Kingsman Motel. A half dozen cars parked in front of the one-story building included a pick-up truck, an old Honda wagon jammed with personal effects, and two semis at the far end. Across the street, accessible by a pedestrian overpass, was a small strip mall containing a hardware store, a veterinary and Le Tigre Lounge.

Josh went inside. Duane registered as Roger Palmer, flashing a fake ID.

"I don't want no parties next door, if you can work it. I need my beauty sleep."

The rotund middle-aged Hispanic woman barely glanced at it as Josh paid cash. Forty-nine dollars for the night.

Josh walked Duane to his room.

"These fuckin' hillbillies with their screamin' brats. I hate that shit."

"Just stay put, huh? You're drunk as a skunk. You're in no condition to do anything. Just lie down and sleep it off."

Duane pointed a finger and winked. "Sure thing, hoss. What time tomorrow?"

"I'll come by around nine."

"You that eager to get rid of me?"

"Nice knowin' you, Duane."

CHAPTER 3

LE TIGRE

Duane sat on the squeaky bed in his shabby motel room and rolled a joint. There were cigarette burns on the carpet and a NO SMOKING sign on the inside of the door. The room smelled of dust and cigarette smoke. A sign in the bathroom said:

Due to the popularity of our guest room amenities, our Housekeeping Department now offers these items for sale: Alarm Clocks, twenty-five dollars. Coffee Maker, fifty dollars. Hairdryer, forty-five dollars. Iron/board, thirty dollars. Pillows, twenty-five dollars. Bath towels, twenty dollars. Hand towels, fifteen dollars. Sheets/per set, sixty dollars. Blankets, fifty dollars. Comforter, eighty dollars.

Each guest room attendant is responsible for main-taining the guest room items. Should you decided to take

these articles from your room instead of obtaining them
from the Executive Housekeeper, we will assume you
approve a corresponding charge to your account.

Thank you.

Duane got on a chair, deactivated the hardware store smoke alarm, lit his doobie, and turned on the television. Some moron interviewing some starlet with a plunging neckline.

"I'd do 'er," Duane muttered, lighting up.

What happened to Leno? Even Letterman was preferable to this new class of low-rent morons. It was only ten o'clock and Duane wasn't sleepy, not even after three boiler makers. He went into the bathroom and pissed all over the seat.

"Gotta take a leak," he sang. "Do it mighty queek. Splatter on the floor, spray around some more..."

A pang of regret insinuated itself in his heart. He had to admit he had not been a good father. He'd failed to see that Josh was exceptional. Maybe he shouldn't have abandoned the boy at a Bosselman's Truck Stop, but Duane had been going through a rough patch and couldn't handle the responsibility. He could barely handle himself.

Still, Josh owed his life to Duane. You'd think he'd be more grateful.

Duane's phone, paid for with a stolen credit card, played "Viva Las Vegas."

It was Merle.

"Hey, baby," he growled.

"Ooh, I miss you so much, baby," Merle cooed in a voice

dripping with southern molasses. "When you gonna come back to me? I'm in Vegas, baby, staying at the El Troubador, out near the airport. You doin' okay?" Bay-ack.

"Well Ryan hasn't caught up with me, if that's what you mean. I'm visitin' my son right now. I should be down there in a day or two. I'll let you know. Can you meet me at the airport?"

"Of course, lover man. I'm wet just thinkin' about you. I'd like to suck your cock and stick my finger up your ass. Would you like that, baby?"

Li'l Duane came to attention. "Watch it, lover doll. You're gonna make me come."

"How about I talk you through it, big boy?"

"Yeah! Hang on. Just gonna get a towel."

Duane dropped his pants, laid back on the four oversized pillows, and listened to Merle guide him through the motions. He came shuddering, squeezing on his knob like the gearshift of a '65 GTO.

"Oh babeeee...that was so good."

"It's even better in person."

Duane wiped himself off and pulled up his pants. He went outside, sat on a weathered bench and smoked a cigarette looking across the Beltline at the gleaming lights of the Le Tigre. Well, all right. He wouldn't mind another drink. Maybe he could score a little blow. Splashing himself with Ax Body Spray, he put on a light jacket and set off down the glass-dusted parking lot, up the frontage road, to the pedestrian overpass. He opted for the bicycle ramp, longer than the stairs but easier on the back. When he got to the top, he saw three youths huddled in the center cupping glows in their hands.

Three no account niggers. Ryan himself referred to low-class blacks as niggers, although Duane had never used the word in his presence. Duane felt around in his pocket for the pistol. Fuck. It was in the trunk of the Camaro. He wasn't expecting trouble, but by god he was ready.

The three young men, wearing hoodies, tensed when they saw him and stood straight, backs to the rail. They cracked wise out of the sides of their mouths. Should they roll this dude or not? Maybe they were high on crack or PCP. Roll the ofay motherfucker and toss his body over the rail. Wouldn't that be a hoot? Run like hell. As Duane approached, they turned inward again and lit the crack pipe. Dude wasn't worth rolling.

Duane reached the group. "Evening, boys."

"Yo," one responded.

A hundred feet on, Duane paused to look at the rushing river of steel beneath his feet. Eight lanes wide open. In the distance, the capitol dome looked like a wedding cake in the floodlights. Gleaming red dots rose and descended from the county airport, across the lake. Duane went down the ramp, waited for a break in the traffic, and walked across Mid-vale. A car exiting the Beltline, unhappy with his progress, beeped at him.

Duane raised a finger. "FUCK YOU!"

The car drove on.

The parking lot was long on American iron, a couple pick-ups, and two choppers. Duane entered the lounge and felt instantly at home. The low lights, the smell of beer, cigarettes, and booze had a comforting familiarity. Tigers everywhere. Framed and ceramic tigers behind the bar, two life-sized fake tigers crouching, tiger-patterned benches in the booths. Tiger beer in the middle of a wide selection of bottles, a framed movie poster, *The Life of Pi*.

It took a minute for Duane's eyes to adjust. A half dozen people sat at the bar, two blue collar types playing pool in the rear, and three middle-aged women in a booth, laughing.

Duane sat at the end of the bar, one stool removed from a woman wearing a *faux* leopard fur, big blonde hair and mucho makeup. Duane guessed she was in her forties. She had a smoker's cough, maybe twenty pounds overweight. The waiter, a balding man with Basset eyes, came over.

"Canadian Club on the rocks and a Miller."

The man nodded and got the drinks. Duane caught the woman's eye in the mirror and smiled. She smiled back. Duane took a swig, walked to the digital jukebox, plugged in a buck. "Stray Cat Strut" filled the room. Duane sat down, caught the woman's eye again and winked. She slid over.

"I love the Stray Cats," she said in a whiskey-soaked contralto.

"Saw 'em once in Boston," Duane said. "They opened for Aerosmith."

"Two of my favorite bands. I'm Stella."

"Duane."

They shook hands. L'il Duane stood at attention. There was no need to go back to the motel alone. He was peripatetic and priapic. Stella loved the Rolling Stones and tacos. She worked as an accountant and had two cats.

"I'm dying for a smoke," she said.

"Me too."

They went out front and lit up.

"Fucking city outlawed smoking in bars. I mean what the fuck?" she groused, her mouth making an odd trapezoidal shape.

"Tell me about it. Like that every city I've been in."

"What do you do, Duane?"

"I'm a lifestyle coach, but right now I'm on vacation. I'm visiting my son. Perhaps you've heard of him, Josh Pratt."

Stella wrinkled her nose. "Why would I have heard of him?"

"Never mind. Anyhow, I'm passing through on my way to Vegas where I'm gonna play a little blackjack. And let me tell you, I know how to play blackjack."

"Why Vegas? You know we got blackjack around here. We got that Ho Chunk Casino off the Interstate on the east side."

"Gonna meet up with some old friends. I'm staying right across the highway there. I have a little reefer, if you're interested."

Stella ground her cigarette out with the instep of her mule. "Fuck yeah!"

Li'l Duane led the way.

CHAPTER 4

HOTCHKISS

Josh got up at seven, nuked a Jimmy Dean egg, cheese, and sausage biscuit, put on the coffee, put on his running clothes, decanted a can of Purina for Fig, ate the Jimmy Dean and went to the door.

"Fig let's go!"

Fig leaped at him barking, tail wagging.

Outside, he headed east up the side of the road toward Madison, jogging easy, warming up before he laid on the gas. Out here where the buses didn't run there were no sidewalks, but the generous bike lanes provided more than ample room. Sunlight slid in between the trees. You could tell a rich neighborhood by the trees.

Josh picked it up, Fig jogging at his side. A jogger on the opposite side of the street waved. Josh recognized Reg Norman, the developer behind White Oaks , as the neighborhood was now known. Josh had been jogging one day while Reg was washing his Ford GT, a rare automobile that drew Josh like a dog to carrion. It took only a few moments for Norman to realize who Josh was.

"You're the guy had the shoot-out in his front yard!"

"I apologize for that, Reg."

Norman laughed. "That was about the most excitement we've ever had around here! What was the name of that gang?"

"The Insane Assholes."

"That's right! The Insane Assholes! I've been thinking about getting a motorcycle. You and me should get together."

Josh gave him the thumb's up.

Passing Norman on the street reminded Josh of their meeting. Reg Norman wasn't a bad guy to know. Name and face frequently appearing in print and on media along with his stunning wife.

Josh ran three miles to his turn around point and went into high gear, Fig running with her tongue in the wind. They got home. Josh parked Duane's car in the garage and moved his Chrysler to the driveway. He slid into the Camaro on the passenger side and opened the glove compartment. Pack of Marlboros, matches, maps, sunglasses, a tire gauge, breath mints, Ibuprofen, Benadryl. He had to give Duane credit. Duane had always stressed the importance of keeping your tires properly inflated. He opened the center console and found a flashlight, some roaches, and a pack of condoms.

In Duane's trunk he found black gloves, latex gloves, a black leather sap, a couple of crow bars, a leather toiletry kit filled with toothbrushes, combs, condoms, keys, change, a baseball bat, a fifty-foot garden hose with duct tape wrapped around one end, duct tape, a blow up doll which Duane used to fool the High Output lanes in cities. Not a sex doll. A straight-looking vinyl guy in a brown plaid suit with orange hair. Maybe a fraternity brother. He also found a thirty-two caliber revolver inside an old shaving kit wrapped in a rag, with a box of shells. Josh left the pistol in its rag, stashed it, the thirty-eight and the shells in his gun safe, showered and checked his email. Steve Fleiss had left him a message. Josh delivered summons for Weiss.

He checked his email.

Hello Dear,

Thanks for your acceptance to listen to what I have to tell you about me. My family. As you know already, my name is Ms. Brigitte Joachim, My father is from ivory coast while my mother is from Russia, well I did not know my mother as my father told me that I lost my mother when I was only 3 year, I grew up with my father in capital city of my country which is Abidjan. I went to primary school in a private school call brighter future primary school in Abidjan, I passed and enter secondary school, Lycee Moderen de Marcory, Abidjan, I do not have brother or sister, I am the only child to my late mother, I have stepmother and sibless but they are treating me bad and it makes me leave my father's house and went to near city and rent an apartment which I am paying monthly. My father when he was alive won prize as best farmer in my country in the year 2013, my father exports cocoa/coffee to foreign countries and he has one of the biggest cocoa/coffee plantation in my country.

I am suffering here since death of my father because my stepmother and her children are very wicked and greedy as I told you earlier, they have mismanaged my father businesses and farms. They are not taken care of me here and I really want to leave here and come and join you over there in your country continue my education and live a better life. I speak English, French and my local language Baouké. I thank you so much for mail and please try all you can to help me because am suffering here due to my wicked stepmother, I am crying every day and night wondering why my father and mother have to died and leave me alone to be suffering in my stepmother and her children hands. I swear with all my life that you will not regret helping me. I will stop here so that you will not get tired reading my long mail. May God guide and protect you always. Before the death of my father, he confidently told me he has money he deposited in a foreign country and he gave me all the papers concerning the money because he know that after his death my stepmother will not look after me as she never like me and see me as a white child from a different country. I do *not know much about investment, I will depend on you concerning investing my inherited money £ 4.4 million pounds in good business there in your country as soon as the bank complete the transfer in any account that you will provide, everything concerning transfer will be legal, I will focus on my education as I will study medicine there in your country while you will invest and manage the business.*

I will be waiting for your respond on my private email:brigittejoachim439@gmail.com

Hoping to hear from you soonest.
Yours sincerely,
Ms. Brigitte Joachim

Josh deleted it and phoned the Kingsman. The phone in Duane's room rang eight times before Josh hung up. Duane wasn't going anywhere. He'd do whatever it took to get his hand on the five thou Josh had promised. More likely, Duane was sleeping it off. He hadn't been arrested because the cops would have notified him.

Fleiss called back. "Got a job for ya."

"Delivering summons?"

"No. How soon can you get down here?"

Josh kicked out in the tiny parking lot of Fleiss' law firm on East Wilson in the shadow of the capitol building and entered the two-story faux Moroccan stucco building. Fleiss' secretary Marsha greeted him on the second floor beneath a dome skylight and pointed to the lawyer's office.

Fleiss looked up from his laptop. He was a middle-aged man with a tight cap of curly white hair and looked like a cross between State Senator Russ Feingold and Larry Sanders.

"You ever hear of Hotchkiss Motors?" the lawyer said in a nasal voice.

"Sure. One of the classic British marques. They were around until the mid to late seventies. Why?"

"A consortium in Abu Dhabi wants to purchase the name, which currently belongs to young Edwin Hotchkiss, who is lost somewhere in the hinterlands of Wisconsin. They have asked me to ask you to find him. Money is no object."

Josh went to the dorm fridge, took out a plastic water bottle and sat on the sofa beneath a photo of Fleiss with his arms in the air atop Mount Kilimanjaro.

"What's he doing here?"

"Hotchkiss studies engineering at the university. Unfortunately, all attempts to reach him have failed. They tried phoning, registered letter, Facebook. Young Hotchkiss has disappeared into the wilderness."

Fleiss slid a manila envelope across the desk. Josh opened it and withdrew several black and white photographs of a young man in a leather motorcycle jacket astride a shiny V-Twin. Another photo of Hotchkiss and an attractive young woman at the Frank Lloyd Wright designed Monona Terrace, their backs to Lake Monona.

"I've listed his address and all his last known contacts.

He doesn't need an engineering degree, he's worth twenty million dollars. Hotchkiss manufactured weapons and heavy machinery. They sold off most of their assets when Lord Hotchkiss died, but Edwin insisted on retaining the marque."

"Lord Hotchkiss?"

Fleiss picked up his coffee mug and extended a pinkie. "Ducks, yass yass. Lord Henry Hotchkiss was the proud scion and heir to the Hotchkiss Empire. He wasted a lot of money trying to win a Grand Prix in the sixties and seventies. The motorcycle was his idea."

Josh looked at the photo again. Hotchkiss trying to look like James Dean. Josh didn't recognize the motorcycle. "What kind of bike is this?"

Fleiss made a *what me worry* gesture. "I'm glad you asked me, because as you know, I'm an expert on motorcycles."

Josh slid the items back into the envelope. "I get five hundred a day plus expenses."

Fleiss clapped. "Now you're talkin'! Abu Dhabi, baby! Okay, you're on the clock. Keep a record of your hours, blah blah blah. The group will be pleased."

"What's the group?"

"Zacharia Motor Sports. Their contact info's in there."

Josh was about to get on his bike when a big man wearing a gray suit and sunglasses approached from the sidewalk. He looked like a Secret Service agent.

"Mister Pratt?"

Josh turned. "That's right."

The big man reached inside his jacket and removed a card. "Franklin Munche. Boyd, Askew and Evans, Miami."

Josh tucked it in his vest. "What?"

"May I buy you a cup of coffee?"

CHAPTER 5

MUNCHE

They walked to Ancora on King Street, across from the Majestic Theater, got two regular coffees, and sat out front on the sidewalk at a round table. Josh pointed to the iron fence demarcating Ancora's territory.

"You're a lawyer. Explain to me how a private business gets to fence off part of the sidewalk for its own private use."

Munche sipped his coffee. "I'm not that kind of lawyer. Would you be able to help us with your father?"

"Help you how?"

"We just want to talk to him."

"Who's your client?"

"Ryan Gehrke."

"Why do you want him?"

"Mister Pratt has been charged with a felony in Miami Dade County, to whit he did steal a valuable original painting from Ryan Gehrke. Mister Gehrke is not a vindictive man, he just wants the painting back. If you can assist us in recovering the painting, there would be a substantial reward."

"I never knew my father. He abandoned me when I was fifteen."

Munche watched two young women walk in front of the Majestic. "I'm sorry to hear that. He doesn't keep in touch?"

"I haven't heard from him in twenty years."

"I admire the way you've turned your life around. I'm a Christian too."

Josh grunted. "You flew in from Miami to ask me that? You could have phoned."

"I have other business in town. I was going to phone. I just happened to be walking by when you came out. You're hard to miss."

Yeah, right.

Josh ran his hand over his buzz cut. He wore a ribbed long-sleeved Tee with traces of dragon tat crawling up his neck. He hated when people shied away from him because of his looks. It used not to bother him. He strove to be polite, lawyers excepted. He looked like every other biker. There were two types of bikers: huge fat guys with beards and barrel chests, and lean, tatted suckers with shaved skulls like Josh.

"I can't help ya."

"Not even for ten thousand dollars?"

"Nope."

"I see. You were imprisoned for atrocious assault. They

called you Chainsaw."

"Full pardon from the governor."

"That makes me curious. How does that work?"

"The guy I used to work for knew him. The guv owed him a favor."

"Daniel Bloom. Wasn't he one of Eugene Moon's victims?"

Josh stood.

"People die around you. You can't be very good at your job."

Josh headed back down King St. to Fleiss' office, where he phoned the Kingsman again.

Duane still wouldn't pick up. Josh took Fish Hatchery to the Belt Line. As he merged with the west-heading lane, three bikers roared by at one hundred and thirty decibels wearing Aces of Spade colors, a black Ace of Spades in a white circle. Josh rode to his house, left the bike, took the car. He parked in front of Duane's room and pounded on the door. He had that cop pound.

"Fuck!" Duane shouted from within. Seconds later the door opened, Duane's hand on the top holding him up. He wore a dirty wife beater and soiled boxer shorts and was drunk tank ready.

"What happened to you?" Josh said.

"I got rolled. Bitch took my roll!"

CHAPTER

6

OLD TIMES

Duane turned, scratching his balls. "She must have put a mickey in my drink. I feel like shit."

"This is like, what, the first time this has happened, right?"

Walking toward the bathroom, Duane held up his left fist and flipped Josh the finger. Seconds later, the shower ran. Josh waited while Duane dressed and came out with his shabby gym bag.

"She took the two bills you gave me."

"Of course, she did. Get in the car."

Duane slid into the passenger's seat and pulled out a cigarette. "Sooner you get me that five, sooner I'll be out of your hair."

"They know you're here."

Duane stiffened, right hand gripping the handle. "Who knows?"

"Ryan knows. Dude walked up to me on King Street this morning. Offered me ten grand if I'd give you up." Josh handed Duane the card.

"That fucker! Fucker's a Nazi!"

"How do you know him?"

"I seen him at Ryan's last shindig, fuckin' cheerleaders in the hot tub." Duane touched his chest. "Got the Maltese cross rightchere. That's a fuckin' Nazi symbol, dude."

They turned onto Ptarmigan.

"Show me the five gees."

"We'll pick it up on the way out of town."

"What the fuck does that mean? I thought you didn't want me around."

"I don't, but I won't be responsible for your death. I'll get you out of town then we'll figure something out."

Duane's chin jutted. He puffed. "I knew it. I knew you wouldn't give your old man the heave-ho. I'm proud of you, son."

"Don't call me son. I'm not doing this because you're my father. I'm doing it because I don't want your death on my conscience."

They pulled into Josh's driveway.

"That's right. You keep tellin' yourself that."

"I need an hour," Josh said.

"You know I'm meetin' my gal Merle in Vegas."

"You can fly to the moon for all I care."

Inside, Josh huddled with Fig. "You're going to the Lowrys. You love the Lowrys. You love George and Gracie, their twin schnauzers. You love Dave and Louise."

Fig licked him effusively. He snapped on a leash, grabbed her favorite chew toy, walked across the street up the Lowrys' winding blacktop to their McMansion. They were his closest neighbors. He'd met them when Lowry hired him to find George and Gracie who'd been kidnapped by a dog fighting ring.

The door opened. Louise was a matronly woman wearing a floral dress, hair cut fashionably short, holding a phone to her ear. Josh stopped on the stoop. Fig sat, tail wagging. Louise motioned them in and shut the door. She hung up.

"You want us to watch Fig?"

"I'm so sorry," Josh said. "I hate to impose on you..."

"Nonsense. We're happy to do it. Fig's better company than most of the people we know. What's going on and when will you be back?"

"Couple days at most. I gotta get a guy out of town. You have my phone number. I'll pay you back when I return."

"There's someone I'd like to you to meet. We'll get together when you get back."

Louise was always trying to fix him up. Married women abhorred a vacuum. Josh ducked her selections because he knew they'd turn out badly, and the story would get back.

"A girl?

"A woman, yes."

Josh grinned. "You never give up."

She waved him away. George and Gracie came around the corner barking, scrambling in place for a second on the polished hardwood floor, finding traction, hurling themselves at Fig. The three dogs took off like a three-element atom, spinning madly through the house.

Josh returned to his office and pulled out Munche's card. A half hour later, he shut his computer down, the bat of paranoia swooping inside his skull. Boyd, Askew and Evans specialized in criminal law. Their clients included Pablo Guzman, head of the Yucatan Cartel, known as "El Cheapo" for his tendency to stiff contractors, and Mario Petruccio who owned a string of nightclubs in southern Florida and was a made man. Duane found Josh's stereo and blasted Luther Allison through the Harmon Kardons. Josh loved the blues, but he wanted Duane out of his house once and for all. He could always look up Duane's criminal record.

He didn't want to know.

He called MPD Detective Heinz Calloway, head of the Gangs Squad.

"Calloway."

"Heinz, you know who the Aces of Spade are?"

"Criminal biker gang with ties to the black separatist movement. Subject of RICO investigation. Three of 'em indicted last year for ambushing a police officer."

"You might want to keep an eye on my place for the next couple of days." Josh told him what happened and what he was going to do. Calloway promised to alert the MPD. The mayor did not want angry phone calls from Josh's neighbors. They donated generously to his campaign and pet charities. They didn't want to hear anything louder than a lawnmower. Josh had met the mayor at one of the Lowrys' parties.

The sooner Josh hit the road, the sooner he'd be rid of his old man.

"You ready?" he said.

Duane looked up from the sofa where he gripped a beer. "I was just startin' to feel human."

"Come on. We'll go by the bank and I'll get you your money."

Josh turned on the 300's radio to WORT's morning blues show. He parked outside the bank on University Avenue and got out.

"Stay here."

Duane pulled out a cig. "I may go into that liquor store."

Josh leaned into his open window. "No. You're off the sauce at least until we get to where we're going."

"Where are we goin'?"

"West. I'll drop you off in Davenport and you can catch a flight to Vegas."

"Why'nt I just fly outta here?"

"You know what face recognition software is?"

"Ryan ain't that slick."

"Maybe I just need to see you outta town for myself."

"Yeah, okay."

Josh went inside. "Hi, Josh!" said the pert brunette behind the counter.

"Hi, Betty. I need six grand out of my checking account."

"How you want that?"

"Hundreds."

Josh turned around and leaned against the counter while Betty got the money. Duane got out of the car and went into the liquor store. Josh put the six gees in his fat biker wallet, connected to his waist by a chain, and got back in the car. Duane rejoined him a minute later, trying to conceal his purchase in his cheap nylon jacket.

"What did I tell you about the liquor store?"

"Oh, come on, man! I'm an adult."

Josh held his hand out. "My car, my cash, my rules."

Reluctantly, Duane dipped into his jacket and pulled out a pint of Four Roses.

Josh waggled his fingers. "Better give me that gun too."

Duane reluctantly handed it over. Josh laid it beneath his seat and next to the booze.

"That's eight bucks you owe me."

Josh kept his eye on the road. He stopped in Mt. Horeb to gas up. If Munche was mob-connected, they could have guys all over Madison. He'd told no one where he was going or when he'd be back. They'd be watching the airport. Within twenty-four hours he would wash his hands of Duane. He reached into the center console, pulled out a pack of breath mints and tossed them in Duane's lap.

"You sayin' my breath stinks?"

Josh pegged the cruise control at seventy.

"How many half brothers and sisters do I have?"

Duane looked out the window, sucking on a breath mint. "Fuck if I know."

"Don't they tell you?"

"Sure, I've had a couple women claim I gave 'em a baby. It's a standard ploy. I don't keep track."

"And you don't take blood tests either, do you? Wham bam, thank you ma'am."

Duane laughed. "Son, I always told you that any time you get a shot at pussy, you take it. I'm just grateful you're not queer. You were such a nervous little boy I thought oh shit, he's gonna be a fag. I'm delighted you proved me wrong."

They rode a hundred miles in silence.

"When can I come back and get my car?"

"When Ryan stops searching for you."

"Man, you don't know what you're talkin' about. He may have come from some high-tone white family, but he's got that ghetto mentality. He's never gonna give up until I'm dead."

"You think he wants you dead?"

"Yeah."

"There's something you're not telling me," Josh said. "He ain't gonna kill you over a lousy painting. What is it?"

"Nothin'. Don't you get it? Sycophants, gang bangers, scumbags, that's his crowd now. He's bitter about not g'tting' picked up. He knows his NFL career is finished so he's a gangster now. He always wanted to be a gangster. Take a look at his rap sheet. He's been in trouble since high school. He'll lose face if he lets me get away."

"I'll talk to him."

"You hate my guts so much, what do you care if he kills me or not?"

"I'd lose face. I'm trying to run a business here."

"Yeah well if you can do that, more power to you."

They crossed the river into Iowa at two-thirty and turned south.

Duane pushed his seat back as far as it would go and stretched.

"Remember those road trips we used to take? Good times."

CHAPTER 7

GENTS

It was eleven-thirty when Josh pulled into the parking lot of the Gilder Motel, a shabby outlier on a frontage road off the interstate, next door to Gents, a topless bar, with a dozen choppers lined up in front. Josh got two rooms for eighty-six forty-eight. When he came out, he tossed the key, attached to a large diamond-shaped brown plastic fob, to Duane.

"I'm zonked. I'll see you in the morning."

Music and boisterous shouts trickled from Gents. Josh aimed a finger.

"I wouldn't."

Duane shrugged. "I'm fagged too. I'll see you in the mornin'."

The room smelled of cigarette smoke and disinfectant and there were cigarette burns on the brown rug. A framed print of dogs playing poker hung over the bed. The tile bathroom needed grouting. Josh turned the shower as hot as he could stand it and stood there, arms to his side, face pointed to the sky, eyes closed, Lakota seeking a vision.

He turned the fan on full blast fell into bed exhausted. Couldn't sleep. Too wired. Duane had never been there for him. Oh, he kept him fed and sheltered, after a fashion, but there were no heart-to-heart talks, no wisdom, no explanation of what it meant to be a man. For half his life, Josh thought there was a secret manual, a behavior guide, and that everybody had a copy but him. As Josh observed classmates and their parents, it dawned on him that parents might be important in preparing him for life.

Duane was only verbose on one subject. Pussy. By the time he was six, Josh had a graphic understanding of the sex act. The word love was never mentioned.

"Every time you have a chance to bang a chick, you take it!"

Duane's conquests had kept Josh up for countless nights, listening to the banging of the headboard against the wall. Some women yowled like cats in heat. Others chanted oh baby, oh baby, oh baby. Duane seldom saw the same girl twice. Most were pale with tats, strippers and whores he picked up in places like Gents, cajoled back to his burrow of the moment with promises of blow, and endless procession of seedy motels that rented by the week, trailer parks, and shabby apartments.

No place was permanent. Sooner or later Duane would screw up at work, say the wrong thing, or screw over the wrong person. Josh wondered if other kids fled in the night. On those rare occasions Duane stayed in one place for a month, Josh had to sign himself up for school. Getting Duane to sign off on the forms was always difficult, best achieved late at night when Duane slumped over from too much alcohol and Josh was able to put a pen in his hand and guide him through a shaky signature.

Skanks came back like boomerangs. Josh overheard Duane talking abortion several times, and he even drove one once to a Planned Parenthood clinic with Josh in the car. As soon as he dropped her off, he headed for the interstate.

Through a series of dedicated teachers, and even a couple of Duane's girlfriends, Josh learned to read, but it wasn't until he went to Waupun that his real education began, thanks to Chaplain Frank Dorgan. Dorgan was more a father to him than Duane had ever been.

Josh feared seeking Duane's criminal record. Sure as shit he had a record. As a licensed private investigator, Josh was obligated to turn him in. He didn't want to know. What was his obligation?

A woman's piercing laughter penetrated the buzz of the air conditioner.

Pins and needles marched down Josh's back. The Lakota had a word for it. *Preska.* Premonition. He got up, pulled on his pants, boots, and shirt, and went outside. Across the parking lot, Gents was a carnival with bikers ripping donuts in the parking lot, a couple humping in the shadows, people laughing, dealing drugs. Josh peered through the shades at Duane's room. Too dark to see. Josh lifted his hand to knock then thought fuck it, there was no point.

Josh walked across the asphalt, boots crunching on broken glass, stepped over the low aluminum rail separating the motel parking lot from Gents, and approached the main entrance. Fellini's *Satyricon West*. On the broad front porch, a man in a cowboy hat, leather chaps and a jock strap dancing spastically with a woman in black fishnet stockings, gut spilling over her three-inch wide white belt, white go-go boots, massive beehive, face like a kabuki mask.

Three Sons of Silence drinking beer and watching a fourth circle his fat-tired Harley around and around, massive rear tire spinning out plumes of smoke. Inside, a short-haired long-legged brunette wearing panties, fishnet stockings, and a pink cowboy hat held in place with a string worked the center pole. The place was packed, AC/DC on the stereo. It smelled of perfume, beer, and testosterone. This was the weekend crowd, blue collar and outlaw. Two brothers with shaved skulls wearing red bandannas sat at the edge of the stage, grinning and cheering.

Josh walked behind them. Black aces on their backs.

Duane sat at the bar, chatting up a girl who looked no older than seventeen. Josh juked through the crowd, touched Duane on the elbow. Duane turned with a shit-eating grin.

"And here's my boy! I was just telling Shelly about you!"

"I told you to stay in the fuckin' motel." He turned to the girl. "How much as he had to drink?"

She held up two fingers. "Boiler makers."

"Ma'am, Duane's an alcoholic. I hope you'll forgive me if I take him with me."

She smiled with horsey teeth. She would be a beauty someday. "No skin off my nose."

Duane stiffened. "You don't tell me what to do. That's not how it works."

Shelley set down her drink. "Oh fuck. Here comes my boyfriend."

Josh turned. The boyfriend was one of those rangy, big-jointed hillbilly types wearing a Case Tractor cap with a face like a shovel. Before Josh could stop him, he reached over, grabbed Duane by the collar and threw him to the floor. He drew back for a kick from his steel-toed work boots. Josh pivoted with a right hook to the kidneys and the boyfriend went down. People laughed and pulled out their cellphones.

Josh reached down, yanked Duane upright, turned to Shelley.

"Nice to make your acquaintance, ma'am."

He bumrushed his old man back to his room and threw him down on the bed.

"You ain't ready to go at seven, you don't get the money."

CHAPTER 8

BROWN PAPER WRAPPER

Josh stood with Duane in line at the Frontier counter at Des Moines International Airport, watched Duane pay cash for a one-way ticket to Vegas. They went to McDonald's in the Food Court for breakfast. While Josh ate his Bacon, Egg, and Cheese Biscuit, Duane phoned Merle on an old iPhone.

"Hi, baby. Coming in today on Southwest four-oh-four-one."

Josh drank his orange juice, waited for Duane to hang up.

"How do you pay for that phone?"

Duane stared at him. "What?"

"I said, how..."

"What the fuck business is it of yours?"

"I'll bet you're using a stolen credit card, am I right? How long can you keep using the same card? And if you start using a new one, doesn't the phone company notice?"

"It's none of your fucking business!"

"Don't call me."

Josh turned and walked away. He'd been angry most of his life without knowing why. Since prison, he knew. And now he was angry again. Why did Duane have to come back? He was doing okay. He didn't have a girlfriend, but that didn't bother him. One would turn up. Of course, no one could replace Fig Newton. That was a once-in-a-lifetime thing. There had been only one Fig.

Sometimes while bouncing, he went home with a waitress at the end of the night. He wasn't a pussy hound like Duane. Sure, he liked women. But he was an honorable man. Since coming out of prison, women came after him. They weren't Rhode scholars. He didn't care. He wasn't looking for a serious relationship. First you had to have the right girl.

He was angry all the way to his car, and he was angry an hour later heading north on the interstate. He reached LaCrosse at eleven, pulled off the interstate onto Highway 3 and drove to Terrier's on Central, a biker bar on the northwest side of town. Josh always ate at biker bars when he could. It was an ingrained habit and the burgers were good. A half dozen chops lined up in front of the full-length wooden porch, on which four bikers in bandannas, shades, and colors, tilted back in wooden chairs, boots on the rail.

Josh nodded and went in. He ordered a burger and a cold draft in a plastic cup and took them out on the porch, finding an empty chair on the other side of the entrance. He tilted back and put his boots on the rail. He ate his burger watching the great American migration. Cars, semis, recreational vehicles, Greyhounds, pick-ups, bikers. He finished his beer and was debating getting another when two bikers pulled into the lot, backed up against the curb showing their colors, split the air and split the ear, and turned off.

The Aces of Spade went up three steps, exchanged nods with the white bikers, and went inside.

This was some serious business, a Miami-based black biker gang showing up in Iowa. You couldn't find a whiter state. Not that it mattered, but two bikers sent a certain message. When a club went on a run, you'd find anywhere from a dozen to two hundred participants. Seldom did you find just two members of a club so far afield. They could be pals out to explore the Upper Midwest.

Or they could have other business.

Josh got in his car and booked. It took him ninety minutes to reach Mt. Horeb where he cut north on M and east on Old Town Road, arriving home a little after two. Even before going inside, he went across the street to retrieve Fig. No one was home, so Josh let himself in through the backyard gate where Fig, George and Gracie were swooping around like starlings. Fig erupted joyously at Josh's appearance, leaping on him and bowling him over. The dogs swarmed him and for a few minutes he wrestled, laughing, before getting up and calling Fig to him.

They went across the street. An immense sense of relief filled Josh as he and Fig entered the empty house. He was a loner by nature. He sat at his computer and looked up The Aces of Spade.

The Aces of Spade is a one-percenter motorcycle club that was founded in Jacksonville, Florida in the United States in 1986. The first chapter outside Florida was the Georgia chapter which was founded in 1988. There are now American chapters in Arkansas, and Colorado. The first foreign chapter was founded in Kingston, Jamaica in 1998.

"The Aces of Spade logo represents the reestablishment of black power symbols appropriated by the White Man, for purposes of keeping the Black Man in chains. We hereby declare the Independence of the Aces of Spade from all games of chance, and rededicate it to its original purpose, the proud symbol of a proud people."

Listed as one of the FBI's ten most dangerous motorcycle gangs, the Aces of Spade are known for their activism and have provided security to Black Lives Matters events throughout the South.

FBI: Gangs provide fertile ground for recruitment by extremist groups, including white supremacists, black separatists, and Mexican reconquistadors. Members of the Jacksonville, Florida-based Aces of Spade, have been indicted for drug smuggling, gun running, rape, assault, and murder. In 2014, Wallace Murfee and Douglas Cienseros were convicted of luring Miami Police Officers Ruth Garcia and Morris Habe to an ambush and murdering them in cold blood. Other Aces have repeatedly been involved in attacks on the police.

Their relationship with black separatist groups such as Africa First, Nation of Islam, and Kill the Pig present special demands on law enforcement. Aces of Spade have provided security at several Kill the Pig rallies, and in Huntsville, Alabama, in 2014, two Aces of Spades were arrested for aggravated assault at a First Amendment rally staged by Young Americans For Freedom.

The Aces of Spade have long been under intense scrutiny by the Bureau's Special Gangs unit and are under investigation for possible violations under the RICO act. If you have information about the Aces of Spade, please contact the FBI at:

Aces of Spade Homepage: We would like to thank for visiting our official website. We appreciate the support. The Aces of Spade MC have been under Federal Indictment for 9 years. The club is staying strong and will continue to fight for the black biker community and every patch holder's civil liberties.

Josh phoned his NSA contact, Roland Stoeckle, and left a request for any and all info regarding current Aces of Spade membership, and any usual activity. Like showing up in Dubuque. He went through the kitchen door to the garage to look at the basket case Harley. It was no longer a basket case. The engine had migrated from his dining room table into the frame itself, a custom soft tail by Zero Engineering. He'd ridden a hardtail to Sturgis and back four years in a row.

Never again.

Duane's Camaro was parked next to the basket case. Josh went through it again, finding seventy-six cents on the floor, numerous cigarette butts, two spent burners in the glove compartment, and a joint stuck between seat cushions.

The back seat was filled with boxes of Duane's clothes. Josh pulled out an iridescent green leisure suit. That might be worth a few bucks. There were twelve pairs of shoes, none of them cheap, and a box of cartridges.

Josh took the box of cartridges from the trunk into the basement, unlocked his gun safe, and put them inside. He was about to leave when he saw a tendril of brown paper extending from behind the safe, which was recessed in an alcove. The safe was heavy. Josh pulled it away from the wall by inches.

Resting against the wall behind the safe was a seventeen by twenty-two-inch rectangle wrapped in brown paper.

CHAPTER 9

GEHRKE, THE EARLY YEARS

The internet revolutionized investigations. Instead of going to the county clerk's office or the newspaper morgue, the modern gumshoe sat in an ergonomically advanced chair pecking at a keyboard or delivering commands by voice.

Alexi, find Wilbur P Wodehouse of Bristol, Connecticut.

Siri, what poisons act fast and leave no chemical residue in the blood?

Laying the brown paper package on his living room table, Josh slit the tape with a knife and opened it, revealing a painting of a Mexican warrior in full Aztec regalia standing over a beautiful, raven-tressed supine woman, orchid in her hair. The warrior held the string of his bow at his cheek, a green and gold cloak falling from his shoulders. The frame was made from gilded wood. Josh turned the heavy painting over and looked at a small white label affixed to the lino-leum back with yellow tape: *Untitled*, Jesus Helguera. Josh turned it around and leaned it right side up against the wall. He turned a lamp on it. It sucked on his eyeballs. It drew him to the Caribbean. He didn't know much about art, but he liked it.

He liked it even more when he learned Helguera drew comics and became a professor at Bilbua Art Institute at the age of eighteen. You couldn't touch an original these days for less than fifty thousand dollars.

No wonder Ryan was pissed.

Duane had played him for a sucker once again, stashing his loot in a place he thought no one would look. Josh had no way of contacting Ryan Gehrke, but research revealed that his parents, Eric and Lily Gehrke both taught at Creighton College in, Creighton, Illinois. Josh called the college, bounced around and landed with a secretary in the history department.

"Professor Gehrke is not in today, Mister Pratt, but I'll see that he gets your message."

"Thank you."

It took Josh ten minutes to find the Gehrkes' land line number in Creighton's White Pages net page. A woman answered on the third ring.

"This is Lily Gehrke."

"Josh Pratt, ma'am. I'm a private investigator from Madison."

"What can I do for you, Mister Pratt?"

"Well you may not believe this, but my father stole something from your son."

There was a minute delay.

"Oh boy. We know something's going on, but we don't know what. Your father, you say?"

"My father is a man of low character who abandoned me when I was fifteen. He showed up on my doorstep out of the blue the other night and told me Ryan was looking for him."

"What is your name again?"

"Josh Pratt. My father is Duane Pratt. That's the only thing we have in common. The name."

"Tell me what happened."

Josh gave her the timeline.

"Hopefully, Duane made it to Vegas. I'm prepared to return this painting he stole if Ryan will call off his dogs."

"We have not spoken to Ryan in a month," Lily Gehrke said in a professorial voice. "I'll give you his phone number, but I don't know if it's still good. Since leaving the Dolphins, his behavior has been inexplicable to us. I believe that woman is poisoning him against us."

"What woman is that, Missus Gehrke?"

"Monique Vigil. Are you familiar with the NFL?"

"Uh, no, ma'am. I'm not."

"I'd like to speak with you at length. Right now, I'm up against it. May I call you back?"

"Let me give you my email address as well."

As soon as he got off, he looked up Monique Vigil.

Monique Vigil is a mixed martial artist and radio person-

ality known for fiery rhetoric. Vigil hosts a late-night talk show on WMIM in Miami called "The Righteous Hour" in which she discusses the need for black separatism. She has advocated both for a nation within a nation, to be carved out of southern states, and a return to Africa.

As a martial artist fighting at one hundred and twenty-five pounds, Vigil is four and oh in the UFC.

Ryan Gehrke, born October 4, 1987, is an American football wide receiver who is currently a free agent. Gehrke played college football at the University of Illinois, where he was named the Western Athletic Conference (WAC) Offensive Player of the Year twice and became the only player in NCAA history to average eighty yards per game. After graduating, he was selected by the Miami Dolphins in the second round of the 2011 Draft.

Gehrke began his professional career as a wide receiver under Dolphins Coach Maynard Speece and became a starter in the middle of the 2012 season after Herman Breyfogle suffered a concussion. Gehrke helped the Dolphins reach the NFC Championship Game. Over the next three seasons, Gehrke switched positions, lost and won back his starting job with the Dolphins missing the playoffs for three years consecutively. He opted out of his contract with the Dolphins to become a free agent after the 2016 season.

In 2016, Gehrke became a national figure after he began protesting what he viewed as racial injustice in the United States by not standing while the United States national anthem was being played before the start of games. His actions prompted a wide variety of responses, including additional athletes in the NFL and other American sports leagues protesting in various ways during the anthem. In 2017, Gehrke filed a grievance against the NFL and its owners, accusing them of colluding to not hire him.

Gehrke was born in 1987 in Elgin, Illinois, to Deborah Lightle, a 19-year-old Caucasion woman who was single at the time. His birth father, an African American man, left Lightle before Ryan was born. Lightle placed Ryan for adoption with Eric and Lily Gehrke, a white couple who had lost their own son to heart failure. Gehrke was the first of two sons they adopted. The Gehrkes live in Creighton, Illinois where Ryan attended grade school.

When Gehrke was eight years old, he began playing youth football as a running back. A 4.0 GPO student at Elliott Reeves High School, Gehrke, played football, basketball and baseball and was nominated for All-State selection in all three sports his senior year. He was the Most Valuable Player for the Illinois Conference in football, leading his school to its first-ever playoff victory. In basketball, he was a first-team all CCC selection at forward and led his 16th-ranked team to a near upset of #1 ranked Oak Ridge High School in the opening round of playoffs. In that game, Gehrke scored three touchdowns and ran for one hundred and eighty-five yards.

Gehrke was baptized Methodist, confirmed Lutheran, and attended a Baptist church during his college years.

In 2016, Gehrke began dating Monique Vigil, a controversial mixed martial artist, radio personality, and black power advocate. Many believe Vigil is at least partly responsible for Gehrke's sudden interest in social justice.

Fig laid her snout on Josh's thigh and whined which turned into a yowl, finishing with a noise that sounded like the text signal on Josh's phone.

"Does Fig-Fig want din-din?"

They danced into the kitchen.

CHAPTER 10

THE HUNT BEGINS

Josh stashed the painting in his gun safe and went to sleep, Fig curled at his feet.

The next day was Monday. An internet search turned up no trace of Edwin Hotchkiss. If he'd had a Facebook or Twitter account, he'd deleted it. The University listed him as a grad student in Engineering, working on his masters, and provided an off-campus address at a rental property in Shorewood Hills.

After his run and a shower, Josh saddled up and rode to 3650 Lake Mendota Drive and stopped at the head of the descending driveway. Frank Lloyd Wright designed the John Pew House in 1939. It had been available for rent for decades.

What kind of grad student rented a Wright House? A wealthy one. Josh rode down the blacktop to the turn around outside the one car port and kicked out. Three motorcycles lurked like ghosts beneath custom covers. Josh peeled back the cover on one, revealing a Suzuki Katana 1000 on a center stand. The second was a new Triumph Daytona, and the third was a classic black Harley Cafe Racer.

He went counter-clockwise to the stairs, up to the front door which was on the second level. Through the vertical window next to the door he saw several days' worth of mail splayed across the hardwood floor. He heard footsteps on the tarmac and turned. A middle-aged, heavy-set man in a Polo shirt and sharply-creased slacks walked toward him down the driveway.

"Looking for Hotchkiss?" he said.

Josh went down the steps to meet him. "Yes sir. Josh Pratt. I'm a private investigator."

The man regarded Josh thoughtfully. "I'm Les Morgan." He jerked a thumb over his shoulder. "I live next door. Edwin asked me to watch the place. What can I do for you?"

"My clients want to buy Hotchkiss Motors."

"Ahuh. Got a card?"

Josh handed him a card. Morgan studied it and slid it into a pants pocket. "I'll see he gets this."

"Thank you. Know where he is?"

Morgan shrugged. "Could be anywhere. He disappears for days at a time on one of his bikes. I used to ride when I was in college. Had a Honda 160. Man, I thought it was the baddest thing on the planet."

"You no longer ride?"

"Nope. My wife wouldn't stand for it. Got two grown

kids and three grand kids."

"Do you know what he's riding?"

"I have no idea. He does meet with a group they call the Crusty Bunkers, but most of them got jobs and I can't imagine they're out riding around."

"Crusty Bunkers, huh? They got a clubhouse?"

Morgan laughed. "They're a bunch of lawyers, professors, realtors. They all ride these fancy cafe racers. You're more likely to find them at the Madison Club than a biker bar. I do know they meet each weekend. I think they have a website."

"Thank you, Mister Morgan."

"No problem." Morgan waited for Josh to leave.

Josh rode his Harley carefully up the steep grade to Lake Mendota Drive, and headed to University Avenue. Across University, Motorcycle Performance occupied a Quonset Hut in an industrial alley. Josh kicked out in front next to an old boxer and a Yamaha 500 single.

Josh entered the shop. A countertop stretched between the corrugated metal walls, and behind that a pegboard wall rose to the ceiling, covered with shelves. The shelves were covered with cases of engine oil, Fram filters, spark plugs, grips, cables, chain lube, chains, and helmets. Racks of tires sat on the black and white checkerboard tile floor. Antique tins and old motorcycle ads in cheap frames hung from the front of the counter. Two racks of motorcycle-covers rose eleven feet from the floor. The place smelled of rubber and engine oil. The sound of grinding metal emanated from the back. A dude in his mid-thirties came out in a blue work shirt that said Motorcycle Performance on one side, Milt on the other. He wore a neat goatee and rimless specs, and a buzz cut.

"Help you?"

Josh handed Milt his card. The man looked up.

"You're a private investigator?"

"Yes, sir."

Milt looked through the streaked glass at Josh's bike out front. "That yours?"

"Yup."

Milt came out from behind the counter, out the front door into the sunlight and regarded Josh's chop. "What all you do to it?"

Josh took a deep breath.

"Engine: 88 with oil cooler. Changed the cams to S&S gear drives with .510 lift. Took out the fuel injection and replaced it with an S&S Super E, Yost Power Tube, S&S manifold and Pingle High Flow petcock. S&S Tear Drop air cleaner cover with a K&N filter. Screaming Eagle Hi Performance ignition unit with a 6200 rpm rev limiter. Accell Super Coil, Fire Wire plug wires and spiral wound metal core wires. Accell Platinum tip plugs. Five speed tranny with Barnett kevlar clutch, self-adjusting hydraulic chain tensioner. Screaming Eagle dualies. Progressive springs in front with higher viscosity, Progressives in back. Changed the rear swing arm bushings to "STA BOW" nylon high density. SBS semi-metallic disc brake pads and the brake lines are stainless steel braids. Went to tubeless wheels."

Milt whistled. "Sweet. You know, we're mostly into crotch rockets and cafe racers, but I appreciate a nice cruiser. What can I do you for?"

"I'm looking for Edwin Hotchkiss."

Milt held his hand up, extended his little finger and said in a Cockney accent, "'Is lordship?"

Josh laughed. "Yeah. I represent a group that wants to purchase Hotchkiss Motors."

"I haven't seen Edwin for about a week. He was in last week to slap some new rubber on The Bro. You know the Bro?"

Josh raised his eyebrows.

"It's the only Brough Superior in Wisconsin, if not the United States. They started making them again a couple years ago. Sweet ride. Only weighs about four hundred and thirty pounds. Costs fifty gees. My name's Milt, by the way."

They shook hands.

"There are rumors that Hotchkiss has some kind of prototype stashed around here," Josh said. "Something they were going to produce in the eighties but ran out of money. Or something."

"I've heard that too. Edwin ain't suckin' air, that's for sure. He always pays in cash. Rides with the Crusty Bunkers."

"I understand I have to wait until the weekend before they gather."

Milt waved. "Nah. Those guys meet every night, soon as they get off from work, at the Essen Haus."

Josh gave Milt his card and asked him to let Hotchkiss know he was looking for him. Outside, he phoned MPD Detective Heinz Calloway.

"Calloway."

"Josh Pratt, sir. I have a gang problem. I wonder if I could buy you lunch."

Silence while Calloway examined his schedule. "I'm in court until about one. Meet me at two?"

"Union Terrace?"

"Where else?"

CHAPTER 11

FREE LUNCH

At ten to two, Josh kicked out in the yard of the Delta Tau Fraternity, next to a new YZF-1. The Delts let him park there since he'd solved the murder of frat member Stan Newton a couple years ago. It was three blocks to the Memorial Union, which had removed the handful of motorcycle slots across the street on Langdon. Although summer school had just ended and the fall semester not yet begun, the place was a hive of activity. Josh walked past tables for the Palestinian Student Association, Feminist Cock Blockers, Queer House, and the Young Socialist Alliance. A young man with a pierced tongue, chin, and cheeks approached with a clipboard.

"Will you sign a petition demanding that the University remove the racist statue of Abe Lincoln in front of Bascom Hall?"

"No." Josh walked on.

The canvasser got ahead of him and puffed up. "Why not?"

"I'm not a student."

"Doesn't matter."

"'Cuz I don't think Abe Lincoln was racist?"

Josh attempted to walk on, but the canvasser got on the steps in front of him. "Are you serious?"

Josh walked around him and went inside, past the Babcock Hall ice cream counter, through the Rathskeller out onto the patio.

The Union Terrace on Lake Mendota was crowded on a hot late August afternoon, grad students, tourists, hipsters, gamers, lawyers and faculty filling the patio, crowding around the giant shade tree with the giant chair, and lined up for brats and beer at the outdoor stand.

Calloway had arrived before him and commandeered a table in the sun overlooking the lake. It was in the low eighties. Both Calloway and Josh wore ball caps with the bills pulled low. Gray seersucker jacket draped over the back of his chair Calloway stood as Josh approached. They shook hands.

"I got you a brat and a beer," the detective said.

"What do I owe you?"

"Ten bucks."

They sat and ate, the sun intermittently revealing Calloway's eyes. His right eye was normal. His left eye stared at Jupiter. The effect was disconcerting, particularly during an interrogation.

Calloway finished, wiped his mouth, and leaned back. He wore a blinding white Cotton Tee, and khakis.

"This about the Aces of Spade?"

"Yeah. They're after my dad."

"Say what?"

"Yeah. My old man showed up the other night on the run from Ryan Gehrke."

"Say what?"

"Yeah." Josh told him what happened, including the Aces of Spade in Dubuque. "You familiar with them?"

"I know what you know. They're bad motherfuckers. Did you inform the FBI that they're up here?"

"I told the Feds."

"'Cuz that's a red flag. I don't recall ever encountering an Ace, and now they're all over the Upper Midwest. This is about a painting, you say?"

"Oh, I'm sure there's a lot more to it than that. Duane hasn't told the truth since he was three. I don't know what he got into, or what happened down there. I reached out to Ryan, but he doesn't talk to guys like me."

"Whyn'tcha sic that Fed on him? What's his name?"

"Roland Stoeckle. He's got better things to do."

"Then why you bothering me?"

"You're the next best thing. Also, I'm looking for a twenty-six year-old Brit named Edwin Hotchkiss who's working on his master's in engineering."

"So?"

"You're in a pissy mood!"

Calloway's phone rang like a rotary. He picked up.

"What's up, cupcake?"

He listened with a concerned look. "Aw fuck. Alright, I'll be right there."

He stood. "I got to go. My daughter Ashley's in the principal's office at Memorial."

"What for?"

"Wouldn't say. And she wants a motorcycle. And she listens to the most god-awful crap. I try to play her the classics: Motown. James Brown. She likes Kanye, Jay-Z, and Doctor Dis. Talk to ya."

Calloway left. Josh went home, fed Fig, checked his messages. The widow of a Nigerian general heard he was a person of character and wanted to transfer twenty two million dollars to his account, if he would only supply the information.

He watched television. A blow-dried blonde breathlessly announced, "UC Santa Cruz has announced Research Justice One Oh One, Tools for Feminist Science..."

Josh turned it off and looked at the Harley clock on the wall. It was five o'clock. He saddled up.

The Essen Haus on King Street had been a Madison institution since 1981. Josh had often stopped in, before or after concerts at the Crystal and the Majestic, to listen to Jamie Cowles hold forth on the history of punk rock. Josh kicked out in back next to five bikes: a BMW 1000 with a black Bell Pro Star resting on the seat, two Bonnies, a Kawasaki 650 cafe, and a bike he walked around twice before figuring out it was an electric. An Energica! Josh heard they were fast, but the idea was anathema. He didn't trust an engine that made no noise.

He entered through the rear and was engulfed in warm, humid air, lights, and music.

Thousands of custom glass mugs hung from the ceiling. Regulars got their own mugs. Josh had no mug. He could count the times he'd been in on one hand. He preferred the Crystal down the street, and biker bars on the fringes. He waited for a break at the oak bar and got his elbows down. The bartender was dressed like a St. Pauli girl.

"What'll you have?" she said, giving him the once over.

"I'll take a Capital lager tap, please."

"Coming right up, big guy."

It was a warm evening. Josh wore a black leather vest with no patches, blue jeans, and black biker books. His Harley wallet jutted from his rear pocket, chain looped to his belt. The waitress placed the beer before him.

"My name's Holly."

"I'm Josh."

"You want anything, you give me a holler, hear?"

"Thanks, Holly."

Josh drank half, turned around, back to the bar. The bikers weren't hard to spot. They were drinking and table racing at a round oak table in the corner, their Joe Rocket and Icon jackets, Sidi boots and five hundred dollar helmets under the chairs. Josh sauntered over.

"Howdy, boys. Are you the Crusty Bunkers?"

A rangy dude who had a grizzled Sam Elliot/Jeffrey Dean Morgan face turned and said, "That's us. Are we in trouble?"

Josh pulled out a card and handed it to the man, who looked at it and passed it on. "Josh Pratt. Mind if I join you?"

"Do you ride?" said the handsome dude.

A lean, bald man with glasses across the table rapped his knuckles. "Of course he rides. I'm Homer Anthony, of Rickles, Anthony, and Holmes. I know Steve Fleiss. Thought of hiring you myself."

Josh forked a nearby chair with his foot and pulled up as the others made room.

The man to whom he'd given the card stuck out his hand. "I'm Jeff Bohm."

"I'm looking for Edwin Hotchkiss. An Abu Dhabi consortium wants to buy the rights to the Hotchkiss Motors name, but I have no way of getting in touch with him. I understand he rides with you."

"That's right," Anthony said. "We're planning a ride this Sunday."

"Mind if I tag along?"

"What do you ride?" said a man with a Beatles cut.

"Modified Road King."

The Bunkers smirked. Anthony sipped a shot of whiskey.

"We meet at nine in at the IHOP on South Park. We ride through Kettle Moraine country. There's a bar we want to check out in Racine. Gepetto's."

"Thanks, boys. I'll be there."

"You gonna run that Road King?"

Josh stood. "Maybe."

They laughed.

It was light out as Josh rode home. At each stop he scanned left-to-right for runaway SUVs, dogs, teens on longboards staring at their phones, and other bikers. Traffic was heavy out Monroe to Odana. At rush hour, Josh preferred to motor through town. He got home a little after seven, keyed open the garage and rolled in, kicking out next to the red Hawk GT Fig Newton had left him. The little 650 gleamed like a jewel.

He went inside where Fig waited, tail thumping, tongue lolling.

Josh smacked his hands together. "How do you want your meatloaf?"

CHAPTER
12

GEPETTO'S

Two dozen bikes lined the curb in front of the IHOP when Josh wheeled in on his red Hawk GT. A half dozen bikers stood outside clutching cardboard coffee cups, including Homer Anthony and Jeff Bohm. Both wore blue jeans and T-shirts, their jackets draped over their seats. Anthony whistled when Josh kicked out.

"Sweet little bike."

Josh got off. "What are you riding?"

Anthony pointed to the BMW 1000, smart phone face-up on the tank bag showing a map. Bohm patted a Bonnie with clip-ons. "Been riding this baby for five years. I have two other bikes, but this is my favorite."

Anthony tossed his cup in a receptacle. "Well, might as well fire 'er up."

Bohm put on his black and red Joe Rocket jacket, strapped on an open-face Bell helmet, drew down a pair of goggles and threw a leg over. "We don't all leave at once. Why don't you ride with us?"

Four other bikers joined them as they revved up and headed for the South Beltline, Anthony in the lead. Josh wore blue jeans, a rawhide leather jacket, an open face helmet and goggles. He usually didn't wear a helmet, but when in Rome.

Anthony rode aggressively, swooping by semis and RVs toting Jeeps, keeping straight on Twelve and Eighteen where they shot to the east, then south on Seventy-Three. The Hawk felt like a minibike beneath Josh, so light he could dismount like a rodeo rider and hurl it into the trees. Others began to catch up. In any group of riders, there are always a handful who want to get out front. Josh let them, riding mid-pack next to Bohm on his Bonnie. They cut east again on One Oh Eight. The air was sweet. It was good to be alive.

It wasn't like a club ride. The bikes were spread out, with at least a quarter mile between the lead and the tail. Anthony led them into the Kettle Morraine, a region of hills and valleys and twisting roads redolent of honeysuckle and the occasional whiff of manure. Sixty minutes later they cruised by Ten Chimneys, Alfred Lunt and Lynn Fontanne's summer home near Waukesha. Josh had taken the tour once with a sorority girl. The docent pointed out Lawrence Olivier's room.

"And this is where Sir Lawrence liked to smoke his marijuana."

They zigzagged southeast for another hour and stopped

for a rest break at City Park in Eagle Lake. Several riders complimented Josh on his ride. For the first time, Josh had an opportunity to look at all the bikes.

He walked the line, admiring a nineteen seventy-nine Honda CB650, a beautifully preserved Norton Atlas and an Aprilia V-4. He wanted them all. He had the money to buy more bikes, but his two-car garage only held so many. He had three: The Road King, the Hawk, and the Basket Case, which would be ready to ride in a day.

Anthony revving up signaled that the stop was over and one by one, they lit up and followed him down the road.

Gepetto's was a one-story tavern with roof tile siding built in the thirties, with a flashing Bud sign in the horizontal window. There were a handful of bikes already there; room in the big lot, which went around back, for everyone. A plaque by the front door informed visitors that John Dillinger, Baby Face Nelson, and Homer Van Meter had stopped in before robbing the American Bank and Trust Company in Racine, November 20, 1933. A half dozen guys sat at tables on the front porch, drinking beer from glasses.

The interior was rustic with pine panels, black and white photos of cowboys and early motorcyclists, a couple with the old Harley factory in the background, and tin signs. The front page of the Chicago Tribune from November 21, 1933 was framed behind glass.

DILLINGER GANG HITS BANK

Dartboard on the wall in back behind the pool table,

where two bikers played while a third watched. These were cruiser guys, in ratty jeans, Tees, tats up the arms, and black boots.

The Crusty Bunkers filled the medium-sized room, flirting with two farm-fresh waitresses who wore Gepetto's Tee-shirts which showed a snap-brim Fedora and a Tommy gun. The Bunkers split into four groups gathered around the round tables, got beer, got brats, and talked bikes.

Josh sat with Anthony, Bohm, and an old guy named Don who rode an old boxer.

"Ain't you the guy had the shootout in your driveway?" Don said.

"I was there, but I really didn't take part."

"Gotcha," Don said.

A young guy with fashionable stubble and pierced ears came up.

"You want to sell that Hawk?"

"No."

"Maybe we could trade bikes," Anthony said. "I've always wanted to ride one. You ever ride the big Beemer?"

"We can do that," Josh said. The thought of riding the lightweight German four cylinder lit his pilot light. He'd never been into crotch rockets but like all bikers, he wanted to try everything. The waitress brought a tray with Anthony's, Bohm's, and Don's lunches.

Anthony looked up. "Aren't you hungry?"

"Nah, I ate before I came."

The bar rang like a cafeteria while Bob Seger sang

"Against the Wind".

"Where's Edwin Hotchkiss?" Josh said.

Bohm shrugged. "Don't know. Haven't seen him in a while."

"What's he ride?" Josh said.

"The Bro," Bohm said.

"The Bro?"

"Brough Superior, the new model. Fancy English one thousand-liter, weighs four hundred and twenty-five pounds. Services it himself. I don't think there's a dealer anywhere in the Midwest."

Anthony wiped his mouth. "It's the modern equivalent of the Hotchkiss."

"Y'know," Josh said, "I'd never heard of the Hotchkiss until my lawyer brought it up."

Anthony poked at his phone, turned it toward Josh, showing an image of a shiny silver bike that looked almost lacy compared to a cruiser. "That's the Brough."

Bohm looked at it. "There's lots of bikes people never heard of. The Flying Merkle."

"Remember when they tried to revive Excelsior Henderson?" Don said. "The CEO spent it all on fancy offices."

"Lawyer says there was a new Hotchkiss in the works," Josh said.

Anthony nodded. "Yeah. There's always talk. This one was gonna be a V-4."

"Hotchkiss ever mention something like that?"

Bohm quaffed beer. "I heard he was working on it here.

I asked him about it and he just winked and put a finger to his lips."

Josh leaned forward. "You think he's working on it here?"

Bohm shrugged. "Hotchkiss says a lot of things. Some of them are true."

Josh handed out his card. "Please tell Hotchkiss to contact me."

From out front came the cacophany of unmuffled street pipes, closer, closer, until they reached a crescendo and shut down, one by one. The door opened and four riders entered. They were the only black men in the place. They smiled and nodded to assure the natives they came in peace. As they approached the bar, Josh saw their colors.

He excused himself, went past the restrooms in the rear, out the back door, around to the front, got on his Hawk and booked.

CHAPTER 13

VEGAS, BABY

Duane took a Frontier flight and arrived in Vegas at one in the afternoon, stood at the back of the plane cursing the feeble-minded taking their own sweet time retrieving their baggage and getting off. Fucking Frontier, man. It was the cheapest. The plastic seats did not recline and were designed for midgets. Duane was six feet and weighed a lean one-eighty mostly due to his coke habit. He was grateful he wasn't one of those fucking manatees he saw on every flight, spilling over the seat rests, assaulting their neighbors with blobs of flesh.

He hated fat fuckers. *Glandular condition my ass*. You didn't get to weigh four hundred by having a glandular condition and drawing calories out of the air. You had to *work it*, baby. You had to suck up those all you can eat buffets. You had to pile your platter high with mashed potatoes and gravy, pork chops, cinnamon rolls, pancakes. He'd sat behind one during the flight. Jammed into her jump seat like a popover. She'd brought hidden burritos in her feedbag and surreptitiously slurped them through the two-hour flight. He wanted to strangle her. He could do it with his belt.

He held his emotions in check with the thinnest veneer of civilization. All his life, Duane had been the last picked, the butt of jokes, a freak, a loser, a weirdo. His mother was an alcoholic nympho and his father disappeared when he was two. Duane fell in with a bad crowd in Pittsburgh and got busted for boosting cars, sent to juvie for two years. First night there he got butt-fucked by three niggers.

Duane never had a chance. Life had a hard-on for him. He always drew the short stick. But he learned a lot in juvie. Burgling, boosting, and the Dixie Drop.

If there's one thing Duane knew, it was pussy. With his bad boy greaser looks, long gray hair brylled in a classic duck tail, he drew a certain type of woman like flies. He was always neat and clean and wore Hugo Boss. He found them in bars and nightclubs, single women on the downside of thirty or forty, getting a little desperate, willing to take a chance.

Merle was like that. Forty-nine, with a body that would stop traffic. Except lately, she'd been looking a little sharp around the edges. Too much blow. They had to cut down. She rode a Shadow 750 and had a four-leaf clover inked on her ass.

Duane met her at Bonita's on Collins Avenue in Miami Beach, sitting at the bar sipping a cocktail with a parasol, legs crossed allowing her red flowered silk skirt to slide, coolly eyeing the crowd from beneath the brim of a straw hat. Duane entered. He was wearing slacks and a sport jacket over a black Tee, from a real estate scam he was working. Their eyes locked. The rest is history.

He banged her three times that night, despite, or perhaps because of the blow. Alas, that proved to be a career high.

They really had to get off the blow.

Which reminded him. First thing he had to do upon deplaning was phone Merle. The second was to score.

Finally, the clowns, manatees, devastated youth, wizened couples headed for the casinos filed out of the airplane and Duane got off. He headed straight for ground transportation, clutching his overnighter like an armored car driver, striding up the left side of the moving walk.

And of course, there was some fat slob in the left lane just standing there, looking around. Duane deliberately bumped him as he passed on the right.

"Hey!" the oaf grunted. But Duane was long gone.

Ignoring the chatter of the slot machines that lined the hallway to ground transportation, Duane exited into hot Vegas afternoon, crossing the ten-lane road to the far side where hotel service vehicles lined up, sun baking, cool shadow beneath bridges, so that Duane experienced hot/cold/hot/cold until he got to the service lane. He paused and phoned Merle. No answer.

"I'm here, baby doll. I'll call you when I get to Fremont."

He went right up to the Luxor van and stepped on board.

"You for the Luxor, sir?" asked a matronly black woman in Luxor livery.

Duane touched his cap. "Yes, ma'am."

He took a seat in the back and waited until all ten seats were taken, three by elderly couples from the Upper Midwest. Duane could spot 'em a mile away. Gramps and Granny stepping out of their comfort zone.

Yeah, right.

A black kid wearing a satin Bucks jacket sat next to the window in front of him. Dude had to be six seven. Two giggling twenty-somethings sat across, oohing over brochures and trying to choose between Cher at the Tropicana, Blue Man Group, or Cirque de Soleil. Couple of sand niggers in six hundred-dollar suits looking for white pussy. Duane had them all figured. He'd seen them all a million times before. Smug assholes. They had no idea how things really worked.

He wondered if he could take the Arabs for a ride. Promise them hot young pussy, get half in advance. Nah. They were too big. They looked mean. Not tall, but thick, like they enjoyed whipping girls.

Man, he thought, that dumb bitch is so busy looking out the window I could lift her phone and wallet right out of her purse.

Duane didn't do it for the same reason he hadn't strangled that manatee. Self-control. Instinctively examining the front of the vehicle, he spotted the discreet camera aimed at the passengers. Mama Pratt didn't raise no fools, which was a joke, because Mama Pratt didn't raise anyone.

As they approached the strip, the passengers oohed, aahed, elbowed one another and snapped pictures with their phones. The Eiffel Tower! Caesar's Palace! The Luxor! The world at your fingertips! An entirely synthetic city that wouldn't exist were it not for the waters of the Colorado.

As the van pulled into the big turnaround in front of the Luxor, Duane rushed to the front and was first off, heading straight down toward the sidewalk and Las Vegas Boulevard. It was hot out! Duane was glad he had a billed cap, even if sweat built up under the band. He took off his lightweight sports jacket and stuffed it in his bag. He looked back at the Luxor. If a fake Egyptian pyramid in the middle of the American West didn't epitomize Las Vegas, what did? The enormous black glass pyramid shot a light beam straight to Mars out of its tip at night.

Duane headed north, past geezers with walkers, gang bangers in hoodies, swivel-necked tourists, past the Excalibur, the Monte Carlo, New York, past Batman, Elvis, and Madonna posing for pictures. *Damn* it was hot!

It took him an hour to reach Fremont Street, which the city fathers had had the wisdom to cover with a tinted canopy.

Bluey's Bar and Casino was on North 7th. The thirty-year-old bar occupied the first floor of a five-floor commercial building that also housed a jewelry store, a Rexall, and an Apple store. The moment Duane entered the establishment, he felt at home. The smell of beer, sawdust, and cigarette smoke, despite the ban. Dino crooning "Everybody Loves

Somebody Sometime" on the juke, and a couple working girls at the bar.

Duane took a booth, set his bag on the bench and waited for the bored, forty-something bottle blonde with too much makeup to saunter over.

"What'll it be, sweetheart?"

"A shot of Jack and a chaser."

"You care what kind of beer?"

"Your choice, pretty lady. And a big glass of water!"

She winked and walked away.

Duane phoned Merle.

"Hello?" she sounded nervous.

"I'm here, baby doll! I'm at Bluey's on 7th."

"Okay. Stay there. I'll be right down."

"Everything irie?"

"Everything is copacetic, big daddy. Can't wait to see you."

CHAPTER

14

ASHLEY

Josh woke Tuesday morning to the sound of a chainsaw. He hoped to hear an explosion, a scream of pain, and then silence.

Forgive me, Lord.

He put on the coffee, pulled on some cut-offs and a sleeveless sweatshirt, and ran five miles with Fig at his side. On the way back, Phil Bass passed him in a silver Lexus and waved through the sunroof. Josh waved back.

When Josh got out of the shower, he saw that Calloway had called. He called him back.

"Josh, I'd like you to come over here and explain to Ashley that she can't just go out and buy a crotch rocket."

"You're her dad, Dad."

"Been meaning to have you over anyway. How's five-thirty sound? Doreen's making linguini. I know it's short notice..."

"What else do I have to do?"

"Great. I want you to tell Ashley how to go about a bike without killing herself."

"What?" Calloway was a law and order guy. He had two kids, the elder, now twenty, was in the Marines. Josh had always assumed Calloway ran his home like a boot camp.

Big sigh. "We cut a deal. She finishes the semester with a straight A average, she can get a bike. Also, no tats or piercings."

"How can she ride a bike without tats?" Josh said.

"Bring some beer."

Mid-morning Josh again cruised Pew House. There was no sign of Hotchkiss. Les Morgan was kneeling in his yard on a garden pad, pulling weeds. Josh walked over.

"Any sign of him, Mister Morgan?"

"Lights were on the other night, but I didn't get a chance to speak with him. You have not caught up with him?"

"No, sir."

"Peculiar young man. Must come from a great deal of money."

"You know of the Hotchkiss Corporation?"

"Not really. But I see how he lives. He has meals delivered all the time, and they aren't Domino's Pizza. Places like The Rotisserie, Second Story, The Brasserie. They don't just slap a plastic sign on the roof of an old Toyota. They each have their own bespoke delivery vans. Plus, he's got all those motorcycles."

"The Hotchkiss Corporation made its fortune in coal.

Lord Alfred Hotchkiss launched a Grand Prix team in nineteen seventy-four. They campaigned a bunch of McLarens
and won a few races before Alfred sunk twelve million into
building his own race car. Then in nineteen eighty-three,
his son Lord Wilfrid Hotchkiss decided they'd make motorcycles."

"Yes, so you told me. I'll tell him you're looking for him
as soon as I see him. Why don't you leave a note?"

Josh aimed a finger at him, went back, took a pad and
pen from his vest and wrote:

*Dear Mr. Hotchkiss: Please call Attorney Stephen Fleiss
(phone number) regarding an offer from the Zachariah Motor
Sports, headquartered in Abu Dhabi, to purchase the rights to
Hotchkiss Motors. You're a hard man to track down. If you
have any questions, please call me.*

Josh taped his card to the note and stuck it in the door
jamb. He rode home, washed the car, mowed the lawn
and played with Fig. He put on a fresh shirt and rode into
town, stopping on the way to pick up a six-pack of Capital's
Autumnal Fire. Calloway lived on the West Side off Segoe
Road in a leafy suburb on a curving street. Housewives
drove by in SUVs. Kids skated by on long boards. Calloway's house was two-level sixties modern with a brick base
and green painted wood, in a leafy yard. An MPD Durango
with a light bar sat in the driveway. Josh wheeled in front of
it and kicked out.

Calloway opened the door before Josh could knock. Calloway wore khakis and a Count Basie Tee-shirt. Josh hefted the six pack.

"Come on in. You want one of those beers or something stronger?"

"These beers are strong enough."

Inside, Doreen, a slim attractive woman who worked as a child therapist, came out and gave Josh a hug. Calloway led Josh into his den, down two steps, walnut paneled, shag carpeted, horizontal windows looking out at the front lawn, pictures of Terry in his Marine dress blues, Terry in the field with buddies, an old faded color photo of Calloway during the First Gulf War. He'd been a Marine sergeant.

Josh popped a can and chugged. "Where's Ashley?"

"She'll be home any minute."

"First of all, she's got to start with a small used bike. Like a one twenty-five or something. Trail bikes are good. You can pick one up for a couple hundred. Who's paying for this?"

"She is. She's been working all summer at Walgreens."

"How much money does she want to spend?"

"She's got eight thousand dollars."

Josh shook his head. You could buy a lot of bike for eight thousand dollars.

"You still having trouble with the Aces?" Calloway said.

"My old man stole a painting from Ryan Gehrke. That's why Gehrke's so mad. Duane stashed the painting at my place. It's in my safe. I'm trying to return it, but I don't know how to contact him."

"Why don't you give it to one of the Aces?"

Josh grimaced. "That might be awkward."

The front door opened and closed. Ashley greeted her mother and tripped down the steps into the den, a graceful, willowy girl with a pageboy, purple earbuds in her ears, smart phone in hand.

She unplugged and stuck her phone in the hip pocket of her denim cut-offs.

"Hi!" she said. "You're the famous Josh Pratt!"

They shook hands. Ashley sat on the sofa next to her father.

"Your dad says you want to get a bike."

Ashley gripped invisible bars. "Vroom, vroom!"

"Have you ever ridden?"

"Just a mini-bike," Ashley said. "And I've ridden on the back a bunch of times."

Calloway's eyebrows went up. "With whom?"

"Oh, Daddy! Brent Forrester. He's got a Honda."

"I thought you were seeing that DeGraff kid."

Ashley rolled her eyes. "Oh, Daddy!"

"Well before you ride," Josh said, "you need to sign up for a rider education course with the National Motorcycle Safety Foundation. They run several here in town. Costs a couple hundred dollars and they supply the bikes."

"Do I need a helmet?"

"Of course, you need a helmet!" Calloway said.

"Yes, you need a helmet. A new one. Get an open face

helmet."

"How was school?"

Ashley, who went to Memorial, said, "It was okay. Mister Flugel went on a rant today on wind turbines."

"What do you want to be when you grow up?" Josh said.

"I'm thinking of studying law."

Doreen appeared. "Come on up. Dinner's ready."

Dinner was peanut sesame chicken in linguine, plus a big salad. Dexter Gordon rolled from the hi fi in the den.

Ashley inhaled her dinner and looked up with a grin, right across the table at Josh. "Why don't you teach me how to ride?"

"I could do that," Josh said, automatically thinking of the Hawk, and how pissed he'd be if she dumped it. "But you really should take the course. It'll mean a discount on your insurance. And when you want to buy, I'll help you find one."

The Hawk was too fast for a beginner's bike.

It was still light out when he rode home. He saw a lone biker straddling his chop in the shadow of the 7/11 on Raymond Road. Watching him.

CHAPTER 15

UNION JACK

Wednesday morning. Josh and Fig ran, Josh showered and nuked a couple of Jimmy Dean Breakfast Sandwiches, one for him and one for Fig. He tracked Professor Eric Gehrke down on the Creighton College website. Gehrke described his work.

My course examines the history of empire and corporeality in the early modern world with a particular focus on Latin America, the Caribbean, the African diaspora and, more generally, the Iberian and Black Atlantic Worlds. My book, Early Explorations of North and South America, *(Chapel Hill: University of North Carolina Press, 2017), explores numerous documented voyages from Europe and Africa to explore the West. I am currently working on a history of the quantifiable body and the development of novel ideas about risk, labor, and disease that appeared in Atlantic slave market.*

Dear Professor Gehrke : Are you in contact with your son Ryan? My father stole a painting from him, and I would like to return it. Please contact me at your earliest convenience. Sincerely, Josh Pratt, Licensed Private Investigator.

He included his contact information.

The beautiful late summer day cried out for a ride. Josh headed west on Valley View to County Road J, up through the Town of Vermont and west through the winding, forested hills created by run-off from the great glaciers a hundred thousand years ago. A moraine was an irregular mass of unstratified glacial drift, the residue of the Laurentide Ice Sheet, which had collided with the Lake Michigan Lobe of a glacier. The moraine was dotted with kettles. They were all over Madison.

With the crisp smell of fall in the air, a hint of manure, the orange and red leaves, it was easy to forget about his problems. This was why he rode, why so many rode. Out on two wheels, away from the city, you forgot your problems. It was the same in martial arts training. Many trained because it was the only time during the day they didn't dwell on their bad relationships, their financial problems, their weight, or their bleak homes.

Josh rode on autopilot, guiding the big Harley in and out of shaded valleys, dodging squirrels, rabbits, and a cat, slowing to a stop on Zwettler Road while a deer and her fawn crossed, stopping on the other side to gaze at him serenely. Josh turned off the engine. He heard a whippoorwill, the breeze sighing through the trees, a tractor a valley over. He inhaled deeply of the fecund air. If only he could do this all day.

Oh well. He couldn't complain. God had been good to him. He had work he enjoyed, a wonderful dog, a cozy home and enough food. All he needed was a girlfriend, but there was no point thinking about that. He dreamed again of Fig Newton, what might have happened had she lived. Would they have kids? Would Josh be a good father? They might have eventually grown tired of one another. Who knew? All Josh had to guide him was personal experience and Duane.

"Hold out your hands. Wish in one hand and shit in the other. Which one fills up?" Duane's wisdom.

Josh's secret sexual history was not something of which he was proud. He'd mistreated women and been mistreated. He blamed no one but himself but he often wondered how things would have turned out if he he'd had a stable home when he was a child, parents who cared.

A frisson of resentment curled in his gut. He hadn't thought of Duane in years and now he couldn't get the fucker out of his head. Duane's dicta were burned into his skull.

"Never turn down free pussy."

"Pussy's like buses, kid. There'll be another one along in five minutes."

Josh couldn't recall hearing Duane refer to women as women.

Duane was not a hands-on dad. There were no games of catch, no signing up for sports, no trips to the Dairy Queen or the movies. Josh watched a lot of movies home alone when Duane had a television. The TVs came and went depending on how much cash Duane had. Give the kid a TV to watch, while Duane was fucking some cocktail waitress in his bedroom or playing poker in some dive. Josh couldn't count the times his father came home with black eyes and bruises, muttering dire imprecations, and he brought it all on himself. Duane thought he was smarter than everyone else and couldn't hold his tongue.

"I speak fluent sarcasm," he boasted.

Josh wondered if there was any point talking to Duane about Jesus. Josh didn't proselytize. He went to church Sundays when he could and prayed every night. He was polite when the Jehovah's Witnesses showed up on his doorstep, and when Seventh Day Adventists handed him brochures at the dog park. But he didn't preach, and he didn't interfere.

Duane wasn't worth the trouble.

Josh had read the Bible in prison and it stuck to him like glue. Mark 2:14 – 17:

"While Jesus was having dinner at Levi's house, many tax collectors and sinners were eating with him and his disciples, for there were many who followed him. When the teachers of the law who were Pharisees saw him eating with the sinners and tax collectors, they asked his disciples: "Why does he eat with tax collectors and sinners?"

On hearing this, Jesus said to them, "It is not the healthy

who need a doctor, but the sick. I have not come to call the righteous, but sinners."

Duane was a sinner. Josh was his son. Was it right for a son to give up on his own father? Josh wouldn't be there were it not for Duane. Well fuck it. A prayer for Duane.

"Dear Lord..."

He didn't know what to say.

A honk startled him. Josh saw a farm truck stopped behind him and realized he'd been sitting in the middle of the road. He waved and rolled the bike to the side of the road. As the truck, laden with silage, passed, the farmer waved back through his open window.

Josh smelled the pong of the departing truck, thumbed his engine into life and headed west. It was just past one. Maybe another hour hooning around. He cut south off Zwettler and west on Sweeney, another perfect road, cruising along at thirty miles per hour. The land was too beautiful to ignore. Josh wanted to travel through it as part of the landscape, not as someone with someplace to go.

He was rising out of a shallow kettle toward bright sunlight when he saw a flash in his rear view. Someone coming up behind him fast. Josh pulled over and made the universal bike signal, left hand down. The rider signaled back as he blatted by, ass in the air, hunched over, on a silver streak. Josh just glimpsed the Union Jack on the back of the rider's full-face helmet before Josh snicked into gear and gave chase.

It could have been any Brit-bike aficionado, of whom

there were hundreds, if not thousands, in Dane County alone. But Josh didn't think so. He hadn't recognized the bike. Looked like some kind of vee twin set up as a cafe racer. It looked like The Bro.

Josh gave chase. By the time he emerged from the kettle, the biker was a quarter mile ahead, bending into a sweeping right-hander, curving toward Spring Green. He was going over a hundred. Josh twisted the throttle wide and the big Harley leaped forward, eighty, ninety, but then he ran out of room and had to brake for the corner. Harleys weren't made for racing.

Josh cruised into the parking lot of the Frank Lloyd Wright-designed Spring Green Restaurant overlooking the Wisconsin River, but there were no bikes in the lot. Josh rode home on Highway Fourteen.

CHAPTER 16

LIVEWIRE

Lily Gehrke wrote, "Dear Mr. Pratt. Please call me at this number."

She picked up on the second ring. "This is Lily Gehrke."

"Missus Gehrke, it's Josh Pratt. Thank you for getting back to me."

"Can you explain to me what's going on with Ryan?"

"Apparently, my father was Ryan's coke supplier. Duane was at a party at your son's place in Miami, probably high and drunk, and stole a valuable painting, which he stashed at my house, without my knowledge. He claims Ryan owes him money for the coke and that's why he took it. He told me Ryan was going to kill him for stealing the painting. I think there's a little bit more to it than that. I found the painting and I'd like to return it to your son, but I have no way of getting hold of him. If you could reach out to him, I would be grateful. Just tell him I'll hand over the painting if he'll call off his dogs."

Silence, in which Josh heard grief.

"Thank you for telling me this, Mister Pratt. We haven't spoken with Ryan since he hooked up with that woman, the radical. I don't know what hold she has over Ryan. He was a very sweet, loving son, and we were all so proud of him. Then he did that thing at the game. It was right after he met Miss Vigil. The number we used to call him is no longer in service. We've tried everything. We sent registered letters. We asked his teammates to contact him on our behalf. He deleted his Facebook and Twitter accounts, so we left him messages on Miss Vigil's page. We have not heard from him in over a year.

"I'm very distressed that he's using drugs. At this point, we don't know what to do."

"I'll find him," Josh said. "It's what I do."

"You're a private detective?"

"Yes."

"What's your relationship with your father?"

"My father abandoned me when I was fifteen. This is the first time I've seen him in twenty years."

"My God. That's terrible."

"I'm over it. I was going to bring you the painting. I'm in Madison. But now I'll just have to find him and hand it over myself."

"Mister Pratt, we would be so grateful if you could effect some kind of reconciliation. We'll be happy to pay."

"That won't be necessary, Missus Gehrke."

"Call me Lily."

"Okay, Lily."

Josh cruised Hotchkiss' place. Empty. He stopped on the way back and picked up some fresh chicken breasts, which he grilled out back on the deck. Fig watched, mesmerized, tail thumping. Josh whipped up a salad with some week-old lettuce and fresh tomatoes and broccoli from the Lowrys' garden. He was no gourmet chef. He knew how to grill.

Using his tongs, he handed a grilled breast to Fig who took it daintily in her teeth and moved away, back to him, guarding her meal with her paws.

"Bone appetite," he said.

After dinner he worked in the garage with the door open, hooking up the electrics to the basket case Harley, which ran an Evolution engine on which he'd replaced the cams and gaskets and polished the ports and cylinder heads. He ran a twenty-three-inch wheel in front, nineteen in back with a fat Dunlop. It was a soft tail, the single shock cleverly hidden so that it looked like a hard tail. Josh wondered why all bikes didn't have single rear shocks. It made tuning and adjustment so much easier.

He wondered why bike horns weren't loud. Harley's were the loudest, but at eighty miles an hour passing a semi on the interstate, you might as well ring a dinner bell. Josh blamed it on the Japanese. They were so damned polite. Simply couldn't bring themselves to install loud horns. And now electric bikes. They were silent.

He wondered why motorcycles were dying. Both *Cycle World* and *Motorcyclist* had switched from monthly to quarterly, become fat, square bound, pricey, and worthless. It took him ten minutes to flip through each issue and find nothing of interest. Long essays on cruising the Baja Peninsula. Appreciations of famous riders and inventors. Artsy fartsy close-ups of cracked asphalt and piston rings. Maybe a road test. Maybe. It wasn't like the eighties, when the manufacturers threw down twenty new models every year. Now appearing every three months, the cycle rags had given up covering the industry in any meaningful way. Sure, they occasionally featured a new bike, like the new V-4 Ducati, but even then, they'd abandoned the spec sheet. If you wanted to know how much the bike weighed, or bore and stroke, you had to wade through reams of tight-packed text.

Cycle dealers were disappearing. Josh blamed it on a risk-averse world where kids were in no hurry to get their driver's licenses, if ever. They had Uber and Lyft. They had self-driving cars. It was a cowardly new world.

At seven, he went on Facebook and asked to join the Crusty Bunkers. They accepted him immediately.

"Thanks, guys! Still looking for Hotchkiss."

Hotchkiss wasn't on Facebook or Twitter. Josh checked the biker forums. The Hell's Angels had sanctioned a TV series. These days they made their money off licensing, rather than drugs and guns. The new series would present a kinder, gentler Angels who did charity runs and protected children and widows.

Two Insane Assholes shot dead at a casino in Henderson, possibly by Mongols, possibly by undercover police. Josh had tangled with the Assholes before. A pox upon them.

Troubling news. Harley was closing its plant in Kansas City, laying off two hundred and sixty workers. It was a sign of the times. Motorcycles were a tough sell for many reasons. There were so many cheap used bikes that anyone who wanted a bike could pick something up at a reasonable price. The average price of a new Harley Davidson was seventeen thousand dollars. You could buy a new Hyundai for that. Even the so-called beginner's bikes, which had ballooned to five hundred cubic centimeters, started at around five grand.

Harley had tried to introduce a new rider-friendly model with the Street line, liquid-cooled seven-fifties produced in India, but everything about it was old hat. The seating position was neither fish nor fowl, cheaper bikes like Yamaha's nine hundred ran rings around it, and it just looked wonky. If only they'd listened to Josh. They'd just recalled one hundred and seventy-five thousand bikes because of a brake problem.

Now they had an electric bike. The LiveWire. Josh didn't know whether to laugh or cry.

He bowed his head.

Dear Lord. Please watch over and guide the Harley-Davidson Corporation to its former glory. It's not for myself that I ask. And also, could you ask them to make the dipsticks white so that it's easier to read the oil level?

Victory had closed its doors. The pioneering motorcycle

company, owned by Polaris Heavy Industries, had introduced model after model during the nineties up through the teens. But their bikes were enormous, the opposite of a beginner bike. The smallest weighed over seven hundred pounds.

Then Polaris brought back the Indian and it was so successful, it killed Victory. Killed a lot of Harleys too. Josh thought the Indian Scout was the greatest American motorcycle ever. He'd ridden them several times and planned to purchase one, but he just hadn't had the opportunity. Money had ceased to be a worry since the National Security Administration had hired him as an independent contractor, due to his involvement with the Jesuit, a CIA rogue agent who had murdered Fig Newton. Every month, a five-figure automatic deposit in his checking account.

He didn't have to work. But a man couldn't just sit around. More than that, he had to have a higher purpose, according to Chaplain Frank Dorgan. For three years, Dorgan had been the father Josh never had. Being a man required a certain generosity of spirit and a willingness to overlook things. Josh resolved to get in touch. He didn't have Dorgan's personal information, and the chaplain wasn't on Facebook. He would phone the prison in the morning. For all he knew, Dorgan had gone to Africa. Dorgan had always said one day he was going to stop administering to cons and go live in another country, one that didn't take so many things for granted.

The sun dipped into the trees and the temperature fell to

the mid-sixties. Josh went out on his deck with a bottle of Capital lager and a joint and sat in the plastic lounge chair as Fig curled up at his feet. He lit the reefer. He uncapped the beer. He was feeling pretty good, listening to some screwed-up mourning doves and the faint murmur of traffic on Ptarmigan Road.

His phone beeped. He didn't recognize the number.

"Josh Pratt."

"Listen, you ofay motherfucker. You got something of mine. And I got something of yours. Say something, Duane."

"Josh! Please do as he says! I stashed something at your place. It's behind the safe in the basement. That's what he wants. Bring it or he's going to kill us."

CHAPTER
17

HINES

Josh remembered seeing Gehrke interviewed when he played for the Dolphins.

"You know about the painting?" the wide receiver said.

"I got it."

"You bring it to me in Las Vegas. Don't fly. Drive. You've got forty-eight hours. If I don't have that painting in my hands in forty-eight hours, I'm going to kill this motherfucker right here, and his whore, and plant their bodies in the desert. You feel me?"

"Where in Vegas?"

"Don't you worry about that. You call me when you get to town. This number. And come alone."

Gehrke hung up.

Josh set the reefer down in an old amber ashtray resting on a telephone company cable spool. He wished he hadn't smoked it. It made him paranoid, running through mental

checklists like a rug-dealer with an abacus. Should he take
a gun? Forty-eight hours? That wouldn't give him time to
sleep.

He needed a buddy.

He called Bobby Hines, Sergeant at Arms of the Jugan,
the most feared motorcycle gang in the Upper Midwest,
not because they killed with impunity, but because most of
them were ex-military, mostly Special Forces and SEALs.
Carl Kuhn, the president was probably still furious at Josh
for blowing the whistle on the Jugan's plan to rob the Fort
McCoy arsenal and sell the weapons to a Milwaukee street
gang.

Josh couldn't blame him.

Who wouldn't be furious? Motorcycle clubs were all
about loyalty. Josh had committed the greatest sin a biker
can commit. He'd betrayed a fellow biker. He'd also saved
Orlok's life when they fought that bull, so maybe it was a
wash.

Josh had met Orlok through Hines. He met Hines by
chance.

The Insane Assholes had cornered Josh and were about
to administer a beat-down when Hines cruised by on his
V-Max, took one look, and pulled over. Hines was six five
and weighed two hundred and seventy pounds. There wasn't
an ounce of fat on him. Following a frank exchange of ideas,
the Assholes left.

"Thanks, man," Josh told the huge black dude in the
Jugan colors. "Why'd you stop?"

"I didn't like the odds."

Josh hadn't spoken with Hines since the incident with the bull. Hines could be in the wind, like several of the Jugan, following a joint investigation by the FBI and AFT. Josh had ratted them out to Roland Stoeckle. He'd earned his money on that one.

Hines picked up. "Pratt! The fuck's goin' on?"

"You ain't mad at me?"

"No. Orlok told me how it was. Finding out you were a spook did kinda rock my world."

"You heard from Orlok?"

"No, man. He's in the wind. I wasn't there when they raided the farm and I'm not mentioned in the indictment. You say something?"

"I told them you were a potentially valuable asset."

"Whatchoo want?"

"I have forty-eight hours to rescue my father in Las Vegas, where Ryan Gehrke is holding him and his girlfriend."

"Gehrke the Dolphin?"

"Yeah. Crazy shit. Can I talk to you about it?"

"Come on down. I'm at the Edgewater. I have a break at eight."

"Thanks, Bobby."

Hines played piano at the Edgewater bar. Earl Hines was his great great grandfather.

Josh whistled for Fig. It was still light outside as they crossed the road to the Lowry's, whose two story house gleamed like a jewel box. There were cars in the driveway:

Lexuses. BMWs. Priuses, Leafs, and Volts. The front door was open and there was a party going on. A fundraiser for the university. Lowry threw lots of parties. Josh went around the house, let himself into the gated back yard where several dozen people milled around holding drinks, chatting, laughing, listening to Bruno Mars on the PA system.

Scholarly types. Tweed jackets with leather elbows. Women in pantsuits with big purses. The Lowrys' schnauzers, George and Gracie, rushed and frolicked. Josh found Dave Lowry at the freestanding bar, mixing martinis in a gleaming silver bullet.

"Hey, we're having a party," he said.

"Dave, I have to go out of town. Can you watch Fig for a few days?"

"Sure. I think maybe I'll put all the dogs in the dog run until people clear out. What's up?"

"Dave, it's too insane to relate on the fly. I promise you I'll explain when I get back."

"How long?"

"Five days."

"No prob."

The Lowrys had been the first to intrude on Josh's neighborhood. Prior to that, Josh had lived in splendid isolation in his small ranch house on Ptarmigan Road, paid for with an insurance company settlement. A little old lady in a Buick ran a stoplight and struck him on his bike. She was horrified. Josh recovered. He bought the house.

He threw together a duff full of toiletries and clothes.

He kept a complete change of clothes in his trunk plus a swimsuit. Downstairs, he unlocked the gun safe, pulled open the door and gripped the painting. He paused, his eyes inevitably drawn to the Sig-Sauer nine-millimeter, or the Taurus Thirty-Eight Special. Although he'd been pardoned and no longer had a record, Josh was forbidden by the court to own any firearms. No question Ryan would have guns.

He stared hard. Moment of truth. He shut the door.

He filled the big Chrysler's tires to forty pounds with an electric compressor. Since building a mail slot in his front door, there was no need to notify the Post Office. He checked all the windows, leaving the one in his bedroom open an inch. He stopped off on the way into town and filled up with premium, raiding the market for Slim Jims, Pure Icelandic Drinking Water, M&Ms, paper towels, and breath mints.

Twilight twinkled as Josh pulled into the Edgewater's underground parking garage, finding a place on the bottom level. He went up the stairs, through the lobby to Augie's Tavern, the buzzing bar, where Hines was laying down ferocious boogie-woogie. The bar was ninety per cent filled with young to mid professionals, splendid in their suits, ties, and hair. Dazzling blondes perched like sundaes on stools. Men of Action with steely gaze, mansplainin'.

Josh ordered a beer and took a table. The glass tip jar on the piano was about to spill over. Hines extended the final chord to applause, got up and sauntered over, unusually delicate for such a big man. Josh stood. They bopped, slapped, and hugged.

Hines settled himself precariously on the wooden chair. "Say what?"

"My old man. I told you about my old man."

"Yeah. A real shitheel bastard."

"Shows up last week claiming Ryan Gehrke wants to kill him. Duane was Ryan's coke dealer. Ryan owed Duane a lot of money, and when Ryan refused to pony up, Duane stole this painting. I've got it in the car."

"Ryan Gehrke? What is wrong with that dude? A slap in the face to every veteran."

"Yeah. He's gone gangsta. He's got Duane, and probably Duane's skank Merle in Las Vegas. I have forty-eight hours to give him the painting or he's gonna ice 'em. Wants me to drive. I think he figures to wear me out so I don't put up a fight."

"This is where I come in?"

"Exactly."

CHAPTER

18

THE SLAB

"Right now?" Hines said.

"Right now."

Placid as Buddha, Hines clasped his hands on the table, lower lip protruding.

"I've got two more sets."

"Can't wait."

Buddha. His gaze drifted over Josh's head. He never blinked. He wore an XXXL Packers jersey number twelve and size fourteen British Knights. His buzz cut emphasized his huge head. His Yamaha V-Max looked like a starter bike between his legs.

"Fuck it. I'll do it to tell Gehrke what I think of him. Let me talk to Jack, grab my bug-out bag and make a few phone calls."

Josh waited while Hines talked to Jack, who wasn't taking it well. Jack grimaced and gesticulated. He swept his arm around the room. He counted on fingers. He pointed at the cash register. With a shrug, Hines turned and walked toward Josh.

"Let's go. I'll call from the road."

Hines retrieved a leather overnighter from the bell hop. They went down the echoing concrete stairs to the basement and got in. Hines lowered his seat and rode it all the way back. His knees touched the padded dash. Josh knew the drill. He'd take State Highway One Fifty-One to DuBuque, cut south on Sixty-Seven all the way Interstate Seventy, through the Rockies, onto Interstate Fifteen into Vegas. Josh headed toward the Beltline while Hines made a call.

"Lecia, baby. How you doin', girl?"

"Doin' fine. How you doin', baby?" Josh heard through Hines' phone.

"Yeah, listen. I gotta go out of town for a few days. You just stay at my place and maintain. I'll be back in about a week."

"What?" Lecia squawked.

"Got to do it, baby girl. It's for a friend. A brother. You know how I am. You knew the deal when you signed up with me. Ain't partyin', ain't chasin' after hoochie. I'm tellin' you straight up, I'll be back in a week and I'll take you dancin'."

Hines hung up.

"Lecia, huh?"

"Oh, she worth it." He poked at his phone and shoved the screen in front of Josh's face. Lecia was as curvy as a mountain road. She looked like the girls who sent him friend requests on Facebook. Josh headed toward the red/orange sunset while Hines made some more calls. Josh stopped for a break in Platteville, went into the convenience store for a hot dog. Hines was right behind him with a DVD of *Roadhouse*.

"Love this movie!" he said, adding two Big Gulps to the tab. They got in the car.

Hines touched the Escort Max glued to the dashboard. "This any good?"

"It has saved me millions. Literally, millions of dollars. Listen, you should get some rest. That chair back lays flat."

Hines twisted. Josh's duffel bag filled the rear foot well. There were blankets, pillows, and the painting, wrapped in plain brown paper. Hines brought it around and set it on his lap.

"This the painting?"

"Yeah."

"What is it?"

"Jesus Helguera. I think he did the cover to the first *Malo* record."

"Mind if I take a look?"

"Go ahead. Just be careful. It's valuable."

Seeing where Josh had already cut the tape, Hines gently eased the heavy painting from its sheath, which he set on the rear seat. He held the painting with one hand, shined his cell phone light on it with the other.

"This is a beautiful paintin'. I wouldn't mind havin' this on my wall."

"Yeah, well it's worth fifty thousand dollars."

"No shit?"

Josh turned on the radio, found KUVO out of Denver laying down some Philly Joe Jones, the one about the vampire. As they barreled into the night nine miles over the speed limit, Hines kept bouncing the painting up and down on his thighs.

"Heavy."

Philly Joe segued into Phineas Newborn Jr. "Manteca".

"Man, I love that cat," Hines said. "You know he recorded his last record with a broken wrist?"

"No shit."

"It's the greatest solo piano record of all time. *Phineas Newborn Solo*. I got it. I got a bunch of copies. I'll give you one."

"Sweet."

Hines kept bouncing. "Too heavy."

"What is?"

"This paintin' and frame. Feels like there's something else in here. Something heavy."

They crossed into Iowa. Turning on a stalk light affixed to the A pillar, Hines began to worry the frame with a pocketknife.

"Fuck you doin', man! Don't ruin it!"

"Dude, I'm tellin' you there's something in here."

"If you mangle that painting…"

"What, is this Ryan Gehrke supposed to be some kind of bad dude? He's a football player, man! An overpaid, spoiled man child. I heard he took up with some far left loonie and she's steerin' him left."

"Monique Vigil."

"Unique Monique. She's the bad ass. She competes in Spartan League."

"You see her fight?"

"Yeah. I watched her fight on Youtube. She knocked the other woman out. Then she did a little jig. Flyweights. One twenty-five."

They crossed the river into Iowa. Josh glanced left, saw the lights of several barges. A little after ten, they turned south on Sixty-seven.

"You really should get some sleep."

Hines fiddled with the frame. "Relax, man. I'd still be playin' if we hadn't left. Maybe we should pull over, I'll drive, and you get some rest."

"Yeah, okay," Josh said, scanning for a rest stop. They were in farmland now, the only lights coming from a half moon, the stars, and the faint lights of farms in the distance. Josh cracked the windshield and inhaled the scent of freshly turned earth and manure.

"There's something in here."

"You'd better be sure."

"I am sure. Pull over. I don't want to do this while we're rollin'. Something heavy."

A road sign flashed by: REST STOP, ONE MILE.

It was just a gravel parking lot with a picnic table and a garbage can, surrounded by a wood fence. A kiosk showed a map of a nature trail and held brochures. Josh pulled to the back of the lot. This wasn't about the painting at all. It was about what was hidden in the painting. Why would someone go to all that trouble? Especially with a painting that was something of a collector's item? Maybe the painting wasn't Gehrke's. Maybe Gehrke stole it from someone else.

At the back of the lot, Josh pulled an LED flashlight from the center console and shined it on the painting. Using a pen knife, Hines gently edged the backing board away from the front. It had been glued in place, but he worked his way all around with the knife so that nothing would tear.

"Okay, here goes."

He peeled off the backing board revealing a slab of discolored metal, eleven inches by fifteen.

"What the fuck is it?" Josh said.

"Don't know. Looks old."

"Turn it over."

Hines turned the metal slab over and set it on his lap as Josh shined the light. Hieroglyph-like figures had been hammered into the slab in an unrecognizable language, as well as pictographs of boats and palm trees.

"What is that, Arabic?" Josh said.

"Fuck if I know. Here. You take it while I take a few pictures."

"Send them to me."

Hines snapped some pictures and sent them to Josh, who forwarded them to Lily Gehrke. "Dear Professor: Can you tell us what this is?"

"I'll drive," Hines said.

CHAPTER

19

AN UNEXPECTED STOP

Josh turned off his phone, lowered the back seat and slept. Hines turned down the volume on the jazz station, set the cruise control at seventy-five and adjusted the fuzz buster, dropping down Iowa State Highway Sixty-Three, through rolling farm country. At this hour the road was deserted.

Hines was wired. He was an adrenaline junkie who'd joined the Army at seventeen with his father's signature and blessings. He'd been playing piano since he was five. His dad paid for lessons from Alice Breakstone, an old black woman who used to play in Nawlins' whorehouses. She didn't just teach, she fed him the whole enchilada, from Scott Joplin and Jellyroll Morton to Eric Reed and Mulgrew Miller. Being a pianist herself, she gave more weight to the piano players. She'd played with the Neville Brothers and the Marsalis Brothers.

"Remember, Youngblood. The piano player gets the

girls!"

Fascinated, Hines would hang out with her afterward while she served cold apple cider and hot Louis Armstrong, Fletcher Henderson, Ellington, Basie, Bird, Diz, Miles, Trane, right up and through the post-modern period to the point where jazz overshot its mark and broke into chaos.

"You ever see Cecil Taylor dismantle a piano?" she asked. "Hmm, mmm, mmm!"

"Who's Cecil Taylor?"

"A man who thinks it's his job to dismantle pianos! Remember, Youngblood! Your first job is to entertain!"

"But, Missus Breakstone, I don't want to be some nigga, shuckin' and jivin' to please the white man!"

Mrs. Breakstone sounded like a donkey when she laughed. "Oh, Youngblood! You don't have to worry about that! You entertain folks, you'll never be out of work. Get a lot of pussy, too. You may not know what I'm talkin' about, but you will."

"I know about pussy!" said the five-year-old Hines.

And he thought about it. Thought about it hard during his junior year, where he supplemented his income by playing in strip bars and jazz clubs in and around Chicago. He was an outstanding athlete, lettering in football, baseball, and track. Northwestern scouted him. But in the end, there was only one path he could take. He had yearned to be a soldier since seeing *Merrill's Marauders* at a local matinee along with *Invasion of the Body Snatchers*. He read about war, any war. From the Crimean to Afghanistan, Hines had immersed himself in its lore and history.

Hines did basic training at Fort McCoy in Wisconsin. He excelled in hand-to-hand combat, and with his base commander's endorsement, applied for Special Forces, beginning training in 1988. During the Gulf War, he was part of a unit that dispatched into Afghanistan to gather intelligence and harass enemy forces. They parachuted in at night, losing one man who impaled himself on a shattered tree branch.

That's how he met Orlok. A friendship forged in combat. They vowed to keep in touch after they got out. Only they really did.

Orlok had been riding motorcycles all his life. When he described the Jugan, named after Genghis Kahn's army, Hines thudded fist to heart.

"I'm in."

The Jugan became one of the most powerful and exclusive motorcycle clubs in the Upper Midwest. Nobody messed with them. They messed with nobody. They did the charity runs, gathered toys for tots, visited the kids in the hospital, and on the outside, farmed ginseng, and a little farther back, in the woods, marijuana.

They also ran a few guns, mostly stolen during break-ins. One of their more reliable suppliers ran his truck through the front window of a gun store in Marshfield, tossed everything in the bed and took off. He was apprehended a mile down the road, higher than Elon Musk's Tesla. After the botched McCoy job, Orlok was in the wind and Hines was only walking around free because Josh had put in a good word for him.

KUVO played Lee Morgan's "The Sidewinder", ending their string of piano players. Poor Morgan, shot by his common law wife Helen in Slug's Saloon. He might have lived, but there was a terrible snowstorm and the ambulance took so long to get there he bled to death.

Hines glanced in the rear view. *What the fuck!* Strobing lights coming up on him fast, and now the state trooper hit the siren. Gut sinking, Hines immediately pulled to the side of the deserted two-lane highway and stopped on the shoulder, running through that cop stop inventory that everyone did, regardless of innocence. License? Registration? Insurance? Drugs? Guns? What?

Worthless fucking fuzz buster. Hines would have tossed it out the window except for the trooper.

The highway patrol vehicle stopped twenty feet from their rear bumper while the trooper communicated via computer. Great. Hines saw that the trooper was alone and knew that he would be able to take him out. But it would never come to that. Hines was a loyal and patriotic American who respected law enforcement despite his criminal past. His only hope was to convince the trooper that he and Josh were innocent of everything except, possibly, speeding.

Hines looked over. Josh slept on.

Finally, the trooper got out of his car, and like most state troopers, he was huge. Bigger than Hines, who rolled down his window and waited with his hands on the wheel. The cop sauntered up and stood a few feet away, shining an LED light inside.

"Sir, may I see some identification?"

"Yes sir. I'm going to reach for my wallet now, is that okay?"

"Go ahead."

Hines fished out his Harley Wallet, removed his driver's license and handed it over. The trooper examined it. "I'll need to see vehicle registration and proof of insurance as well. Please wake up your companion. I'd like to see his identification too."

Hines nudged Josh. "Hey man."

Josh opened his eyes, squinted. "What's goin' on?"

Hines held out his hand. "Driver's license."

Josh raised the seat back and forked over his license, which the trooper examined.

"This is his car," Hines said. "Wants the registration and proof of insurance."

Josh opened the glove compartment and pulled out a manila envelope.

"Do you know why I stopped you, sir?" the trooper said.

"Speeding."

"That's right. You were doing seventy-five in a sixty-five mile an hour zone. Would you mind getting out of the car, please? Both of you. Keep your hands where I can see them." The trooper walked back and took up position ten feet behind the bumper, his hand on the butt of his auto-matic. When Josh got out, he motioned.

"Both of you on the driver's side, feet spread, hands on top of the car."

"What's the problem, officer?" Josh said.

"You two just wait right there."

The trooper went back to his car and talked to his dispatcher.

"We gotta get moving, man," Josh said.

"I know."

"Where are we?"

"We're about twenty miles north of Missouri."

"What if he wants a dog or something?"

"Hush up. Here he comes."

"Turn around and face me," the trooper said. When they turned, he handed them back their licenses. "I was going to call in a drug sniffing dog. Hines, let me see that tat on your left bicep."

Hines lifted the short sleeve exposing the Airborne logo, three lightning bolts over a sword on an arrowhead. The trooper put his flashlight in his mouth and lifted the short sleeve of his crisp brown uniform exposing the same tat.

"Where'd you serve?"

"Gulf War. Afghanistan. Where'd you serve, brother?"

The trooper grinned. "Same place, twenty years later. I ain't even gonna give you a ticket. Slow it down, boys. Y'all have a good night."

CHAPTER

20

THE MOUNTAINS

Josh went back to sleep until Hines pulled over at a truck stop outside Kansas City.

"Okay. I'm ready to crash."

Hines pulled up at the fuel island, released the gas cap, got out, walked inside to hand over a deposit, came back out and filled the tank with premium.

They went inside, used the restroom. Hines picked among the DVDs while Josh bought some fresh fruit. Bananas a buck apiece. A couple of apples. He went outside into the cool morning sun and sat on a bench waiting, remembering he'd turned off his cellphone. He pulled it out and powered up. Lily Gehrke had phoned him at eleven-thirty the night before. He called her back.

"Josh, I'm so glad you called. I showed your pictures to Eric, I hope that's all right."

"No prob."

"What is it, if you don't mind my asking?"

"We found it inside the stolen painting from your son's house. It looks like a bronze plaque, only really old, with weird markings."

"Yes. Some of them look familiar. We'd like to take a closer look at it."

"We're on our way to Vegas right now to return the painting to your son, but we're keeping the bronze. I'll hit you when I get back. What is it?"

"Have you heard of the Mali Empire? They ruled vast sections of Africa in the fourteenth century."

"Nope."

"Well it may have come from there, and even that's taking a leap of faith. We're very eager to take a look at it in good light, use some spectroanalysis, and carbon-dating. Please don't take any chances with it. It could be valuable. In fact, I'm going to go out on a limb here, it is valuable. Maybe priceless."

"We'll take good care of it, Professor."

"Yes. Please keep us updated, and we would love to talk to Ryan, if you see him."

Hines came out with a grocery bag tucked under one python-like arm, chugging a chocolate milk. "Let's go, hoss."

Hines got in the passenger seat, set the groceries between his legs and put the seat back down flat, oozing catlike into a curled position that included front and back seats.

"Lily Gehrke called," Josh said. "Said the slab might be valuable. Says it has something to do with the Mali Empire."

"The Mali Empire, huh?"

"You heard of them?"

"Prince Abubakari was a bad motherfucker."

"What did he do?"

"Unified the motherfuckers, then one of the shamans told him there was a great land across the sea, so he put together a fleet of four hundred ships. Every kind of ship. He invited a huge ship-building competition to see who could build the best ships and rewarded them with gold and pieces of the new land, if any. Then they all took off."

"How do you know all this?"

Hines pumped his fist. "Black history. I read a lot in the sand. Everybody thinks Africa is a shithole, 'cept for Wakanda, of course. And it kinda is mostly a shithole. But it had its moments, and the Mali was one of 'em."

"Then what?"

"That's it. Nobody ever heard from them again. I got to nod off, hoss."

"Mind if I play a little jazz?"

"Fuck no. Helps me sleep."

Josh headed west on Interstate Seventy. He'd been this way before, several times. It was hard to believe that a couple hundred miles down the road, the boring, ruler-straight highway on which he drove turned into one of the most spectacular drives in America as it twisted and snaked up through the Rocky Mountains. KUVO was playing some old Weather Report. With a speed limit of seventy-five, most traffic was doing a little over eighty. A county deputy sitting in the center didn't raise an eyebrow as vehicle after vehicle streamed by over the limit.

He couldn't pull everyone over, so he pulled no one. Josh passed semis, SUVs, old bikers and their old ladies on Gold Wings with Teddy bears bungeed to the sissy bars, recreational vehicles towing cars, motorcycles attached to the rear bumper, boats on top. He cracked the windows to inhale the rich scent of corn and wheat as a rumble intruded from behind. Bikers on the move, dozens of headlights gleaming in his mirror. Josh put on the blinkers and pulled into the right lane between two Mayflower moving vans.

The head rider waved as he passed, the roar of the unmuffled Harleys drowning out everything else. Their colors said Sons of Silence, an outlaw gang from Colorado. Josh had partied with them at Sturgis one year. With the sun behind him, Kansas loomed. He drove west past endless farmland, the land gradually rising until his ears popped outside Limon, where he pulled over at a visitor's center and hit the head.

Hines woke and used the restroom, got back in the car and resumed his sleep. Josh ate a couple Slim Jims and washed them down with a Mountain Dew, shut the door and drove on.

The only thing wrong with KUVO, was they frequently stopped the music for soft-voiced lectures on introducing your children to anal sex and the threat of global warming. As the hushed host welcomed listeners to his station, Josh switched to the CD player. Son Seals' *Midnight Sun*. Josh figured the blues was as good as jazz to a sleeping giant. Josh had learned about jazz in the joint from Chaplain Dorgan, who invited Josh into his office where they would listen for hours.

"Lecia baby," Hines mumbled in his sleep. "Lecia. Where is it? Where's the feather duster?"

Josh turned up the radio. They rolled through increasing settlement until Denver loomed in the distance, its cluster of downtown towers back dropped by the Rockies. The rise was precipitous. Josh's ears popped twice in the next half hour as they climbed past Arvada, up the canyon past million-dollar log cabins perched on peaks, up and up until the mountains closed in. It was dark out, but Interstate 70 was brightly lit as they passed Silver Plume and entered the Eisenhower Tunnel.

Hines woke, rubbed his eyes, crawled into his seat and brought the seat back up. "What's going on?"

"We're going through the tunnel. I thought we'd swap at Glenwood Springs."

"Yeah, that's cool. I gotta hit the head."

"There's a place just past the tunnel."

Josh pulled off in Frisco, gassed up in a Kum & Go, stretched, hit the head. They had thirty hours to make Las Vegas, no problem if they experienced no delays.

Vail was an upside-down Christmas tree, lights spreading as you went higher. The ski resorts had figured out how to make money off season years ago. Tourists rode ski lifts to the top of the peaks, then strapped themselves into little wheeled plastic carts to ride down through a twisting chute. It looked like fun. At times the mountains spread out to reveal broad plains, but mostly, they crowded the road. Signs warned about rock falls. They passed a semi pulled over on the narrow shelter, orange cones and flares out, while the driver stared at a blown tire carcass. They pulled into Glenwood Springs a little after midnight, turning south on State Highway Eighty-Two, pulling off at Bern's Roadhouse, a rustic, rambling ranch-style bar and grill with several dozen bikes parked in front.

As they walked past the line of bikes on the sidewalk, Josh noticed three Florida license plates, one Harley and two Victories. He pulled his ball cap low on his head. Inside, a party atmosphere prevailed as one contingent watched a baseball game while the other watched mixed martial arts. There were bikers everywhere, including the Sons of Silence who'd passed them earlier. Three Aces of Spade were at the bar. Bern's was decorated with Western bric-a-brac including stuffed lynx and wolf over the bar, a moose's head looming over a dormant cast iron stove, and framed posters of Lilly Langtry and Oscar Wilde.

Josh pulled Hines into the restroom alcove.

"The Aces are here. I'm going back to the car. Get me a hamburger. See if you can get a look at those photos."

Josh photographed the Florida license plates and sent them to Stoeckle. He waited on the porch in shadow. He looked like half the guys in there.

Fifteen minutes later Hines came out, ramrod straight,

carrying a brown paper bag.

"Let's book." Hines opened the rear door, slid something out of his belly and laid it down.

Josh got in the shotgun seat and chowed down. By the time they got back to the Interstate, that burger was gone. "What'dja find out?"

"Lookin' for some guy. Old photos taken from the newspaper. Kinda hard to identify."

"What's that you pulled out of your gut?"

"Take a look."

Josh swiveled in the seat and picked up a cast iron slab, similar in size and weight to the bronze tablet.

"Got that off the stove."

CHAPTER

21

THE SOUTH POINT

Duane and Merle slept fitfully on sofas in the living room of Ryan Gehrke's suite at the South Point Casino. The suite had two bedrooms and three baths and was comped by management because Ryan was a high roller and a celebrity and brought people to the tables. Malachi Shabazz, Aces of Spade's War Counselor, tossed two blankets at them earlier. Shabazz slumped in a big chair, wearing a pork pie hat, feet on an ottoman, a "Fuck Da Police" shirt stretched tight across his gut, snoring like a portable generator.

Duane's bladder nudged him awake. He got up silently and padded toward the bathroom, eyes on the main door which was barred shut with a table shoved against it. Glasses all over the table. Shaky as he was, he didn't think he could move those glasses without making noise. The drapes were pulled shut to keep out blazing afternoon light.

Poor Merle. She was a dental technician. Duane's teeth

were bad. She pointed that out on their second date. The last time he'd visited a dentist, eight years prior, the dentist had told him he needed fourteen thousand dollars' worth of replacements. He didn't have a thousand. He agreed to see Merle, who rented space in a strip mall near the airport. Merle rode a Shadow 750 and slept in her office. An Army veteran, Merle was about fifty, short and vivacious with long, buttery hair, a butterfly tat on her wrist and a four-leaf clover on her ass.

After examining Duane's teeth, Merle said, "You have about ten teeth left. You need implants. I know a clinic in Monterrey that does good work. Costs one third of what it would in the States."

"I'm a little short on cash," Duane explained. "Would you like a bump?"

Indeed she would. Merle had lost her certification for abusing cocaine.

Duane looked at the door to Ryan's bedroom. It had a separate exit into the hall, but Monique was in there. She might be sleeping. She might be sticking pins in dolls. She claimed to have supernatural powers and Duane believed it. Look what she'd done to Ryan, who used to be a sweet guy. And she'd put a beating on Duane like he hadn't had since he pissed off some cops in Boston. His ribs were on fire from where she'd spin-kicked him, and his left eye was half-closed from one of her lethal punches. Duane had never seen a woman move like that and hoped he would never see it again.

Silent as a professional burglar, Duane opened the door to Ryan's room. Monique lay on her side snoring, her nostrils drawing serrated breaths. Ever so gently, Duane shut the door behind him and stood in the semi-gloom sweeping the room with his eyes. Gold and jewels on the dresser drew him like the scent of blood. He padded over shoeless, and gazed at the collection of gold chains, jewelry, rings, amethysts, diamonds, rubies, pearls, a Rolex, a Chinese panda money clip, two Chinese pandas worth three thousand dollars. Every room had a safe in the closet, but *nahhh*. All those gold chains. Probably put them on all at once. They all looked alike.

He let himself out, softly closing the door, and went into the bathroom off the living room, leaned over the toilet, forehead against the wall for support, and pissed. There was blood in his urine. He looked at himself in the mirror. He looked like shit. He had the crackle finish and jaundiced skin of a heavy smoker and a three-day stubble. He looked like a shit bum. He picked up a jumbo amber plastic pill bottle prescribed for Malachi Shabazz. Valium. Well, all rooty. Duane shook out a dozen and downed two.

He returned to the suite, stood in front of the huge picture window, parted the drapes and looked out over baking flat lands punctuated here and there by gleaming glass cubes, the mountains a purple sine wave behind them. The view would have been terrific but there was nothing to see. The sun hung low in the sky. Duane had been to Vegas many times over the years. Once you got past the glitz of the strip, the fake Eiffel Tower, the Pyramid et al, you realized that it was an artificial city, kept on life support, pumped full of dollars by hedonists who wouldn't know a tree if it bit them in the ass. The skyline was mostly flat stretching west save for a few modest clusters where rose an outlier hotel and casino, like the South Point, which was famous mostly for the annual Stock Horse Show, and the Mecum Auctions. Directly opposite on the northwest edge of the city sat the Golden Nugget, in perfect balance.

Before Ryan met Vigil, back when he was a star wide receiver, beloved of millions, and had not yet weighed in on global crisis, he was a great guy to be around. He'd turned his Miami mansion, in the same neighborhood as Desmond Pow, the kung fu actor, into party central with hot and cold running babes, champagne, chicks, food and coke.

Duane had been his coke supplier.

It was the closest Duane ever came to success.

Duane got the blow from the Goat Heads, an MC from South Miami with close contacts with the Aztecs and other Latino groups, who brought it in via boat, or ran it in from Texas. Many nights Duane had spent at Ryan's place, watching the big man dance, sing, party, and wonder how he could maintain his health and attitude.

Even Duane knew you had to stop doing that shit sooner or later.

One night, Monique Vigil appeared among them like an avenging angel, wearing black yoga pants and a black tank top, snapping and popping like a live wire. She sang and she danced. She'd talk politics at the drop of a match, and she clung to Ryan like a big game hunter clings to his trophy.

Next thing you know, Ryan's kneeling for the National Anthem, he loses all his sponsors, the Dolphins put him on waivers. Vigil tried to get him off the blow, but it was no use. His will was as ferocious as hers, when it came to his addictions. By the time Duane worked up the nerve to say something, Ryan owed him fifty gees, and Vigil was an addict.

"Yeah, yeah, don't worry about it! Make sure you come through for tonight! Gonna have a sweet little Jamaican gal here with your name tattooed on her ass!"

He met Ryan's parents when they came down for the play-offs. They wouldn't remember. It was at the game. They seemed like nice people. Just went to show that even nice people could produce a certified fuck-up, with the best of intentions. All that class and money couldn't buy class and money.

Of course, Ryan was adopted, so it may have been genetics. It had always been Duane's opinion that blacks weren't as smart as whites, and here was proof. You didn't need to be a genius to catch footballs. Ryan had won the lottery of life by being adopted and being the right skin color. As a black athlete, doors opened for him that had never opened for Duane.

Of course, Duane never went out for athletics. He'd dropped out of school in the ninth grade to earn a living.

Now Ryan was gonna flush it all down the toilet because

of that insane Vigil broad. The coke didn't help.

Duane heard voices in the corridor. Seconds later, someone fumbled at the door which banged into the limit of the brass safety guard, knocking glasses to the floor. One shattered.

Pounding.

"Hey! Open the fuck up!"

Shabazz sat bolt upright, went to the door, pulled the table straight back into the room and released the latch. Ryan, Slob, and Malcolm boiled in like bulls in a chute. Slob, the Aces Vice President, weighed four hundred and fifty pounds and rode a Boss Hoss, a huge bike with a V-8 engine. Aces President Malcolm was a bald monster who reminded Duane of Tommy Lister.

Slob and Malcolm wore black leathers. Casino management didn't allow colors on the floor. Ryan wore a turquoise and gold dashiki, gold chains visible around the neck, five pounds of gold on his wrist and hands. He reached into his pockets, pulled out a wad of cash and a bindle of coke.

"SCORRRRRRRRRE!" he sang. "Slob, chop some up, willya?"

Merle sat up, rubbed her eyes and went into the bathroom. Seconds later, Vigil appeared in the door wearing gray sweats with blue stripes.

"The gods are with us!" Ryan exalted, rolling up a hundred-dollar bill.

Duane and Vigil eyed the coke hungrily. When Vigil first showed up, she was all, *oh no you don't! The revolution*

will not happen if you snort that shit up your nose! Within a
week she'd succumbed to coke's siren call and now she was
just like the rest of them. She couldn't wait for her next line.

Duane hovered at the fringes. Ryan looked up, a white
rime around his nostrils.

"What, fuck face, you want a hit? Why the fuck not? I'm
feeling lucky. Give fuck face a line."

Duane hovered over the smeared kitchen plate while
Malcolm rubbed his nose. Ryan's cell phone chimed. He
pulled it out, looked at it.

"Well, well. Look who's here. It's your boy! He musta
done a shit-load of meth."

CHAPTER 22

UP THE ELEVATOR

Josh dreamed he was stuck in France with Fig Newton and the airline kept delaying their flight. One day. Two days. A week. Finally, they got on the plane. The ride was turbulent.

Josh woke up to Hines' prodding.

"Up and at 'em, General Saddam. We're forty miles out of Vegas."

Josh sat up, rubbed his eyes, put on his sunglasses, and looked out the window at the baking expanse. Hines had cranked the AC and the CD, blasting Duke Ellington's "Daybreak Express".

"That music would wake the dead."

"Like your collection, hoss. IHOP next exit. IHOP, si. Hip-Hop, no. I'm hittin' the head and then you can drive."

It was three p.m. when they pulled into the IHOP with four hours to spare. They took a booth and had breakfast.

Josh compulsively stacked plates and jars on the table.

"They won't be expecting you."

"Yeah. What if they see me and say, 'You know what? We told you to come alone so we're just gonna off your old man, how about that?'"

"They ain't gonna do that. Not with what we got."

"Yeah and if they did you wouldn't feel that bad."

The waitress took their orders and called them babe. Josh had lost his appetite. Hines' words were like a punch to the gut.

Lord, I try to be a good person.

Hines jolted as his cell phone beeped. "Goddamn! Every time!" He pulled it out and looked at it. "Gotta take this, hoss. It's Lecia."

Josh pulled out his own phone and turned it on. Lily had left a message. "Please call as soon as you can."

Josh dialed her back. A man answered. "This is Eric Gehrke."

"Professor, it's Josh Pratt returning your call."

"Yes, thank you, Mister Pratt. I want to apologize for any hardship you're experiencing with our son and thank you for reaching out to us."

"What can I do for you, Professor?"

"Well we've had a little time to look at those photos you sent, and I'd like to tell you why it's so important, and why you must turn it over us."

"I'm listening."

"Depending on where it was found, it provides proof that Africans were the first to reach the new land. I don't have to explain to you the implications of such a discovery."

"Do it anyway."

"Given today's heightened political climate, the news that Africans discovered the New World a century before Columbus will lead to social unrest."

"What does it matter if they reached South America first?"

"They may have reached North America first. We won't know until we have an opportunity to examine this monument in person. As Professor of Latin American and African diaspora, I am uniquely suited to analyze such an artifact."

"Why didn't Ryan give it to you?"

Josh heard a slow exhalation.

"That's a legitimate question, and it has to do with his recent radicalization. Lily and I are lifelong registered Democrats and have supported every Democratic initiative. We stand for social justice. He knows I would disseminate this news far and wide. Perhaps he's withholding it to spite me. I don't know what we did to alienate him, Mister Pratt, and that's God's honest truth."

"Are you religious?"

"We attend Trinity Lutheran Church regularly."

"Professor, we're in Las Vegas now and hope to see your son shortly. With any luck, we'll give him the painting and he'll release my father and his girlfriend."

"You're not going to surrender the artifact, are you?"

"We don't plan to, no. I will give your regards to your son."

Josh hung up. His food had arrived. Hines inhaled a four-egg omelet and a rasher of bacon. Hines came up for air.

"Who dat?"

"Ryan's father, history Professor Eric Gehrke. He wants the slab. He wants it bad. Says it may prove Africans discovered North America a hundred years prior to Columbus, and that will lead to war, famine, pestilence and death."

"How dat?"

Josh shrugged. "Fuck if I know."

Hines reached in his pocket and proffered a quarter, head side up. "Lookee here."

"Yeah. So? Is that your tip?"

"Turn it over."

Josh picked it up and turned it over. DISTRICT OF COLUMBIA, with an embossed portrait of a man standing next to a grand piano. "Duke Ellington" was written on the piano.

"Sweet. I'm waiting for Hendrix."

"No, mon, you don't get it. That's a magic quarter. We're going to arrive early so I can play the slots."

"Are you shitting me? The slots are your worst odds! Blackjack is the best."

"I know that, but I won't be gambling. Trust me."

When the waitress brought the check, Hines tried to grab it, but Josh was too fast for him. "You're my employee. You don't pay for anything."

"Well then let's stop by the Harley-Davidson place."

Their drive took them down the famous strip. It was stop and go traffic all the way. Tourists, hustlers, and trade persons filled the baking sidewalks. Batman and Superman worked diagonal corners. Elderly women walked tiny dogs, stooping to retrieve their droppings. A compact Elvis huckstered outside the Hard Rock. It was Elvis in a funhouse mirror, about five and a half feet, thick neck, thick torso, thick legs, and a pompadour that rose like a mighty wave.

"Tonight only, the world's greatest Elvis tribute act, endorsed by Graceland itself, starring the one, the only, Slack Joseph, tickets are going fast! Thank you very much!"

They pulled into the South Point two hours ahead of schedule and parked way in back. A uniformed security officer rode up on a bicycle.

"You gentlemen visiting the casino or staying at the hotel?"

"We're here to try our hands at games of chance," Hines said.

"Very good." He pedaled off.

"Hmm, mmm, mmm," Hines said.

He tucked the painting under one arm, the cast iron grill in his grip. They walked around to the main entrance, past a Bugatti Veyron sitting on the lip. Inside, the casino stretched before them, a video game come to life. Ready Player One. Josh wondered what it would be like to drop acid and just watch.

"Ahmina visit the shipping office to repackage this, make it look it wasn't opened."

"Okay. I'll be over there in that lounge."

The Grandview Lounge, behind one of many bars, featured Wes Winters, a combination Little Richard, Jerry Lee Lewis, Barry Manilow and Bette Midler. Josh got a Coke from the bar and sat in back, surveying a field of blue hairs, lounge lizards, and cowboys.

Wearing a gold lame jacket, Wes Winters played "Good Golly Miss Molly" standing, shaking his booty, singing to a table of four little old ladies near the stage who blushed and cooed. He sang "Summertime Blues", "Walk On By" and "Sea Cruise".

Josh got a refill and looked at his watch. He could phone Ryan anytime. Hines returned with the painting and a shit-eating grin.

"Wha'd I tell you? After I got this baby ready to go, I hit the quarter slots, primed it five times and when the stars aligned, I played my Duke. Well guess what?"

"You won the jackpot."

"Correctomundo! Nine thousand dollars!"

"In quarters?"

"I cashed 'em in. But I kept this." He held up the shiny quarter.

"Is it the same one?"

"Does it matter?"

"I'm phoning Ryan now. You ready?"

"Do it."

Josh walked out of the lounge, out the side door and made his call from the parking lot. It was dusk and in the sixties.

"Yeah?"

"Josh Pratt. I'm here."

"Did you bring the painting?"

"I said I would."

"Come on up. Suite One Two Two Four."

Josh nodded. The casino was an unreality game, a candy war zone, all flash and hustle. They passed lizard-skinned veterans with paper cups filled with tokens, ashtrays overflowing with butts, construction workers in CAT hats, kids on college break, old bikers wearing Harley Davidson shirts. Santa Fe Harley Davidson. Thunder Road Harley Davidson. Lake Mills Harley Davidson. Josh and Hines got on the elevator with five other people. It stopped on the third floor and a man smoking a cigarette got on. Hines reached over, plucked the fag from his lips and crushed it between thumb and forefinger. The red-faced cowboy rounded, got a look at Hines, and turned his back. He got off on the tenth.

"Thank you," a woman said, getting off on the eleventh.

The twelfth-floor lobby was Southwest elegant with Kachina dolls, Navajo rugs and pottery. Only ten doors extended from this wing.

Josh knocked on 1224, which opened in the hand of a huge black man wearing a black leather vest. He motioned Josh and Hines inside.

Gehrke looked up from the table, nose dripping, and glared at Hines.

"Who the fuck is this?"

CHAPTER 23

A TENSE EXCHANGE

"Did you expect me to drive non-stop for forty-eight hours?"

"What the fuck is he doing in my suite?" Gehrke said, rising. He was even more intimidating in person than on television, a huge guy with a long Roman nose, high cheek-bones and a wide mouth, sporting a mid-sized 'fro.

Hines handed him the wrapped painting. "I'm Bobby Hines, National Enforcer for the Jugan."

Gehrke stared, dumb and furious. Malachi Shabazz tapped him on the shoulder and whispered something in his ear. Josh turned to Duane.

"You okay?"

Duane pointed to Vigil, standing hip shot, radiating attitude. "That bitch beat me up."

Josh laughed.

Gehrke set the package on the table. "The Jugan, huh? I hear you're some kind of bad ass dudes."

"We have a code, same as you."

Gehrke dipped into the pocket of his hoodie and brought out a compact automatic. "I told this dumb motherfucker to come alone. I ought to kill you both right now. What's to stop me?"

"Look here, Ryan," Duane said. "You said you wanted the painting back! You don't got to turn this into murder."

"Shut the fuck up, you fuckin' cocksucker. We wouldn't be in this situation of you hadn't ripped me off."

Duane got hot. "We wouldn't be in this situation if you'd paid me what you fuckin' owe me!"

Vigil slapped Duane hard. Josh stood cold as ice. Duane touched his cheek and gave him a what the fuck look.

Shabazz took off his hat and held it upside down. "Phones."

"What?" Josh said.

Shabazz shook the hat. "PHONES!"

"He don't want you recordin' shit," Duane said.

Josh and Hines dug out their phones and dropped them in the hat. Shabazz left the room with them.

"Hey man," Hines said. "Watched you rush for one hundred and ten yards against Pittsburgh. I was a big fan 'til you took that knee."

"Fuck you. Yeah, I've heard of the Jugan. You're all veterans, so what? All veterans of foreign wars where you bomb mosques and weddings and send drones after children. How many children you kill, big man?"

"I only killed enemy combatants. I don't expect you to

understand what the national anthem means to a patriot. I don't expect you to be grateful for your blessings. But is it too much to ask you to show a little respect for your fans?"

"Fuck you talkin' about?"

"Most football fans are decent patriotic Americans. They tune in to see a game. They want to have fun. It ain't the place for your signifyin'."

"Yeah, fuck you."

Josh wondered if bringing Hines was a good idea.

Gehrke smirked. "You know what? You a house nigger."

"Put that gun down and lets you and me go at it."

"I'd be lyin' if I said I didn't want that. But right now is all about business. Maybe you and me can hook up down the road." He turned to Duane. "Get the fuck outta here. I better not see you again. Take that skank with you."

Josh held out his hand. "Phones."

Gehrke nodded. "Oh yeah." He went into the next room and returned with their phones.

Duane and Merle grabbed their bags and left with Josh and Hines. They got on the elevator.

"If he thinks this is over," Duane said, "he's got another think comin'. No one can treat my girl like that."

"Can it, Duane," Josh said.

Duane grinned like a Lotto winner. "Wha'd I tell you? Did my boy come through big time or not?"

Josh slugged him in the jaw. Duane fell to floor of the elevator and looked up, anger sparking.

"Whadja do that for?"

"That's for using my house to hide your stolen shit."

Merle helped Duane to his feet. "Don't be like that, Josh. Duane loves you. He told me all about you." The elevator stopped on the fifth floor for an elderly couple. Nobody spoke the rest of the way down. The couple scrunched into a corner, as far as they could get from the others. The door opened on the main floor and the couple fled.

Josh strode toward the casino. "We'll drop you some-place down the road. I'll give you some money. I don't want to hear from you again."

Merle, a short plump woman with a pretty face, blonde hair in a ponytail, struggled to catch up. She put her hand on Josh's shoulder.

"I know he's not perfect, but he's a good man! He's changed! He told me how you changed, why can't he change?"

"He hasn't changed." They strode through the casino past the blackjack tables, the roulette wheel, the poker corral, and hundreds of slot machines: *Mega Moolah*, *King Cashalot*, *Game of Thrones*, *Gonzo's Quest*, *When Pigs Fly*, *Voodoo Candy Shop*, and *Big Bad Wolf*.

Hines stopped at *Jimi Hendrix*. "Hold on, man, omma pitch a buck."

"Bobby, we got to get out of here before they open that painting!"

Bobby slid a dollar into the slot. "One second." He pushed the button. The icons swirled round and round and stopped on two Jimis and a Janis. The slot sang and flashed and registered two hundred and twenty-five dollars. Hines pushed the button for the receipt.

"Come on!" Josh said.

"Go on, I'll catch up with you."

There was nothing Josh could do except grab Duane by the arm and march him toward the exit. They were halfway across the lot when Hines caught up with them, panting slightly, waving a wad of cash.

"Is this a great country, or what?"

Josh beeped open the car and opened the trunk. Duane put his and Merle's bags in. Hines got in front, while Duane and Merle got in back. Hines brought his seat forward six inches to make room for Merle's feet. They left the parking lot, got on State Highway Ninety-Three and headed for the Hoover Dam.

"Duane tell you how he saved all your news pieces? He printed them out and keeps them in a big folder."

"Yeah," Duane said. "What happened to all those articles? I wanted to show a friend what a big stud you are, so I went on the internet and they'd all disappeared."

"I had a friend delete them."

"Delete them? You can do that? Could you delete, like, my credit history?"

"I can't do shit. I had a friend do it. I really don't want to hear from you, Duane."

Merle leaned forward and swatted Josh on the shoulder. "Shame on you! The Lord says you should honor your mother and father!"

"I never knew my mother, and my father dumped me at a Bosselman's truck stop when I was fifteen. He tell you that?"

"The Lord wants you to forgive him."

Josh white knuckled the wheel and kept his eyes on the road. Hines turned on the radio and searched until he found a jazz station out of the University of Nevada playing Oscar Peterson, "Nica's Dream."

"My man Oscar," Hines said.

"Christ, what is that cocktail music? Find some country," Duane said. "Find some Hank Williams or Johnny Cash."

Hines swiveled in his seat and looked at Duane who tried to meet his gaze, then looked out the window. "You'd best zip it, my man."

A half hour later they approached the dam. Even at this hour of night, there were tourists parked on either side, out of their cars taking pictures. The dam was lit up like a Hollywood premiere. Since nine/eleven, there were NHP cars parked on either side. They crossed without incident, pulled off the Interstate in Henderson and went through a Wendy's drive through. Josh paid the bill. The car smelled of fresh French Fries. Josh gulped his cheeseburger, slugged his coke, and pulled back onto the highway. The sooner he got to Denver, the sooner he'd be rid of Duane. They barreled east through the night, stars gleaming in the distance. How brighter would the stars be if all the vehicles turned off their headlights? Lights streaming toward them on the left side of the highway showed a half dozen hues from familiar old yellow to the cool new blue that had become the standard for modern vehicles. The Chrysler had cool blue headlights.

Josh was still chewing when he looked in the rear view. At least a half dozen motorcycle headlights loomed, coming up fast.

"They opened the painting," he said.

CHAPTER 24

HIGHWAY JOUST

Josh wasn't certain they were Aces until two pulled up on either side of the car and wanged on the fenders with hammers. He floored it, the big Chrysler bellowed and surged ahead. In the rear view, the bikes all pulled over to the right to make room for a pickup truck coming up fast on the left with its brights on. They weren't stupid enough to try and stop a two-ton car with bikes alone. It was a Dodge Ram riding on oversized tires and wheels with the hood scoop and the hemi. The passenger side window lowered, and a shotgun barrel rested on the sill.

"Shotgun," Josh said, braking and swerving to the right as a flash ignited the night and pellets pinged off his A pillar.

"Did you bring a gun?" Hines said.

"No. Did you?"

"It's in the trunk."

Ahead, the truck slowed to the right. Josh couldn't

stop. The bikers were right behind him. In the mirror he saw two semis hauling ass at eighty miles per hour to pass. As they pulled adjacent, only twenty feet separated them. Both trucks were painted with red and yellow Continental Movers livery. Josh waited for the first to pass, stood on the accelerator and jerked left, pulling in five feet from the first's rear bumper, using the truck's wake to pull him along. The truck behind him leaned on the air horns and flashed his brights, but for the time being they were shielded from the bikers. That wouldn't last long. The driver in the second truck saw the Aces swooping and veered into the right lane just ahead of them, forcing the bikers to brake hard. One ran off the highway into the ditch.

"How'd they find us?" Hines said.

"They must have planted a bug on Duane," Josh said.

"A bug? Where?"

"Search your shit," Hines commanded. "It may be in your bag."

"My bag's in the trunk."

Merle raised the center armrest, opened her purse and set items on the seat between them. Tissue, keys, phone, lipstick, compact, lighter, pack of American Spirits, two pens, some cat treats, her wallet. She unzipped the little side pockets and pulled out more tissue, aspirin, an amber vial and a bottle of Mydol. She held up a black plastic rectangle the size of a stamp.

"What's this? This isn't mine."

Hines held out his hand.

"Pliers in the glove box," Josh said.

The truckers had had enough. They both started pulling to the side of the road and had probably called the police. Josh veered into the left lane and gunned it, watching the needle climb past one hundred miles per hour. Where was a cop when you needed one? The bikers and the Ram convoyed directly behind, the truck's passenger side window still open.

Hines crushed the black rectangle revealing tiny circuitry. He threw it out the window.

"We're still gonna have to search the rest of their shit."

Josh checked the rear view. He checked it every couple of seconds. He'd always done that. He saw the red and blue strobing lights an instant before he heard the wail and whoop of sirens. There were too many cop cars to count. The Ram gunned it, blowing past the Chrysler at over a hundred. It had no rear lights. Josh slowed and pulled over a hundred feet ahead of the Aces, who all pulled over as other police vehicles arrived. A sheriff's deputy stopped in front of Josh. Another rolled to a stop behind him. He counted at least four more vehicles back with the bikers.

He had the window down and his license ready when the deputy approached, covered by his partner who stood behind and to the right, hand on the butt of his gun.

The lead deputy shined his light just below the driver's window. "Please lower all your windows."

Josh complied. The deputy shined the light on Hines, Merle, and Duane before returning to Josh. "License and registration."

Josh handed them over. The deputy looked at them, then to his partner behind the car. "Carl?"

The deputy, whose name tag said Ruiz, handed the items to Carl. "Run it."

As Carl returned to the squad car, Ruiz said, "Do you know why I stopped you?"

"We were trying to get away from those bikers, sir."

"Any idea why they were chasing you?"

"No, sir."

"Do you know how fast you were going?"

"No, sir."

"Everybody please step out of the vehicle and stand on the passenger side with your hands in open sight. I need everybody's identification."

"Why?" Duane whined. "We ain't done nothin'. Sure, you can ask the driver, but what probable cause do you have to hassle us?"

Josh wanted to kick him, but Hines and Merle stood between them. The deputy shined his light in Duane's face.

"You first."

"Fuck," Duane muttered, and Josh knew he had outstanding warrants.

Josh should have checked. The truth was, he didn't want to know. Now they were in for it. Now the deputies would call for the drug dog, search the vehicle, find the slab, find Hines' gun. They'd arrest Duane for sure, and possibly the rest of them. Hines hadn't said whether he had a CC permit and Josh hadn't asked. He wondered if Fleiss would be up by the time he was allowed to make his phone call. It was already past ten at night.

Carl returned scratching his head, spoke quietly in his partner's ear. Taylor eyeballed Josh. Josh hoped to God they didn't know who he was.

Finally, Taylor spoke. "All right, this is how it's going to be. We're going to call for a drug dog, and we're going to wait here outside the car for it to arrive. You may or may not have anything to do with that biker gang, but we're going to find out."

"Who are they, officer?" Josh said.

"Well maybe you've heard of them since you're a biker yourself."

Fuck! Josh thought.

Taylor turned toward Hines. "And you, Mister Hines. You're a member of the Jugan MC, isn't that right?"

Hines nodded. "Yes, sir, I am."

"I see that you have a distinguished service record. I respect that. But when I look at this little group, I just have trouble picturing you all in the same car." He shined the light on Duane and Merle. "Especially you two."

"He's my father," Josh said.

"Ahuh. Well he's under arrest."

"What for?" Duane howled.

Taylor pulled out the cuffs. "Failure to pay child support, income tax evasion, and cruelty to animals, among other things."

"I never shot that fuckin' dog!" Duane howled.

Two reports, like lady fingers, occurred behind them, by the side of the highway, followed instantly by a half dozen more. White flares pierced the darkness as the Aces of Spade drew down on the Arizona Highway Patrol. It was the Fourth of July. Let freedom ring.

Ruiz looked at Carl, back at his prisoners. They ran toward their squad car.

CHAPTER 25

FLAGSTAFF

Josh, Hines, Duane and Merle leaped into the Chrysler. Josh peeled out, unconsciously counting off the gear changes in the five-speed automatic. Whirrrrrrrr, ka-chung! Whirrrrrr-rrr, ka-chung! It only had five speeds. Soon they were going one hundred and forty miles per hour, flashing around other vehicles while more emergency vehicles strobed the other way. The fuzzbuster wailed like a banshee. Hines wrenched it from its perch and tossed it out the window.

"Slow the fuck down," Hines said.

Josh took his foot off the accelerator.

"I say we get the hell outta here!" Duane declared. "Them po-po ain't payin' attention to us. They're all runnin' to the shootin'."

"Maybe," Hines said. "But we don't have to tempt fate."

Josh slowed to seventy-five and let a hotshot in a Lexus pass.

"I taught that kid how to drive!"

"You didn't teach me shit. The Bedouins taught me how to drive. The Bedouins were more of a family to me than you ever were. You couldn't even get your shit together to come down to the school and sign a fuckin' paper, so I could be a student!"

Merle put a hand on Duane's arm, knowing from experience how futile that was.

"That's a fine way for you to talk to your father! I clothed you and fed you up until that time you left me..."

"You left me?!"

"Whoah there, hoss," Hines said. "You're veering all over the road. Maybe I should drive."

They traveled in silence, save for the thrumming of the big Continentals on the pavement. A green highway sign said REST AREA, 1/2 MILE. Josh took the exit and pulled into the brightly lit parking lot of an Arizona Department of Tourism Rest Stop. Pulling between a massive Winnebago and a Coronado towing a Corolla, Josh got out, slammed the door, and stalked toward the facility.

Hines turned and pointed his massive finger at Duane. "You keep your fuckin' mouth shut, or I'll shut it for you."

Duane glowered and cowered. "Fuckin' coon," he muttered.

"What did you say?"

Merle opened the door. "Come on, Duane. Let's take a break." She pulled him from the vehicle and marched him toward the desert.

The adobe-style visitor center had a sand garden punctured with cacti. The night smelled of mesquite and creosote. You couldn't see the stars because of the glare. Josh stormed through the brightly lit foyer, where a half dozen travelers were eying brochures or watching videos, went in the men's room, found an empty stall, went in, shut the door, and relieved himself, fuming. Gangbangers had engraved their handles on the stainless-steel walls. MURDRINC, SASK-WATCH, SHRED HUSTL.

"Why am I even doing this?" he said.

He owed his father nothing, except life.

"Well my daddy left home when I was three," Josh sang. "And he didn't leave much to my momma and me."

He zipped up, stepped out and washed his hands. "Well, I grew up quick and I grew up mean.

My fists got hard and my wits got keen. Roam from town to town to hide my shame. But I made me a vow to the moon and stars. I'd search the honky-tonks and bars. And kill that man who gave me that awful name."

An old trucker one sink over, wearing a Ford cap, looked over. "That's damn good!"

Josh smiled and stopped singing. "Thanks."

He tore off a paper towel. *Bzzzt*. He tore off another. *Bzzzt*. He tore off another.

"You sing it like you mean it!"

"I do mean it," Josh said, tossing the towels into the bin. He went out the exit opposite the highway, across the parking lot, past the bikes and cars, past the semis in the outer circle, past a drainage ditch out into the desert. He walked a hundred yards into the desert and stood with his back to the visitor center staring up at the sky, listening to the swoosh of traffic. At least out here, you could see the stars. The Milky Way splashed across the sky reminding Josh of his insignificance.

He heard someone cough. Turned and it was Merle, lighting a cigarette.

"You're a good son."

Josh barked. "You mean I'm a good son for not killing him."

"You talk tough, but I can see you're a good man."

"You see that in Duane?"

She sighed. "He's all I got."

"You can do better."

"Duane took me in when no one else would. I have two kids, you know. The ex got sole custody because at the time I was having a lot of problems."

"Merle, sooner or later, everything Duane touches turns to shit. You'd be smart to walk away."

"I know you believe that. I wish I had you in my life. How bad can Duane be if he has a son like you?"

Josh took out a card and handed it to her. "Let me know if there's anything I can do that does not involve Duane."

She tucked it away.

As he walked back to the truck stop, Merle joined him, ditching her cigarette.

When they returned the car, Hines was sitting behind

the wheel and Duane was in back.

"Where the hell you been?" Duane said to Merle as she got in the car.

"Just catching a smoke, Duane. Don't get bent out of shape."

"We got enough gas to get us to Flagstaff," Hines said, backing out of the place. "Try to get some sleep. All of you."

"They gotta know about this car," Josh said.

"Yeah, but we ain't a priority right now so let's get the fuck outta Dodge."

Hines set the cruise control at two miles over the limit, while other cars routinely passed them. He twisted the radio this way and that, swore softly at the dearth of listenable music, and cued up the six-disc player in the dash. Toby Keith. So be it.

Josh turned around. "How much of that five grand you got left?"

Duane eyed him suspiciously. "Why? You want it back now?"

"He blew it all," Merle said.

Duane stared out the window.

"You better not be using stolen credit cards," Josh snapped. "You dumb son of a bitch, you are, aren't you? You think the owners haven't reported those? You think they ain't keeping track of you?"

"Not your problem. Maybe you could give your old man another five grand and I'll get out of your hair. I promise you, you'll never hear from me again."

"You sound like my ex-wife," Hines said.

Josh slept. When he woke it was four-thirty in the morning and Hines was pulling into the Satellite Truck Stop amid the land yachts and honking semis. Josh sat up, turned around. Duane and Merle were slumped together like two bananas. Hines pulled up next to a fuel island. When he shut off the engine, they could hear Duane and Merle snoring. His was a snork, hers was a sigh. Hines used his credit card to free the premium, stood with arms crossed while the car sucked forty nine dollars out of his pocket, replaced the nozzle, got back in and parked the car in shadow next to a dark blue Chrysler that was nearly identical.

Hines got out. "Let's go."

"Better not leave Duane here with the slab. Better take him with us."

Hines thought a minute, then nodded.

Josh pulled Merle's leg.

"Huh?" she said, opening her eyes.

"Come on. We're going in the restaurant. I'll buy you an early breakfast."

Duane dutifully followed them inside. While Hines hit the head, Josh, Duane and Merle grabbed a booth. A waitress named Lucille took their orders. Josh ordered Hines a four-egg omelet and when the big man returned, Josh hit the head. He always checked the floor for the urinal with the least pooling.

Seconds later, Duane followed him in, took the next urinal, and stood there pissing.

"You have a right to be mad at me."

Josh looked around. They were alone. "Tell me something."

"What?"

"Did you know there was something inside that painting when you stole it?"

"Huh?"

They went to the sinks. "You heard me."

"I don't know what you're talkin' about. I took it 'cuz I knew he liked it and it was worth a lot of money."

"You didn't think the painting was a little heavy?"

"What are you talkin' about?" The light went on in Duane's eyes. "Wait a minute. What was in it?"

The door opened inward and a trucker built like a bulldozer, wearing Osh Kosh B'Gosh coveralls, walked in quickly, took a stall and locked the door.

Josh and Duane got out of there.

"If there's something in there, I want a piece. I deserve a piece. It was my idea."

Josh was afraid to look at him, afraid what he might do. "I'm dropping you and your girlfriend in Denver. You can take a flight anywhere. If I ever see you again, I'll phone the cops. You know I've killed a shitload of men. That's my gift to you as a son."

They ate their meal in silence.

CHAPTER
26

BEGINNINGS

Heading north on Twenty-Five out of Albuquerque they passed and were passed by numerous motorcycle clubs. No Aces. The firefight at Boulder City instantly shut down all Spade activities. Every Ace that wasn't in police custody had gone to ground.

The black Ram had passed them doing one forty.

Ryan was still at large, or they would have heard about it. Newscasters described it as a "coordinated bust against outlaw cycle gang Ace of Spades, in the planning for months." Josh laughed when he heard that.

"It's Aces, you morons."

Josh pulled into Egan's Truck Stop and Restaurant in Pueblo, Colorado, at four in the afternoon. It had sixteen islands and every one was busy. Josh and Hines stood by the pump while Duane and Merle headed for the rambling structure.

"They might have another bug," Hines said.

Josh spat. "You want to strip search him?"

"He ain't stupid. He can search his own damn self."

"We're dropping them off in Denver and then I don't want to ever see him again. I have work to do."

"What's this job?"

Josh told him about Hotchkiss.

"Oh yeah. They was s'posed to be building a vee-four mystery bike way before Ducati, back in the nineties or something."

The pump clicked to a halt. Josh printed out a receipt and stuck it in his back pocket. Force of habit. He saved every receipt and put them in a big plastic box as soon as he got home. His accountant loved him. He moved the car to a spot and he and Hines went into the store, the standard formica-floored, glaring, garish display of souvenir key chains, post cards, Slim Jims, Trident chewing gum, greasy dwarf peanuts, mouthwash and engine oil with adjunct restaurant, visible through Spanish arch in *faux* adobe wall, where truckers sat at rustic tables and read from laminated menus with cacti on the covers.

No Duane or Merle. Maybe they were still in the restrooms. Josh bought a chocolate milk, picked up an auto flyer with a bike section, went back to the car to wait for the others. Out of the corner of his eye he saw Duane come around the corner, a hundred feet distant, wiping his nose, followed seconds later by Merle. Like they were fooling anyone. Duane's lack of self-control disgusted him, not to mention that Josh used to do a lot of meth and blow, and that it made you crazy, you had to piss all the time, and you had to have a new bump every hour.

Hines was last, with a six pack of energy drinks and a couple magazines in a bag.

"Duane says you have a dog," Merle said. "What kind?"

"Fig is a German shepherd/border collie mix."

"I love dogs. I had one up until last year when my dear Nellie died. She was a Labrador, twelve years old. I want to get another one, but I don't know where I'm going to live."

Duane put his arm around her shoulder. "Don't you worry about that, little lady. I got a few ideas."

"I got Nellie from an animal shelter. Where did you get Fig?"

"Jerell Moore. Dude I know in Milwaukee."

"Oh, I wish I could see her."

"I've got pictures on my phone. I'll show you when we stop."

"She's a real sweet dog," Duane added. "Took to me right off."

Josh held his tongue.

"I taught Josh everything he knows about fighting."

"Oh, for fuck's sake!"

"Didn't I tell you to always stand up to a bully? Didn't I tell you to get in the first shot?"

"You taught me shit! I learned more from a Chuck Norris movie! *The Hitman*."

"I distinctly remembering teaching you how to box, me

down on my knees..."

"Oh, blow it out your ass, Duane! You scored meth back at the truck stop, didn't you? I can see it in your fucking eyes. After I asked you to keep it clean? You just can't help yourself, can you? I did that shit for about two years before I wised up. I got my brains from my mother, but neither one of us knows who she is, isn't that right, Duane?"

"I don't know what you're talking about. I was snuffling because I'm allergic to something."

"Yeah. Work."

Hines swiveled slowly, aimed a knackwurst-sized finger at Duane. "Shut the fuck up."

"Or what? You gonna hit me? I been hit by better men than you."

Merle put her hand on Duane's shoulder. "I think you've said enough."

Duane shrugged her off, crossed his arms, and stared out the window at the sere landscape. They were in Colorado, but the mountains were a long way off. Hines gently lowered his seat back and dozed. Josh found KUVO, Cedar Walton live in Rome. They were still on that piano kick.

Josh nursed an ember of hate for his old man, not hearing the music, driving automatically. Yet the Lord told him to honor his mother and father and turn the other cheek. Bam. Paradigm shift. So he had a shitty dad, so what. At least he was alive, healthy, doing what he liked.

Thank you, Lord, for my manifest blessings.

He'd bounced around from foster home to foster home.

It was at his third foster home that he decided he wanted to be a biker. The Workas were decent, hard-working, Lord-fearing people who'd taken him in despite three kids of their own, including Johnny Worka, his own age. And Johnny had a friend. And his friend had a mini-bike, one of those fifty cubic centimeter deals the Shriners rode, and he rode it up and down the dirt road past the Worka house, and Josh wanted it so bad he ripped the friend right off the bike as he rode by, sending the bike into the ditch where it died. Josh was on that bike in an instant, pushing it down the road to jump start it.

The Workas traded him in the next day.

He'd been kicked out of his last foster home and been living on the streets since he was seventeen. He was eighteen, sharing a flat with a teenage male hustler on Ninety-First Street in Milwaukee, in an old four-story brick building called The Shelton, across the street from Schlotzky's Tavern, making rent by breaking into parked cars, stealing and fencing whatever he could find. He rolled drunks as they came home from the bars late at night. As he shoved them to the ground or tripped them, he saw Duane.

One night through open windows he heard that highway sound, the shriek of straight pipe vee-twins coming down the street, revving outside his second-story balcony, backing up to the curb in front of Schlotzky's. There were four chops already there when they pulled in. Six more backed up to the curb. Josh leaned over. Josh gaped. He looked up, seeing the tower of St. Patrick's Cathedral, and beyond that downtown Milwaukee lit like heaven's mirage. Milwaukee was a Catholic city. Milwaukee was a blue-collar city. Milwaukee was the most segregated city in the United States. Milwaukee was home of Harley-Davidson. Josh threw on his cheap tennies and flew out the door.

In the excitement and confusion of a typical Friday night, he entered Schlotzky's, got a beer, and eavesdropped from the end stool, ten feet from where the Bedouins played pool. There were four of them wearing colors. Their design showed an Arab in flowing headdress riding a chop. They smelled of fuel, engine oil, body odor, tobacco. They joked and joshed and used a secret language all their own.

A tall Bedouin with Goose stitched in red script on his filthy denim vest plugged the juke. Smokey Robinson and the Miracles sang "Soulful Shack". A hulking dude in a leather vest with an exaggerated Elvis-like pompadour, got up from his booth halfway to the front, sauntered back, and kicked the jukebox which skipped, segueing into the next selection, TOP's "In the Slot". The dude canceled it, fed in his own coins. AC/DC's "Highway to Hell".

"Don't play that nigger shit in here," snarled the dude, returning to his seat, showing his back. His colors said Road Rascals. The bottom rocker said Racine. The design showed an Ed "Big Daddy" Roth type monster on a bike with a hand shifter.

Goose's jaw dropped. He looked mouth opened. *Can you believe this shit?* Brick held up his hands. *Watcha gonna do?* Larry, the fourth Bedouin, laid his pool stick on the table and stared hard.

Goose was ready to go. He took off his vest so it wouldn't get blood on it and headed toward the front when a man with close-cropped hair, a face like a clenched fist and a denim vest that said PRESTO/SGT AT ARMS, gripped him and pulled him back. Thick. Presto was thick. With his castle-top cut, he was a walking rock formation. They conferred. Goose looked in the mirror at the booth where the hulk sat with three more Road Rascals, eying him back. Goose and Presto had words. Presto threw his arms around Goose's shoulder and led him back to his table, the way a good cattle dog herds a bull, joining two other Bedouins. Josh followed like a spotlight.

Presto turned to Josh.

"What are you staring at?"

"How do I get to be a Bedouin? Do I gotta have a bike?"

CHAPTER
27

INITIATION

The Bedouins laughed. Presto gazed open-mouthed, at a loss for words. "How old are you, bwah?"

"I'm eighteen."

"So, you want to be a Bedouin, huh?"

"Yeah. The moment I heard you guys coming up the street I thought, that's it. That's what I.want to do. Ride a chopper and raise hell."

"Just now?"

"Yeah. I'm at that age, y'know, where I got to consider what I'm going to do with my life."

"All of us have real time jobs. I own a body shop. Goose is a roofer. Being a biker doesn't pay the rent. You even ride a bike?"

"Well yeah, I've ridden bikes."

"What'd you ride?"

"I rode a Honda 400."

"That's a mighty big bike."

"You guys all ride Harleys?"

"'Cept for Bear, who rides a Victory, 'cause he's a rebel, AIN'T THAT RIGHT, BEAR?"

Bear, a scrawny fucker bending over his pool cue, looked up. He had sideburns and a nose like a conning tower.

"WHAT?"

"I SAID YOU WERE A REBEL."

"FUCK AN A, BOB."

Presto turned back to Josh. "What's your name?"

"Josh Pratt."

Presto examined Josh's face the way you might a painting. "Where'd you get those scars?"

Josh unconsciously ran a finger down the line splitting his brow. "I was in a fight."

"Well, Josh Pratt, let me buy you a beer and we'll talk about it."

Presto and Goose sat at a round table on a round base that still managed to wobble. Presto caught the pert brunette bartender's eye and signaled for three beers. She nodded.

"What are you ridin'?"

"Ain't ridin' shit," Josh responded. "But it's what I want to do."

"Well what are you gonna do about that?"

The waitress set three big glasses of dark beer on the table. Presto gave her twenty.

"Thanks, Debs."

"Anytime, big guy," Debs said, breezing back behind the

counter.

Presto picked up his beer and drained half. Josh did the same. Presto set down his beer with a thunk. Josh did the same.

"The question is, how do you intend to obtain a bike? You got any money?"

"No."

"You got a job?"

"No."

"How do you support yourself?"

"I hustle."

"One thing you need to know, we're men of character. We may drink, smoke, and snort a little, but we're all about helping people. First, we help ourselves. Then, we help others, especially those who can't help themselves. So, what in God's green earth leads you to believe that you should ride with the Bedouins?"

Josh projected his gaze like a laser to the back of Presto's skull. "It was what I was born to do."

Presto tried a stone-face but cracked after a few seconds. Goose laughed too. Everyone looked over.

"What?" demanded Brick.

Presto pointed at Josh. "See this kid? Says he was born to ride with the Bedouins! How do you like them apples? Tell 'em your name."

"Josh Pratt."

"So how you gonna get a bike."

"I ain't chose my hustle yet."

Presto swiveled beaming. "HE AIN'T CHOSE HIS HUSTLE! And tell me what you'll do, Josh, to get with the Bedouins?"

"Anything you say."

"JOSH WILL DO ANYTHING I SAY! Brethren, I put it before the council. What should Josh do to join the Bedouins?"

Goose nudged Presto with an elbow like the corner of a Saarianan end table, whispered something behind his hand and winked at Josh. Presto's eyes lit up. Everyone in the bar was watching. The television hummed in the background, some basketball game. You could hear the sportscaster's excitement as Mike drove for the lay-up.

"You see that big greasy fuck who doesn't like Motown? Throw him out."

Josh looked at the hulking dude, who looked back, his greased hair reflecting the light behind the bar. The Road Rascals said things out of the sides of their mouths while hands reached into jacket pockets. The rest of the bar waited in a state of muted excitement. This is why they came. Money changed hands. Josh got that feeling he always got before a fight, equal parts excitement and fear. A black playground pal had taught him a few moves derived from kung fu movies and magazines. Josh was always looking for an opportunity to try his moves.

Presto and the Bedouins eyed him expectantly.

Josh stood and walked straight for the exit as if he'd been rejected. He stopped abruptly at the Rascals' table like he'd just remembered something, turned and stuck out his right hand to the pompadour.

"Josh Pratt," he said.

The dude, who looked like a tall Spain Rodriguez, took his hand. Josh gripped the man's index and middle finger with his left hand, rotated them counter clockwise while popping the man's right elbow up with Josh's right hand, controlling the big man like a forklift until he stood on his toes, trying to relieve the pressure in his fingers.

"FUCK—OW!"

Josh led him out of the bar onto the broad front porch, the bar boiling out behind them. As soon as Josh released the man's fingers, he swung, but Josh ducked under, throwing his elbow into the dude's liver, grabbed him by his duck tail with his left hand, and slammed his face into his knee. As soon as the music lovers moved to get Josh, the Bedouins were all over them, kicking in their knees from behind, grabbing their heads, shoving them into each other.

The pert brunette came out. "Boys, Hank says if you don't knock it off, he's calling the cops."

The Road Rascals formed a tight little group like snarling pit bulls, but they were outnumbered, and the crowd was not with them.

"Fuck off, you racist pigs," somebody said.

The Road Rascals left, holding their extended middle fingers behind them.

The guy with the pomp cupped hand to mouth. "This ain't over, you cocksuckers."

"We'll catch you down the road, camel fuckers," said another.

They got on their chops, rose up, jumped down, shook the earth and departed.

The Bedouins back-slapped Josh into the bar. Somebody thrust a drink in his hand. He stared at his left hand where he'd grabbed that guy by the hair. Someone handed him a napkin. A girl with blonde hair, wearing a short denim dress smiled at him and ran her tongue along her teeth.

"Where'd you learn to do that?" Presto sprayed.

"Dude did it to me once. I learn something every time I fight."

"You get in a lot of fights?"

"Some."

Presto looked up and around. "Whaddaya think? Should we make this guy a prospect?"

"Fuck yeah!"

"Why not?"

"Lookin' good."

"Soulful Shack" blasted from the juke.

Presto turned back to Josh. "Well I guess we'd better find you a bike."

CHAPTER

28

DENVER, THEN STERLING

Sullen and brooding, Duane hadn't said a word in hours while Merle fussed over him like he was a long-haired cat, dividing her attention between Duane and her smart phone, on which she was constantly texting. Josh kept the radio on KUVO while Hines provided commentary.

"Oh yeah Ray Charles. I saw him once in New York. They bring this old dude out onstage, looks like a pile of sticks, got two guys, one at each elbow. Sit him down and I'm thinkin', etude time. Then Charles hits the keys and it was like a bomb hit the building. He's up off his ass booge-yin', all over the keys, shaking his ass, it was like, *whoah*. Yeah, I saw a lot of the old cats 'cause my old man played piano. Runs in the family."

"He still alive?"

"No, he passed on some years ago. Ron Carter and Wyn-ton came to his wake."

Josh kept his eyes on the road. He was doing eighty, five miles over the limit, and getting passed every second. A string of Nissan GTs roared by. Four squids blew by, asses up, heads down, followed by a fifth squid who must have been doing one hundred and twenty miles an hour. A mile down the road, Josh saw a State Patrol bike going the opposite way, brake to a slow turn through the access available to police and take off heading northeast.

A minute later, Josh spotted the errant squid in the opposite lane passing vehicles like a mad man. It reminded him of old Road Runner cartoons. They hit the turn off to the airport.

"Omma jet home, boss," Hines said. "I got to get back to my gig."

"Thanks, Bobby. I couldn't have done it without you. Send me your receipts. I'm payin'."

"Oh, you'da found a way."

"Duane, you got any money left?"

Duane wasn't talking.

"He's broke, sugar," Merle said. "That ol' blackjack took it away."

"All right. I'll go in with you. I'll pay for the tickets. No Miami or Chicago. Merle, you got someplace else to go?"

"I got family in Dallas. Wouldn't mind gettin' down there. I can work anywhere."

"You're going to Dallas."

Denver International appeared on the horizon, a series of gleaming white tents that reminded Josh of the Bedouins.

It wasn't until he had been with them for a month that he asked where they got the name.

"I don't see any Arabs."

Presto grinned. With his tanned skin and dark hair, he might have passed for an Arab. "It's on account we're nomads. Harleys are our camels."

As they neared the main terminal, Blucifer, the fourteen-foot sculpture of a demonic blue mustang with gleaming red eyes, loomed, red eyes glowing.

"Oh my god," Merle said. "What is that?"

"That's Blucifer," Hines. "It fell on its creator, killing him."

"It's horrible. Why would we have something like that outside an airport?"

"Blucifer is a loving god who brings good luck."

"My ass," Merle said. "Are we almost there? I'm dying for a cigarette."

Josh parked in the outside lot. When Duane got out, Josh held out his hand.

"Gimme your wallet."

"Fuck you."

"Turn it over. I'm not letting you out of here with any stolen credit cards."

Duane got right in Josh's face. "Well whaddaya gonna do about it, tough guy? Search me? Hold me upside down and shake me? Listen—after this, we're through. I mean it. I just need a little seed money."

"We'll hit an ATM."

Duane looked disappointed, as if he knew the airport ATMs were limited to five hundred dollars. Hines hung back with Josh while Duane and Merle purchased two tickets to Dallas with Josh's money. While the clerk was punching her keyboard, Duane threw an arm around Josh's shoulders.

"Well it was great seein' you, son."

Josh aimed a mock fist at Duane's chin. "You bet, Pops! We must do it again sometime!"

Duane grabbed his bags and headed for the escalator followed by Merle, who looked sadly over her shoulder. Josh went back to where Hines waited with a black leather gym bag.

"Dad doin' okay?"

"Compared to what?"

"Well listen, old son, it's been absolutely thrilling but I have to get back. You got my gun in your trunk, don't forget."

"What gun?"

"Three fifty-seven. I told you!"

"Oh yeah."

They hugged and slapped each other on the back. Hines left to buy a ticket. Josh returned to his car. Parking was twelve dollars. He drove all the way to Sterling before calling it a day, turned in at a three story Best Western on a strip that included a Burger King, a Taco Bell, and a Chick-fil-a. He was so exhausted he ignored those savory eateries, took a room on the second floor. Inside, it was like a million other rooms. The very inoffensiveness of the bright colored framed abstract above the bed was offensive. A pamphlet declared *Discover Sterling*. The only thing Josh knew about Sterling was that they had a maximum-security prison.

He phoned Eric Gehrke. It was six-thirty in the evening.

"Hello," Gehrke answered.

"Sir, it's Josh Pratt. I'm in Sterling. I have the artifact. I'd like to bring it by your place."

"Yes, hang on a sec." He turned away and called out, "Lily, it's that private detective! He's bringing us the artifact." Back to Josh. "When will you be here?"

"Not sure. Sometime tomorrow evening. I've been up for three days and now I have to sleep. I'll call you."

"Do you have a pen? Let me give you the address."

Josh grabbed the pen and pad off the desk. "Shoot."

We are at Three Six Six Plimsoul Street in Creighton, Illinois."

"Got it. I'll call you when I'm near."

"We look forward to seeing you."

Josh was so tired he didn't even take a shower. He crawled into bed and fell asleep to the sound of traffic on the highway. It sounded like the surf. He fell into a deep sleep. The dreams didn't come until near dawn, when he found himself on a mountain meadow alive with wildflowers, white-capped peaks in the distance, that great dog bounding toward him with tongue in the wind like a pennant. Josh stooped to embrace his dog. Fig leaped into his arms.

She turned into Fig Newton. She was alive. In his arms.

It was the happiest dream he ever had. They rolled in the flowers. She sat up, whipped off her shirt, reached down and took off Josh's. They fumbled with each other's pants. They lay in the grass. Josh woke up. He'd slept nine hours. He had a woody.

He clapped it between both palms. A nurse taught him that. They were drinking one night, and she said that she sometimes came across comatose patients with erections. She smacked her hands together. "You just slap them like this, see?"

Josh rose, showered, threw his stuff in the car and drove down the strip to an IHOP, where he ordered coffee, orange juice, Belgian waffles and bacon. He was on the road by nine.

CHAPTER

29

THE GEHRKES

Josh drove east on Eighty. Sunglasses, check, cap, check, cruise control pegged at seventy-five, passing Nebraska State Patrol crouching in the median past North Platte, joining the great migratory river. Land of the free. Free to get rich, destroy your life, pull up stakes, move somewhere else and do it again. The land of reinvention. How many hours had he spent staring out the window while Duane chain-smoked, bitched, and painted a rosy picture? Yeah that sumbitch who fired him was dumber than a bag of hammers. Yeah, maybe he shouldn't have helped himself to those tools. Yeah, he really screwed the pooch that time. But don't worry. The next town will be better. The next town won't know him. He ran a decent con when he was straight and sober. He was a roofer, a carpenter, a mechanic. He really could do all those things he just chose not to. Work was demeaning. Duane would rather work the con.

But it was no glide. Duane's life was one disaster after another. You'd think, at some point, he'd learn, but when Josh looked back on his own life, he realized that he had been set on the same path, and the only thing that had saved him were the Bedouin. He loved motorcycles. But then the Bedouin went bad and started dealing meth, got in a brawl and Josh cut off a man's arm with a chainsaw.

He went to prison, and that's where change happened, thanks to Chaplain Frank Dorgan.

If Duane hadn't wakened by now, it would never happen. Duane was doomed. Josh didn't want to be around for the end.

A sign announced The Great Platte River Roadway Arch at Kearney. Josh never understood the arch. It was only accessible from the north side via an access road. It had a restaurant, a tub full of jellybeans, and some art depicting the wide-open spaces. Some bronze sculptures. It wasn't like Nebraska was Colorado or Mississippi, with stunning visuals. There were some interesting sandstone formations in the northwest, but they were far from the interstate.

He reached Omaha at one, pulled off the Interstate to a Bosselman's Truck Stop. Josh gassed up, re-parked, went inside, bought a hot dog, chocolate milk and a dollar banana.

Creighton was seventy miles northeast of the Quad Cities. It was six when he pulled into the Porter Motel and entered the office, where a twenty-something clerk with curly hair was reading a book. As Josh approached, the kid set the book down. *To Die in California*, by Thornton Newburg.

"Yes sir!"

"I'll take a room for the night."

"Just you?"

"Just me. How's the book?"

"Feckin' bril!"

It was forty-eight dollars for the night. The kid gave him an old-fashioned key on a green plastic fob. "Second floor, take the stairs right outside."

Josh thanked him and headed out, stopping at the fliers to pick up a copy of *Used Autos* on the off chance they had some interesting bikes. Not that he was in the market. Flipping through he saw the usual Harleys and Victories. He glanced at an *Omaha World Herald* on a table by the door.

NO ANSWERS IN DEATH OF FAMILY OF FOUR.

He picked it up, turned around. "How much?"

The kid waved him off. "Just take it."

Josh took the newspaper up to his room, opened the drapes and sat in the chair.

A *week later, Rockford Police are stymied as to what caused the death of a family of four. The mother, father, and two children, a girl of four and a boy of two, were discovered dead in their room at the Hardison Motel on Cambray Boulevard in Rockford the morning of August 19th. An autopsy report indicated they had died of carbon monoxide asphyxiation. Although the windows were closed, neither the air conditioning nor the heat was on.*

Josh held the newspaper a long time before he set it on

the table. A nickel of pain appeared behind his left eye.

He dialed the Gehrkes.

"This is Josh. I'm in Creighton."

"Please come over, Josh. We hope you'll join us for dinner."

"I'm on my way."

Three Six Six Plimsoul Street was a spacious, two-story on a wooded lot in a toney neighborhood sheltered by Midwest old growth hardwood. Josh pulled up the broad asphalt driveway, parked on the flagstone turnaround in front of the two-car garage, got out, and retrieved the slab, wrapped in a pillowcase, from the trunk. A lawnmower droned in the distance. Fall was in the air. There was a fifteen-speed Trek leaning against the brick facade on the step-up porch, which held a swing, a couple of steel lawn chairs, and some potted plants.

Josh rang the doorbell.

"I'll get it!" sang a youthful voice from inside.

The door opened in the hand of a tall, bright-eyed kid, the color of cafe *au lait*, with tennis ball frizz on his head. "Hi! I'm Adam."

Josh smelled garlic in the flagstone entryway. An Arnold Palmer golf bag leaned against the beige wall next to the front closet as a man wearing a Perry Como V-necked sweater, tweed pants and suspenders came out of the living room.

Professor Gehrke was fiftyish, balding, sloping shoulders, no discernible paunch. "Mister Pratt. We have so looked forward to meeting you and seeing this extraordinary object."

They shook hands.

Gehrke reached for the package. "Is this it?"

Josh handed it over.

"Woah," Gehrke said. "Heavy. Come on in the living room. Lily's cooking right now. We expect you to stay for dinner."

Josh followed Gehrke into the living room with a sliding glass door looking out on a patio, hooded stainless steel grill, garden bursting with violets and gardenias, shaded by mature elm, oak, and alder. Gehrke carefully laid the slab on a free-form maple table and unwrapped it, setting it on the pillowcase.

"Would you like a drink, Josh?"

"I wouldn't mind a beer."

Gehrke looked up where Adam hovered. "Adam, would you get Josh one of those Tyranena Ales from the fridge?"

"Sure thing."

Lily entered, all smiles, holding out her hands for Josh. She had a great head of gray hair, smelled of lavender, and wore a chef's apron decorated with Tiki faces.

"Josh. Thank you for coming. So, this is the fabled slab."

Husband and wife examined it from opposite sides of the table. Lily's finger graced a hieroglyph that might have been a ship with her finger, without touching the bronze. "Oh my. Oh my. You know what this looks like?"

"Mali," Gehrke said.

"Mm-hmmm." She looked up. "Will you leave this with us?"

"Of course we'll give you a receipt and assume full responsibility for it."

Josh sat in an old recliner. "But who's the real owner? How did Ryan get this?"

Adam returned, handing Josh a frosty brown bottle, carrying a lemonade for himself. Josh took the beer.

"You can have it. What am I gonna do with it? I hope this is the end of this whole sorry affair."

"Is your father all right?"

Josh tilted back the bottle and glugged three times. "I put him on an airplane to Dallas yesterday. I pray to God I never see him again."

"You don't mean that," Lily said.

"Ma'am, he is a wicked man."

"How did Ryan seem to you?"

Gehrke looked up. "We don't know. We just don't know with Ryan. We started to lose him last year when he started protesting. Don't get me wrong. There's plenty to protest, but we didn't feel that was the proper place."

Lily nodded. "Tell us what happened. Tell us what he was like."

Josh recounted his encounter with Ryan verbatim, sparing nothing. Adam sat rapt in the background on a sectional.

Lily shook her head sympathetically. "I'm so sorry you had to go through that, Josh."

"Your father sounds like quite a piece of work," Gehrke said.

Josh held up his hands. "I'm through. I made that clear."

Adam piped up. "They actually tried to run you off the road?"

Josh turned around, one elbow over the back of the seat. "They were trying to blow our heads off."

Adam's eyes showed all white. "Ryan did that? Did you see him?"

"He was driving the truck. They were snorting a lot of powder. You haven't heard from him?"

Lily stood. "Not a peep. Dear, would you like a cocktail?"

"I'll take a bourbon. Josh, anything stronger?"

"I'm good."

Lily headed for the kitchen, Gehrke addressed the slab. "For decades scholars have been searching for evidence that Africans may have reached the new world before Columbus. This isn't definitive, of course, but it substantiates the hypotheses."

"You know what it is?"

Gehrke looked up intently, finger on the glyph. "This is the symbol of the Mali empire. These ships indicate a fleet, and this tree, not of a kind found in Africa. I'm not sure, but this could be a date using the Pan-African calendar which was invented by the Egyptians, and is based on cycles of the Nile. It could have profound consequences, not just in the scientific world, but politically."

"What do you mean, professor?"

"I don't remember a time when we were as divided as we are today. It's like two completely irreconcilably tribes. I fear we're headed for civil war. The announcement of such a discovery will fuel the passions of those who are seeking to inflame the country, particularly those with a racial grudge. I'm afraid Ryan's mixed up with these people. We've always voted Democratic, but we don't think the police are evil."

"I'd like to know how he got it," Josh said.

Lily leaned in. "Let's eat."

CHAPTER
30

THE SLAB

White linen covered the dining table, with a floral arrange-
ment in the center: gardenias, marigolds, lilacs in a vase. The
rectangular table had four settings. Lily gestured from the
kitchen. "Come in here and help yourself, Josh."

Josh used tongs to lift a chicken and ham roll onto his
plate, along with macaroni and cheese and steamed broccoli. There were four salad bowls already set and a lazy Susan
with several types of dressing. Josh sat opposite Adam on
the long side, his back to a window. Adam chowed down at
once. Josh waited for his hosts.

Lily went to the stove. "Don't wait! Don't wait!"

Adam barked. "That's what the guy said in *Jaws*! 'Don't
wait for me!'"

"Ma'am, this chicken is first rate."

"*Cordon bleu*," Adam said with a French accent.

"Huh?"

"That's what they call it. *Cordon bleu.* I may go to France next summer."

They ate.

"What do you do, Adam?"

"I play basketball and skate. I'm going into pre-law when I graduate."

"Adam's captain of the Creighton Warriors," Gehrke said. "Some teams are looking at him."

"As if. I'm not going to play ball all my life."

"You want to be a lawyer?" Josh said.

Adam looked at him earnestly. "That way I can really help people. I hear those lawyer jokes. Dad tells them! But some of the greatest men in history have been lawyers. Thurgood Marshall. Lincoln."

"Nothing wrong with it," Josh said. "If not for my lawyer, I wouldn't be sitting here tonight. He got me a full pardon."

"Is it true you killed all those guys?"

"Adam!" Lilly snapped.

"Look. If I'm going to be a lawyer, I have to study criminal law. I have to study criminals."

He held his hands up in supplication. "No offense!"

"No prob," Josh said.

"I researched you. There was some kind of shoot-out in your yard."

"That was a long time ago."

"Two years!"

"Adam!" barked Gehrke.

Adam withdrew his head and stuck down his chin. "There was this big article about him on some biker blog."

"It's a lot of nonsense," Josh said.

"But you ride."

"Yeah, I ride."

"I have a Yamaha 250 Scrambler but I want to get a road bike. The parents are guardedly optimistic. I repeat, *guardedly optimistic*."

Josh nodded his head. "I've heard that before."

Gehrke pointed at his son. "If you can hang on to your grade average until you graduate, we'll get you a car."

"But I don't want a car, Dad. I want a bike!"

Josh finished off his beer. "You gotta have a car. If you really want a bike, you gotta take an AMA learner's class. I'm sure they have one around here and they supply their own bikes."

"How much do they cost?"

Josh shrugged. "I don't know."

"Did you take one?"

"No, but I wish I had."

After dinner Lilly and Adam cleared the dishes. Gehrke stood. "Let's go to my office."

On the way, Josh paused in the open doorway to what was obviously Adam's room, noticing the wall posters: Bruce Lee, Malcolm X, Spike Lee, Black Panther. Gehrke's office in back had a window looking out on the back yard, patio, free-standing charcoal grill, and a covered hot tub. Gehrke set the plaque on an old pinewood desk with a thump and pulled out his phone.

"I'm going to just take a few pictures. Give me some of that Buffalo Trace on the bar there. Where you staying?"

"The Porter." Josh poured a couple fingers into two tumblers, handed Gehrke one.

Josh looked around. The usual collection of citations, doctorates, achievements, family photos, photos of the professor in some jungle. Africa, Josh supposed.

An entire wall was dedicated to Ryan, including photos of him as Homecoming King, Pop Warner Champ, State Division Champ, Player of the Year, a faded color photo of Ryan with a young lady decked out in prom duds, framed headline: DOLPHINS DRAFT GEHRKE. Running stats, honorifics. Up until recently, Ryan had been involved in charities, and often visited children's hospitals, handing out comic books, stopping to chat.

"I looked you up. You're an interesting guy," Gehrke said.

"Not really."

"How'd you come to be a private investigator, if you don't mind my asking?"

"I accepted Jesus Christ into my heart and soul while in prison."

"Seriously?"

"I was a monster. Then I found Jesus."

Gehrke raised his glass. "I'll drink to that. We're not that religious, but we do go to services every Sunday at Calvary Lutheran. I don't know if there's a god, but I know that you have to accept something bigger than yourself if you want to be happy."

Josh raised his glass. "Amen."

"But you still haven't explained. Why a private eye?"

Josh shrugged. "It seemed the best job I could get, legally, given my skills."

"What were you in for?"

"Assault. I was in a biker gang. The only reason I'm out, I had a great lawyer who got me a pardon."

"Adam thinks you're some kind of bad ass."

"Really, I just want to be left alone."

"Are you working on anything now?"

Josh thought guiltily of Edward Hotchkiss, not that there was any rush. It was his OC kicking in. "I'm trying to locate someone. Adam seems like a great kid."

"He does. He volunteers, his grades are good, he's already been accepted at Creighton. We're waiting to hear from some others. Wants to study law. You got any kids?"

"No, sir."

"They can be your greatest joy and your deepest pain. I don't know what's going on with Ryan. He was a great kid too. I know what you're thinking. Here's this white couple who adopted two black kids to prove how liberal they are."

"That's not it at all."

"The questions began in junior high. We got a little hate mail from the usual suspects, but fortunately Creighton is a forward-thinking community which has embraced us and our children."

"Did you try to have kids on your own?"

"Can't. I had a vasectomy when I was in college. I was convinced that the only way to save the world was to cut down on population. Lily and I talked it over at great length before adopting. We are both active in the civil rights movement. Ryan never had trouble adjusting. He was only one when we got him. Adam was six. Ryan developed an interest in politics in high school, started getting involved. Young Socialist Alliance. Canvassing for Jane Whitman for governor, that sort of thing. We weren't too alarmed because Lily and I have always supported progressive causes."

Lily entered, went to the sideboard and poured herself some bourbon.

"I don't see how you can teach these days without being politically involved. What about you, Josh? Who do you vote for?"

"Ma'am, as an ex-con, I can't vote."

"Oh. I'm sorry. And I think we owe Josh an apology for even bringing it up. He's not a political animal like we are."

"Like every member of the faculty and staff," Gehrke said. "There's really no choice. If you don't fight for yourself and your beliefs, who will?"

Here were these good people, Josh thought, who had given their son every advantage, had lifted him out of the circumstances of his birth like the finger of God picking him out of a litter, raised him in a warm, loving, intellectual family where he excelled at school and sports. Went on to become an NFL superstar before running aground on his girlfriend's radical shoals.

And here was Josh, whose father abandoned him at a truck stop, fell in with a bad crowd, did bad things, went to prison, and through a series of blessings and sheer dumb luck, emerged at peace with himself.

Go figure.

"Where did Ryan play college ball?"

"University of Illinois. They wanted him bad. He graduated with honors in political science."

"He's always been socially conscious," Lily said. "What was he like when you saw him? What about that woman?"

"He was doing lines. She seemed pretty hard to me." The bourbon was starting to hit. Josh felt as if he could drift off into a nap.

"He wasn't like this before," Lily said. "It's that woman. That radical."

"Ryan has always been socially conscious."

"He kidnapped Josh's father."

A minute buzz insinuated itself into the atmosphere, a mosquito from a long way off. Only Josh heard it at first, but as it rose in intensity, there was no mistaking the racket of straight pipes.

CHAPTER
31

ELVER PARK

Calloway arrived at the scene at six-thirty while there was still plenty of light. Kids from the Prairie Ridge neighborhood hovered on their long boards and BMXs, necks craning, holding their cellphones high and slowly turning, like they might catch a glimpse of an alien. A couple had shinnied up the basketball poles and were sitting precariously on the hoops. Calloway hoped he wasn't there when one of them fell on his head. Three MPD cruisers and two Town of Madison Dodges sat jumbled by the curb.

A half dozen cops spread crime tape from the swing set one hundred feet to the sidewalk. The rectangle encompassed over five thousand square feet. Lying on top of the recycled rubber tire shingles that covered every public playground in Dane County lay two dead bangers, both wearing white wife beaters to display their inked, vein-popping arms. Garlands of thorns, tribal bands, dagger-pierced skulls, Che Guevara,

Mao, and a woman with devil's horns and tail covered the arms of a dude wearing a red bandanna around chopped black hair. Two prison tear drops dripped from one eye. You couldn't tell much about the other dude's face. Blood spatter radiated from the remains of his skull toward the canvas swings, congealing in the rubber treads. He too was covered in ink.

A cop named Morrisey held a brass shell with his latex-covered hand. "We think they used a MAC-10. Several witnesses heard automatic gunfire."

"IDs?"

Morrisey, a big, thick Irishman, pointed to the one with the bandana. "Ferdie Macineau, twenty-seven, seven priors, known gang member, been a resident since 2012. The other's Esau Provincio, twenty-two, no priors, fresh off the boat. He's only been here about a month. Both from the Dominican Republic."

"I arrested Macineau last year for stealing a woman's purse. Knocked her down and gave her a concussion. His PD insisted it was just his culture, and that charging him over something like this was racist oppression. Started the local DFL chapter."

"DFL?"

"Dominicans For Life."

Calloway looked around. The crowd had grown to over a hundred, mostly neighborhood kids, elbowing one another, feigning a sophisticated ennui, learning the lessons of the street, watching the freak show. This was better than

Avengers: Infinity War. Madison, Wisconsin. If you had told Calloway twenty, or even ten years ago that Madison would have big city crime problems, or that the City Council would annually conduct racist witch-hunts throughout the department, he would have laughed in your face.

Madison was a liberal college town like Cambridge or Berkeley. Madison, the Committee City. Madison, Four Lakes, More Flakes. Madison, two hundred square miles surrounded by reality. When he'd moved up with Doreen, in the nineties, Madison was the Midwest Athens, a sophisticated city of intellect and the arts. Parents entrusted their children to the University of Wisconsin and the Dane County School System because it had been vouchsafed, in word, song, and *Money*, consistently one of the Top Ten Best Small Cities in the nation. Arts! Lakes! The Capitol! The University! Who wouldn't want to live here? Chicago had been busing their homeless to Madison for thirty years. But the gang violence, this was new.

Hardly a week went by the City Councilperson didn't tender a bill requiring the police to give up their guns, announce their policy vis-a-vis Kenya, or attempt to ban drinking straws.

"We got a witness says he saw a car go by, and a guy leaning out the window..." Morrisey mimed shooting a machine pistol while blowing through his lips.

Calloway wiped an eye. "Did you get a statement? Who is it?"

"I wrote it down. Some old guy, walking his dog. Been

living in this neighborhood for fifty years. I felt bad for him. What's that like, to watch your neighborhood turn to shit?"

"Any video?"

"Naw. They don't have the new cameras up, and it happened so fast."

Calloway headed to the perimeter where a half dozen homies bunched, separated from the Dominicans by ten feet of no man's land. Some kids who participated in the police boxing program called out. Two boys had pit bulls straining at their leashes. Half were smoking cigarettes. Calloway smelled weed.

"What's up, Chief?"

"Who done it, Mister Calloway?"

Calloway looked at a tall kid with a skinny neck wearing a hoodie three times too big. "Tell me, Morton. Anybody see anything?"

They looked at one another and shrugged.

"I was inside trippin' on *Call of Duty*," Mort said. "First I thought it was the game, 'm sayin'? Rat-tat-tat. I thought it was the fuckin' game."

"Anybody see the car?"

"It was a Jeep Wrangler." A stubby girl with short black hair wearing a Packers jersey.

Calloway zeroed in. "Come up here. What's your name?"

She sashayed forward. "Monica Stubbs. I saw it. It was a Jeep Wrangler, one of them new jobs, with four doors."

"What color?"

"I dunno. It was dark. Mighta been brown."

"Would you come downtown and make a statement?"

Monica started laughing and waved him away backing up. "Aw fuck no. My mama would kill me."

Some kids laughed.

Calloway put his hands on his hips and surveyed the crowd. No help here. *Omerta*. These kids grew up playing *Grand Theft Auto* and listening to Doctor Dis. They feared retaliation. It made Calloway weary, thinking about their future. The city, county, state and federal government could offer instruction and encouragement until the Marines came home, but it made little difference so long as the kids came from broken families, cultures that didn't value learning, or placed the highest premium on physical prowess.

Calloway had been lucky. He and his two sisters had been raised by a loving mother and father in Rockford. His mother was in Attic Angels on the west side. His father had died at age eighty. He and his sisters got together most holidays, either at Calloway's house in Madison, or at Carol's house in Milwaukee. Pauline lived on the west coast, although they'd met there once for Christmas, five years ago. It was crowded, expensive and bewildering.

Thank God he'd adopted their values. Some of these kids were older than Ashley. Most of them were doomed. Sure, it was possible for people to turn their lives around, but it was hard, and rare. The recidivism rate among heroin abusers who entered treatment programs was eighty-seven per cent. Yet it happened. God knew, he and Doreen had done most things right. Ashley was popular, focused, and motivated.

His cell phone rang. It was Doreen. "What's up, Dee?"

"Please come home. Your daughter has been smoking marijuana."

CHAPTER 32

THAT HIGHWAY SOUND

Josh got up. That highway sound. The Gehrkes stood as well.

"What is it?" Lily said.

Josh put up a hand. "Let me look."

"Screw that!" the professor said. "This is my house. Let's go together."

They left the office just in time to see Adam fly out the front door. Josh and the Gehrkes followed him into the darkening evening to find three choppers kicking out on the flagstaff turnaround, as a lissome babe dressed all in black leather got off behind the lead chopper, pushed her goggles up to her forehead. Vigil.

Ryan barely had time to get off the bike before Adam threw himself into his big brother's arms. "RYAN!"

Ryan lifted him effortlessly as he hugged him. "Little brother! You ain't so little anymore."

Lily approached, beaming. Ryan let Adam go and hugged his mother. "Ryan! We've been trying to reach you!"

The other riders were Malcolm and a huge guy with a bland baby face, both on Harleys. Josh wondered where they got the bikes. The last he'd seen of them they were fleeing the highway patrol in a Dodge truck. Malachi Shabazz had died in the shoot-out. Ryan was now *de facto* president of the Aces of Spade.

"Mom, I've been tied up with all sorts of shit. I shoulda called."

Gehrke approached. "Son."

They embraced, stepped back. Malcolm and Baby Face took up position behind them, hands on their belts.

"Dad. Want to introduce you to Monique."

Vigil shook her hair like a Marvel heroine and extended her hand to Gehrke, who took it.

"Very pleased to meet you," she said. "Ryan speaks highly of you."

Gehrke plastered a faculty smile across his face. "Thank you. And who are your friends?"

"Malcolm and Baby Face." Ryan looked at Josh. "And here's our old friend Pratt. Where's the old man?"

"Fuck if I know."

They stared at one another.

"Ahuh."

Lily turned toward the house. "Well why don't you all come inside. I'll make some iced tea."

Josh thought about lingering, getting the gun. But he

didn't know where it was in the trunk and it would look suspicious. He kicked himself for not digging it out earlier. Then what? Shootout in the driveway? Malcolm and Baby Face did not appear to be carrying, but they could have heat in their saddlebags. They hardly needed guns.

Everyone went in the house. Malcolm and Baby Face conscientiously wiped their boots on the jute welcome mat in the foyer. Malcolm looked at his boots, bending his feet up at the knee, then sat on a wicker chair and pulled them off. Baby Face followed suit.

They went into the living room while Lily entered the kitchen. "You folks make yourselves at home. We're just so happy to have Ryan back! This is a real treat. I've got plenty of iced tea and some soda."

"What kind of soda?" Malcolm asked.

"Diet Coke and A&W root beer."

"I'd love a root beer, Missus Gehrke."

Ryan and Vigil sat on the big sofa, with Malcolm. Baby Face, Josh, and the Professor took chairs, all clustered around the coffee table. The floor to ceiling glass sliding door reflected the room. Night had fallen.

The professor leaned forward. "Why the long silence?"

Anaconda arm draped over Vigil, who reveled in his armpit, Ryan said, "I'm sorry about that, Pops. I just got so wrapped up in things. You know me. I've always been about social justice. But lately, I see things more clearly. I just couldn't continue as I had, dancing on a string for the benefit of my corporate masters."

"Your white corporate masters," Vigil added.

"Baby, my folks are white, in case you ain't noticed."

"Oh, I know. No offense, Professor Gehrke. There are a lot of right-thinking white people out there and we welcome your support."

"Ryan's our son. We'll support him no matter what he chooses to do with his life. But realistically speaking, how to you propose to replace the salary you made in the NFL?"

"Oh, I'm not worried about that. I've got all sorts of ideas. Money won't be a problem."

Lily came in with a big platter on which sat seven glasses, a pitcher of iced tea, a ceramic bowl containing sugar, and several cans of root beer.

"Where's Adam?" the professor said.

"He's playing one of his games. Leave him be."

Ryan zeroed in on Josh. "I believe you have something that belongs to me."

"What?"

"Just hand it over, there won't be any trouble."

"I don't know what you're talking about. Can you describe the object?"

Ryan fixated Josh with his death stare. Josh gazed blandly back. Monique stared lasers, her mouth a slit. Everyone knew what they were talking about, but for Ryan to describe the object would lead to questions. Questions led to trouble.

Professor Gehrke crossed his arms. "He doesn't have it. I do."

"Well Pops, I'd like it back."

"Do you know what it is?"

"He knows," Vigil piped up. She was just bursting to run the show. "And he is fully aware of the significance such a document would have on the world, how it would boost black hearts and destroy the myth of white supremacy."

"How do you know it's a document?" Lily said. "Have you seen it?"

Vigil pursed her lips. "That item rightfully belongs to the black community."

"Where did you see it?" The professor asked.

Vigil tossed her hair, impatient. "I don't see where that's even relevant. The picture, and everything that came with it, belongs to Ryan. He bought it."

"From whom? Do you have a bill of sale?"

Vigil stood and strutted, hands on hips. "I don't know why we're wasting time with this shit. Just grab the thing and let's go."

"I bought it from Monique," Ryan said.

"Well how did you get it?" the professor asked.

Monique puffed up. Everything was a challenge. "It was left to me by my grandmother. I had every right to sell it."

"Do you have a bill of sale?"

Vigil rolled her eyes and turned to Ryan. "Can we get going please?"

"Baby, I haven't seen my parents in over a year. Why don't you wait outside? I'll only be a minute."

Vigil rose, her back rigid.

Malcolm looked at Baby Face. "Come on. Let's give 'em a little space."

Vigil pointed at Josh. "What about him? Is he part of the family?"

Josh put his hands up, picked up his iced tea and followed the others through the foyer out into the front yard, lit lamps on either side of the big oak door. As soon as they exited into the warm evening, Vigil stalked away, pulling a cigarette from the pocket of her black leather jacket, lighting up. She looked like an angry mantis.

Malcolm and Baby Face looked at each other and shook their heads.

"Mmm, mmm, mmm," Baby Face said.

A dog started barking, a couple more joined in. The faint whoosh of traffic in front of the house, the distant brapp of a motorcycle in the distance. Single cylinder.

Malcolm fished a fat joint out of his vest and lit up. After inhaling, he offered the joint to Josh, who took it, drawing the sweet smoke into his lungs. He passed it to Baby Face.

"Whatchoo ride?" Malcolm said.

"Ninety-seven Road King."

Baby Face made a fist. "Respect."

Josh bopped the fist.

Malcolm shook his head. "Insane Assholes. They came to Daytona a couple years ago, got in our face. We taught 'em some manners."

Baby Face smiled at the memory. "We sure did."

Shouting from inside. Something shattered. The front door flew open and Ryan stepped out. He pointed at Josh.

"YOU MOTHERFUCKER!"

CHAPTER
33

CONTRITION

It was after nine when Calloway parked his MPD Dodge in the well-lit driveway of his house on the near west side. Doreen met him at the door, her mouth a slash with parenthesis, deep furrows in her brow.

"Fran Holder phoned me this afternoon. They found marijuana in Ashley's backpack."

Calloway followed her in and closed the door. The lights were on in the living room, but Ashley was nowhere to be seen.

"Hold on. How did they find it?"

"She reached into her backpack for her wallet to get a snack from the vending machine and a joint fell on the floor. One of the teachers was walking by and saw it and reported it to Missus Holder. She called Ashley into her office and asked her for an explanation and Ashley gave her some bullshit story about holding it for a friend."

"Where is she?"

"She's in her room. Sulking. I took away her phone."

Calloway followed his wife into the dining room where she headed for the bar and poured herself two inches of rum.

"You took away her phone?"

"That's right, and I went through her calls. It's very interesting stuff."

"Pour me one of those and let me see."

Doreen brought him a tumbler and a printed sheet of calls, on which she'd underlined the name Scipio in red ink. Ashley had dialed the number ten times in the past week.

"Who's Scipio?"

"I've been waiting for you to settle that one. I tried her computer, but I don't know the password."

"What did the principal say?"

"She told me that possessing marijuana anywhere on school property was grounds for expulsion, but considering Ashley's outstanding academic record she is going to handle this on the QT. She wants to meet with us on Friday."

Putting hands on knees, Calloway heaved himself to his feet, walked up the stairs to the second floor where a balcony overlooked the living room, and went down to his daughter's closed door. He knocked softly but knew she wouldn't answer. He could hear the thump of gangsta rap coming from her earphones. He opened the door. Ashley was at her keyboard, earphones on. Now Calloway could hear the lyrics.

"Fuck you inna ass, that's how I show class..."

He tapped her on the shoulder, and she jumped, turned, took off the earphones and faced him, resentful, guilty, defiant.

"What?"

"Would you come down to the living room please?"

"Okay."

Calloway spotted the CD on her desk and picked it up. The art showed a bare-chested black man with fifty pounds of gold chains around his neck, wearing leopard-skin trousers, legs spread, arms akimbo, the obligatory sunglasses, standing in front of a beach with a pristine jade '59 Caddy convertible behind him, with three women wearing skimpy bikinis, one of them white.

Dr. Dis: The Business.

Ashley went down the stairs hugging herself, took up position on the edge of the piano bench.

Calloway sat on the sofa. Doreen sat on the arm next to him.

"Well?"

"Look," Ashley said. "I made a mistake. I never should have had that joint in my backpack."

"You told Missus Holder you were holding it for a friend."

Ashley shrugged and looked down. "It's mine. Everybody gets high, you guys! Everybody has it at school! Some kids sneak out at lunch to get high. My grades are good. I don't see what's the big deal!"

"The big deal is, you're not mature enough to handle

marijuana. It can seriously affect your thinking and your life. You're living in our house you will follow our rules. You know that's not allowed."

"Your father is a police officer, Ashley! Did you ever think you were putting his career at risk?"

"Oh, come on! The mayor smokes dope! He's said so! Look at all the millionaires who smoke a little reefer!"

"When you get to be a millionaire, you can smoke all the reefer you want," Doreen said.

"Where'd you get it?" Calloway said.

"Brent Forrester."

"That boy you've been seeing?"

"Yes! And you know what? His folks don't care. They even get stoned together!"

"What does Mister Forrester do?"

"He's a psych professor at the university."

Doreen made a face. "Of course, he is."

"Who's Scipio?" Calloway said.

Ashley's mouth formed the oval of outrage. "You raided my phone?!"

"We have every right to monitor your phone. So long as you're living under this roof..."

"I know! I know!"

Doreen got up and sat next to Ashley. "Look, honey, we love you. We only want what's best for you. You're a smart girl. You must realize how this looks."

Ashley hung her hair. "I'm really sorry. It won't happen again."

"Who's Scipio?"

"He's a self-help guru. I met him online."

"And now you phone him several times a week?" Calloway said. "Have you met him? Are you planning to meet him? How do you know he's even who he says he is?"

"He's very smart. He created a crypto-banking system and is worth millions, but he's not about the money. He wants to create a more perfect society devoted to spiritual pursuits, while not neglecting our physical needs on earth."

Calloway showed his teeth. "You ever ask what possible interest he could have in a high school student?"

"I'm not like other students! You've said so yourself. My SAT scores are at the top. I have a four-point average! Scipio is about building a community of the mind. Why wouldn't he go after the brightest young minds he could find?"

"Listen, young lady, this is a very serious business. From now on you're going to have zero contact with this person, do you understand me? We're taking your phone. If you need to call us, ask to use a school phone."

Ashley stared at him in abject horror. "What?! How do you expect me to function without a phone? My whole life is on that phone! My papers!"

"Use your home computer. Now we're not going to take away your computer privileges. I know it's important for school, but we expect you to respect our wishes and do not have any contact with this Scipio person whatsoever."

"That's so unfair! You don't even know him!"

"Neither do you."

"I've talked to him!"

"That means nothing. You're a policeman's daughter. I expect you to be a little smarter about this sort of thing. Understand—you may have been targeted because of my position. A lot of people would like to compromise me and get me out of the department."

"It's not always about you!" Ashley said.

Doreen looked at her. "That's unfair and you know it."

"Is Missus Holder going to pull me out of girl's basketball?"
"I don't know. That's up to her. Now I have to go in and talk to her."

"You know what the court wants," Calloway said. "Some kind of contrition."

Ashley hung her head. "I know. I'm sorry. It won't happen again. Can I go now?"

CHAPTER

34

SACKED

Ryan Gehrke rolled toward Josh like the defensive end he'd played in high school, before they found out he could catch. Josh walked backwards, hands up and open, the universal gesture of "Whoa, baby!"

"What?" Josh said.

"None of this shit would have happened if you hadn't meddled. Why couldn't you leave it alone? Now you got my family involved. Omma teach you to mind your own business."

"Fuck him up!" Vigil, returned from the shadows, urged.

Malcolm and Baby Face looked at one another and backed off.

"None of this would have happened if you'd paid Duane!" Josh said.

"Fuck that shit! I turned that motherfucker onto a life he could only dream about! What I owe him? A lousy five, six grand? And he goes running to you! Now it's down to you and me."

Josh took off. He ran five miles every day, but Gehrke was an NFL wide receiver. Josh dashed across the lawn toward the street, hidden behind a massive shed, and tripped on a water sprinkler that had been left down. The world fell on him. Gehrke threw himself down in a classic sack. Josh felt a rib crack. That made six. They hurt like a motherfucker and took months to heal. He rolled over on his back, drew his hands to his head and swung his legs around Gehrke who rained down heavy blows. Josh caught one on his elbow and heard Gehrke grunt and curse.

"Mother FUCKER!"

Malcolm and Baby Face each grabbed an arm and pulled Gehrke off.

"What the fuck you doing?" Vigil raged. "That motherfucker has it coming!"

"Yeah, well Ryan's old man just called the cops so maybe you better think twice about this shit."

Gehrke shook off the boys. "Fuck. We'd better split." He aimed a bratwurst at Josh. "We ain't finished, motherfucker."

Josh propped himself up on his elbows. "Ouch."

The Gehrke gang saddled up. The brutal crack of engines shattered the night. Before they could turn the bikes around, red and blue strobe-lights lit the underside of the tree canopy and the first Creighton PD cruiser wheeled into the drive followed by another. A big man with a belly wearing a blue police uniform got out of the lead car and sauntered over, hands on his belt.

"Turn 'em off, boys," he commanded, while two police piled out of the second and third cars, hands on their guns.

Vigil fairly leaped off the pillion and rounded on the cop like an aggressive terrier. "Why are you here?"

"We received a call from the professor that a fight had broken out."

The big cop looked around, saw Josh painfully picking himself up off the lawn.

"IDs, everyone," the cop said.

A lady cop with a buzz cut came up to Josh. "Are you all right? Do you need medical care?"

"I'm fine."

She stared at the swelling under his left eye, twin tracks of blood from his nostrils. "What happened?"

"I tripped on the water sprinkler."

She stared at him. "Uhuh."

Behind her, the big cop was talking to the professor and Lily.

Vigil was in Valkyrie mode. "You have no right to detain us, you have no probable cause, we are not obligated to show you our IDs."

Ryan put his hand on her shoulder, and she shook him off. A cop got in her face and said something Josh couldn't make out. Trembling with rage, Vigil controlled herself with a visible effort that left her shaking. A cop named Ramirez with a Pistol Pete mustache asked Josh for ID and told him to wait while he ran a check. Everybody stood around while Ramirez ran the checks. The big cop motioned Josh up on the porch where he stood at the end opposite the Gehrkes. His badge said Morris.

"What are you doing here?"

Josh told him the story from finding Duane in his living room.

"Okay, that backs up what the professor said. That your car?"

"Yes, sir."

"You want to press charges?"

"No."

"Okay. Just hang here for a minute."

"Yes, sir."

Morris conferred with Rodriguez. The cops arrested Malcolm and Baby Face, but not Ryan. Officers cuffed the two Aces, placed them in separate cars and departed. Morris came back to the porch, motioned for the Gehrkes and Josh to gather.

"Perkins and Jones have warrants out. Mister Gehrke, you're free to go, but please. No more brawls."

Ryan spread his hands. "I'm sorry, officers. I was irate."

"Where's Adam?" the cop said.

"I believe he's at the library," the professor smoothly said.

Morris turned to Ryan. "You staying here?"

Ryan looked at his folks.

"Of course," Lily said. "Ryan is always welcome here."

Morris jerked his head. "What about the girlfriend?"

Lily's mouth tightened.

"No worries," Ryan said. "We'll get a room at the Porter. It's right down the street."

Morris looked at Gehrke Senior. "Anything else, Professor?"

"Thanks, Chief. Thanks for understanding the situation."

"Sir?" Josh said.

Morris stopped.

"Why did you arrest them?"

"Perkins for child support and bank fraud and Jones for assault. They're serious felonies. Keep out of trouble."

Morris went down the steps and headed for his car. Vigil stood at the edge of the lawn, back to the house, arms crossed, staring off into the trees.

"Where's Adam?" Josh said.

"Well there's a problem," the professor said. "He took the slab and took off. Come on in. You too, Ryan."

They reconvened in the living room where their iced tea had left water circles on the table.

"Did you tell them about the artifact?" Ryan said.

"No. Where did you really get it?"

"I told you. I bought it from Monique."

"Do you have a bill of sale?"

Ryan crossed his arms and looked away.

"It's stolen," Josh said. "Isn't it?"

"Not by me. I paid cash money for it."

"Whydja buy it, Ryan? Are you a Helguera fan?"

"Yeah in fact I am. I always wanted one, ever since I

toured an art museum in Mexico City when I was a senior in high school. This one was presented to me and I snapped it up."

Josh crossed his arms. "Oh my ass."

Ryan focused on him. "You callin' me a liar?"

"Yeah, among other things. We're not here about the painting, we're here about the slab. And the reason you want the slab is to prove the black man got here before Columbus, and that changes everything."

Ryan got up and went to the sideboard in the dining room. "I'm having a bourbon. What are you having?"

"Do you have any ibuprofen?" Josh said.

Lily went out and returned with a bottle of ibuprofen. Josh took three.

Eric handed Josh, Lily, and Ryan tumblers of bourbon, resumed his seat on the sofa. "Josh is right. Sure, the painting's beautiful, and worth a lot of money. I'd like to know how the artifact got in the frame, that's what I'd like to know. We need to track this back until we find out where it came from."

Ryan rolled his massive shoulders. "Fuck if I know."

The front door softly closed, and Vigil stood there a moment, looking around, before beelining toward Ryan. She sat on the arm of his chair.

"Ryan, you don't need to say a word to these people."

Lily looked at her. "Why are you even in my house?"

Vigil fixed her with the death stare, stood, and headed for the front door. "I'll wait out front. If you're not out in five minutes, I'm outta here."

Ryan raised his eyebrows. "How she gonna be outta here? She don't ride."

Josh checked his watch. He could be home in two and a half hours. He waited.

Ryan squirmed, grabbed his hands and looked down. "Mom, Pop, you know how it is. I love Monique and she loves me."

"Son," Lily said, "we're worried that she's using you."

Ryan stood. "She's not. Trust me. I gotta go. I'll talk to you soon."

Seconds later, they heard a bike rev up and leave.

CHAPTER 35

HOME AGAIN

"Josh, you're welcome to stay here for the night. We have a guest bedroom."

"That's very nice of you, Lily, but I think I'll head home. I can be there in three hours. What are you going to do about Adam?"

"I tried calling him," Lily said. "He's not picking up."

"He'll come home when he's bored," the professor said.

"But why would he take it?"

Lily shook her head. "Who knows what goes on in his head?"

"Folks, I would love to stay and chat, but I have to get back. Please call me if anything happens."

They all got up. Lily hugged Josh. He gritted his teeth at the pain. "Thank you so much, Josh. I'm so sorry you got dragged into this."

Josh drove through Rockford a little after nine. Something about Rockford was wrong. It bugged him, but he couldn't put his finger on it. After that, it was a straight shot up the Interstate to Madison, boring through the tunnels of the night, boring through the tunnels of his mind. No one really knew what went on in families, but the Gehrkes had impressed him as good people. Sure, they were libs. You had to be to teach college these days, but they seemed to be people of good will, genuinely concerned about the state of the world, their students, their family and each other.

Ryan with his family was very different than Ryan with his homies, including the she-devil on his shoulder, Vigil. The contrast between the two Ryans was striking. The Gehrkes had done everything they could for their children, Josh could see that. They weren't hiding sociopathy. Josh felt he was a good enough lay student of deviant behavior to spot a sociopath. He'd been one. He'd always thought like a criminal, which was one reason he was a good detective.

Or was he? He'd been unable to prevent the violent murders of two girlfriends and a client, but then, he was dealing with extreme sociopaths. Not your garden variety. Men who were steeped in rage and violence and used it to get what they want. Ryan wasn't like that. Was he so weak that he would permit someone like Vigil to control him? H*a!* Josh had to laugh. The things he'd done for pussy. But he'd never hurt anyone.

Duane said, "Pussy is like voodoo. It can make a man do anything."

Maybe so. Josh gripped the wheel in both hands and

kept his eyes on the road.

He passed a Greyhound bus and thought of the time Duane took him to Boston, and they were on a bus, Duane at the window, Josh next to him, looking around, absorbing Duane's fears. That black man with the comb in his hair. Looking around for an easy mark. That guy with gleaming hair, obviously a fag. That fat woman taking up two places on the bench with her many bags. Obviously, some kind of welfare leech. Duane was mad that he never could get on the government gravy train, what with his questionable employment, constant shifting of social security numbers, and no permanent address. Two punks got on, pegged jeans, shaved skulls, took the two seats ahead of them. Duane forcefully shoved the window forward, letting in fresh air. The punk in front of him shoved it back just as forcefully. The other punk looked over his shoulder, raised eyebrow.

As they approached the next stop, Duane pushed Josh. "Come on. We're getting out."

The got out. The door hissed shut. As the bus pulled forward, Duane drew back within himself and hawked up a loogie the size of a jawbreaker, sending it unerringly through the open window to land in the punk's lap. Those punks practically crawled out the window to get at him but there was nothing they could do; they were now lost in traffic.

"That's how you do it," Duane said.

A night-glow white and green sign marked the state line.

WELCOME TO WISCONSIN. Attention Criminals,

Terrorists. Over 170,000 Wisconsin Residents Have A Legal Permit To Carry A Handgun. They Are Armed And Prepared To Defend Themselves And Others Against Acts Of Criminal Violence. YOU HAVE BEEN WARNED. ILLINOIS AND CHICAGO, HOWEVER, HAVE BEEN DISARMED FOR YOUR CONVENIENCE.

Second Amendment supporters kept putting them up. The highway department kept taking them down.

Duane was sociopath. A failure as a human being and a father. But somehow Josh had come through the nightmare of his childhood and young adulthood to emerge with a sense of self and balance. He considered himself a fair man given to courtesy and decency. More importantly, he considered himself a man. There were millions, maybe billions of human beings who'd had it worse than he, but not in the United States. He'd only been out of the country a couple times, once to Mexico to retrieve someone, and once to Brazil and Paraguay, and Brazil didn't really count, since it was only the airport.

He couldn't speak for other cultures. He didn't watch the nightly news except when it concerned him, and he only read the *Wisconsin State Journal* because he felt he should at least support his hometown newspaper. He had no opinions on the governments and worth of other countries, but he could see that some cultures were better than others.

It was close to midnight when he pulled into his own driveway, one light in the living room on a timer. Fig must have heard him pull up because she launched a fusillade of barks from across the street, behind the Lowrys' cedar fence. Before even going in the house, Josh went across the street, slipped in through the Lowrys' latched gate, stooped and subjected himself to Fig's dance of joy and flopping tongue. George and Gracie were happy to see him, swept away by Fig's mood.

Josh got out of there as silently as he could, Fig beside him wagging her tail as they went into the house. A delta of mail fanned out from the slot in the entryway: bills, *The Horse*, the latest *Cheaper Than Dirt* catalog, some personal correspondence. Josh left it on the floor, stripped off his clothes, brushed his teeth, and knelt by his bed.

"Dear God, please watch over the Gehrkes and protect them from harm."

Beat.

"And God, if it isn't too much trouble, could you throw a little good fortune toward the Harley Davidson Corporation?"

He crawled into bed, Fig beside him.

He held her close, listening to her breath. Occasionally her tail thumped.

Is this all there is? he thought. *Me and this dog?*

It could be worse.

He went to sleep.

CHAPTER

36

A STEAL

Fig had had enough. She hadn't been fed they hadn't gone for their run. Sun streaming in through the blinds, she licked Josh awake. Josh looked at the clock.

"Holy shit!"

He pulled on some pants, fed Fig, nuked a bacon egg and cheese hot pocket, the best of a bad selection. Why couldn't they make a decent frozen breakfast sandwich? Where was McDonald's, Burger King, and the rest? Jimmy Dean's were sad excuses for breakfast and Walmart's Great Value frozen breakfast foods looked like something you threw in the trash.

Josh checked his phone. Louise Lowry was glad he was home safe and invited him to a party at their house that night. "There will be plenty of food," she said. Josh had to get them something for housing his dog. He was lucky to have neighbors who would take in Fig. He'd cruise by

Woodman's.

Fleiss' secretary Marsha had called. The attorney wanted a progress report. Josh put on a pair of runner's shorts, a Garbage Tee-shirt and his new Nikes. Running close to noon was different than running in the morning. It was warmer, but there was less traffic. Ptarmigan still lay on the fringes, and with the land subdivided into three quarter and full acre lots, there wasn't likely to be a lot of traffic, but Madison was on the march. It was astonishing how quickly the landscape changed. Downtown had turned into an urban canyon land with high rises crowding University Avenue and Johnson Street. Hilldale was in constant motion. Time lapse photography would show buildings rising and storefronts changing. Hilldale used to be a modest, low-profile shopping center, but now it resembled a city center of its own.

Josh was drawn to odd little neighborhoods in the country, three or four households clustered together sharing the same dead-end street with septic tanks. His own home had been such a place when he'd moved in, but now it was surrounded by million-dollar McMansions and the sewer line was to die for.

Josh showered and checked his messages. Nelson invited him to a Brazilian barbecue. More mail had come. Anderson Renewal Windows was offering a terrific deal. The new quarterly *Motorcyclist*, which took five minutes to read and contained nothing of interest. *Range* magazine. More bills, his energy rating as compared to his neighbors, a Humane

Society pitch. He opened his energy rating. He was far and away the most energy efficient person on Ptarmigan Road. He only had five rooms and no swimming pool.

He called Fleiss. "What's up?"

"Zachariah wants to know if you've made any progress."

"Dude's a ghost, but I'll get him. I'm heading out now."

Josh put on gray carpenter's pants and a shocking pink Tee-shirt. When he thought back to what the Bedouins wore, it was a miracle any of them were alive today. They'd worn black, brown, and more black. Most of the bikes were black, brown, or black. These days, Josh wanted to be seen. He'd thought about electric sneakers that flashed ground effects when you walked, but he wasn't trying to attract attention. He just wanted the cars to see him.

A blue Leaf was parked in the driveway of the Frank Lloyd Wright house on Lake Mendota when Josh kicked out. Not a vehicle he would associate with a Hotchkiss, but stranger things had happened. He went up the wooden steps to the front porch and knocked.

"Just a minute" sang a woman.

The door opened on a cutie pie brunette in a white blouse and sharply-creased slacks.

"Yes?"

"Josh Pratt, ma'am. I'm a private detective. I'm looking for Edwin Hotchkiss."

"Well you just missed him. He took off on his bike. What's this about?"

"A consortium in Abu Dhabi wants to purchase the

rights to Hotchkiss Motors."

"Oh my. Why is this being entrusted to a private detective?"

"He's a hard man to find, ma'am."

"May I see some identification?"

Josh showed her his private investigator's license.

She came outside and shut the door. "Let me call him."

She pulled a phone from her hip pocket, zipped her finger around, put it to her ear, frowned, took it down and stared at it. "Well he's not picking up."

She put the phone to her head. "Eddie, baby, this is Sheila. There's a private investigator here who's trying to get in touch with you. Everything's fine, some people want to buy your company. His name is Josh Pratt."

"I left my card here before," Josh said.

Sheila put her phone away. "Would you like a cup of coffee?"

It was in the mid-seventies. "Do you have any ginger ale?"

"Let me look. I'll be right back."

Josh sat in an Adirondack chair and gazed up the hill at Blackhawk Country Club, which surmounted the ridge. There were several effigy mounds on the property. Shorewoods Hills was heavily wooded, one of the tonier neighborhoods. As always, waterfront houses were at a premium, but Mendota was not the once pristine spring-fed lake it had been. Decades of agricultural run-off had polluted the lake so that every year, especially in hot weather, there were huge algae blooms which precluded swimming. Josh could hear motorboats out on the lake, on the other side of the house.

The door opened and Sheila came out holding a cup and a Mountain Dew, which she handed to Josh. "That's all we had."

Josh popped the can. "This is fine. Any chance he'll be back soon?"

Sheila made a raspberry. "I love him, but God knows he is difficult. Eddie's a genius. They're not like normal people. The other night he woke me up. I think it was around two AM, and I'm all, like, 'What? What? Are we being invaded?' And Eddie says, 'I just had the greatest idea! An airline that charges by the pound!' and I'm like, 'You had to wake me up to tell me that?'"

"So you don't know when to expect him?"

Sheila raised her arms in a 'what me worry' expression and made another raspberry. "He's working with some guy on his big new secret project, which will resurrect the Hotchkiss marque and make her..." Sheila lowered her voice. "A force to be reckoned with! Which may be one reason he's not responding. Oh, there are a thousand reasons. He's terrible on time, forgets things, sometimes he forgets to brush his teeth and I have to slap that boy silly."

"What secret project?"

The shrug. "It's secret."

"You have no clue?"

"That's right. Engineering talk bores me to death."

"What do you do, ma'am?"

"Call me Sheila. I'm a realtor. In fact, I found this house for Eddie."

"It's Frank Lloyd Wright, isn't it?"

Sheila smiled brightly with a blank-eyed stare. "Frank Lloyd Wright's finest Usonian house located on beautiful Lake Mendota in Madison, Wisconsin. The Pew House, designed by Frank Lloyd Wright and built by his right-hand man, Wesley Peters, a civil engineer in 1940. Built of red tide water cypress and local limestone, the house is cantilevered over a natural ravine and is often compared to Falling Water. Updated and refurbished for modern living but not changed from the original, this is a rare jewel that has had only two owners in sixty-six years. Included are three original Wright designed tables. It is located in the most desirable residential area in Madison on an eight thousand-acre Lake. Yet, it is very close to the University of Wisconsin, downtown, shopping and the new two hundred fifty-million Overture Center For The Arts. A very rare opportunity."

"How much?"

"Two point five mil. It's a steal."

A motorcycle downshifted through the trees, grew louder, and turned into the driveway.

CHAPTER
37

HOTCHKISS

The lope of a vee-twin reverberated as Hotchkiss descended the steep driveway on a sleek silver motorcycle. Josh couldn't quite put his finger on the sound, as he'd never heard it before. He could tell a Harley from an Indian, a Knucklehead from a Panhead, a Ducati from a Victory. But this sound was new. He went down the stairs as Hotchkiss swung a pencil-thin leg over the seat of the gleaming Brough.

Hotchkiss wore an open-faced Arai with goggles and a Wild One black leather jacket. He wore pegged jeans and black cycle boots. He took off his helmet and goggles revealing a youthful, handsome face with silky blond bangs that might have belonged to a matinee idol of the thirties.

"So!" he said in a plummy accent. "The famous private dick! Edwin Hotchkiss, at your service."

They shook hands.

"Nice bike," Josh said admiring the Brough. "Where did

you get it?"

"I brought it over from Jolly Old, along with my mechanic, Waffles, currently apprenticing with a master craftsman of your country."

Hotchkiss put his hands on his hips and walked around Josh's bike like a connoisseur admiring a sculpture. "This is so American. What did you do to it?"

Josh drew a deep breath. "Engine: 88 with oil cooler. Changed the cams to S&S gear drives with.510 lift. Took out the fuel injection and replaced it with an S&S Super E, Yost Power Tube, S&S manifold and Pingle High Flow petcock. S&S Tear Drop air cleaner cover with a K&N filter. Screaming Eagle Hi Performance ignition unit with a 6200 rpm rev limiter. Accell Super Coil, Fire Wire plug wires and spiral wound metal core wires. Accell Platinum tip plugs. Five speed tranny with Barnett Kevlar clutch, self-adjusting hydraulic chain tensioner. Screaming Eagle dualies. Progressive springs in front with higher viscosity, Progressives in back. Changed the rear swing arm bushings to "STA BOW" nylon high density. SBS semi-metallic disc brake pads and the brake lines are stainless steel braids. Went to tubeless wheels."

"Very nice. Very nice. Sheila tells me some bloody Arabs want to buy my company."

"Zachariah in Abu Dhabi."

Hotchkiss stroked his chin. "What do they want with a bloody old wreck like Hotchkiss?"

"My guess is, they have a lot of money and probably a

design, but they want to purchase the cachet associated with an old-line English racing firm. The way Polaris purchased Indian."

"And how do I get in touch with these fine chaps?"

Josh handed him Fleiss' card. "Steve Fleiss is the attorney who asked me to find you. He has all the details. Please call him."

"Another bloody shylock, eh? Well thank you so much. I promise to call him as soon as I get a chance."

"Would you do it this week?"

Hotchkiss sized Josh up. "Well you're a bit cheeky."

"I'm a bloody American."

Hotchkiss laughed "Well of course you are! Would you like to come inside?"

"Yeah. I'm a big Wright fan. That would be great."

Sheila looked at her coaster-sized watch. "I have a showing. It was nice meeting you, Mister Pratt. I'll see you later, Eddie."

She stood on tiptoes to kiss him, went down the stairs, got into her Leaf and blew.

Carrying his helmet, Hotchkiss held the door for Josh. The tiny foyer gave way onto a jewel box of polished tongue and groove cypress, more the interior of a superbly crafted ship than a house, a warm but chaotic living room on which lay Navajo rugs, Persian carpets, student housing furniture, several laptops, cast-off clothes, a big TV. The built-in bookshelves were crowded with scholastic journals, mostly about engineering. A long coffee table was heaped with books, empty cups, notepads, pens, *Architecture Journal*, *Popular Mechanics*, *Cafe Racer*. A long-haired cat meowed from the worn sofa.

"It's only sixteen hundred square feet," Hotchkiss said, "but perfect for a bachelor like me. I like the peace and quiet, except when those bloody motor boaters are out there. Come out here. The view is lovely."

Hotchkiss opened the sliding glass door on the porch that ran the full width of the house facing the lake. Shaded by massive oak, elm, and ash, they stood in dappled sunlight looking out on the clear blue of the lake, on which white sails danced, and motorboats pulled skiers.

"I'll spare you the bedrooms. Sheila says if I don't get a cleaning service, she's moving out, but I don't fancy the idea of a group of strangers pawing through my dirty laundry, and I mean dirty laundry."

"This place isn't that big. Why don't you clean it?"

Hotchkiss looked at Josh with astonishment. "What? I don't think so! We'll just call it my Bohemian lifestyle and leave it at that."

Hotchkiss might be a little paranoid about his research. His stuff was pretty safe. Shorewood Hills was as about as low crime as you could get. It was only eight tenths of a square mile housing some of Madison's wealthiest citizens.

"Are you building a new bike?"

Hotchkiss took a pack of English Ovals from inside his jacket, shook one out, offered the pack to Josh who declined. Hotchkiss lit his cigarette with a gold Dunhill. "Now why would I do that?"

"Because you're a mad Englishman."

Hotchkiss grimaced. He was laughing. "Mad dogs and Englishmen, eh?"

"Sheila says you're working with someone on an invention that will revolutionize the world."

"Hardly. I'm working on a bunch of ideas, none of them exactly earth-shattering. I say old chap. Make yourself at home, I've got to visit the loo."

Josh leaned on the rail looking out at the lake while Hotchkiss went inside. A moment later, Josh went in, sat on the sofa next to the cat and began casually leafing through the magazines, papers and reprints which covered the table like a Sao Paulo slum. Josh had never before seen a magazine on soccer, but here it was. He uncovered a trove of unopened mail including what he took to be entreaties from charitable organizations including the America Red Cross, Realities For Children, and the United Way, a laundry receipt, a pharmacy receipt, and a brochure for the The House On the Rock. A corner of white foolscap with pale blue printing peaked out from the bottom of the pile. He drew it out.

It was a blueprint of a five-cylinder engine displacing one thousand cubic centimeters named the Hotchkiss Avenger with the words TOP SECRET stamped in red, like a government document. Josh heard the toilet flushing and quickly reinserted the page back into its pile. Hotchkiss ran the sink, reentered a moment later without the jacket

,wearing a Bucky Badger tee-shirt.

"Mister Pratt, thank you for delivering the message."

Josh knew it was a signal and rose. "Call me Josh."

"And you must call me Eddie."

"Will you contact Fleiss?"

"Oh, by all means. I can't wait to hear what these camel jockeys have to offer. In the meantime, I'm afraid I must get to work. That's the thing about being self-employed, i'nit? If you don't crack the whip, who will?"

"Well it's nice to finally meet you. Let's go for a ride sometime."

"By all means."

CHAPTER

38

RAY

Josh stopped at Woodman's and picked up a bottle of Glenmorangie for the Lowrys. He put a Nato Coles disc in the little Bose in the kitchen and did the dishes. He looked at the floor. Fig tufts rolled like tumbleweeds. He retrieved the twenty-gallon Craftsman shop vac from the garage and went to work. It was hard to believe one dog could produce so much fur. If he started saving, he would have enough for a sweater by Christmas. He'd tried one vacuum cleaner after another. The bagless Dyson. The masterful Shark. The robotic Neato. None were capable of keeping up with one mixed-breed mutt. The Craftsman sucked coins out of the cracks in the sofa. It sucked birds out of the air. Josh loved his Craftsman.

He took it out through the garage, attached an extension cord and went to work on the 300, vacuuming out every trace of Duane. Fast food wrappers, cigarette butts, lint, bad vibes. Let this be the last of him. If Duane called about the Camaro, Josh would drop it somewhere where Duane could pick it up. Maybe he'd just send Duane eight hundred bucks, which is what it was worth.

He got Hines' pistol out of the trunk and locked it in his gun safe.

He phoned the Gehrkes. "Did Adam show up?"

"No," Lily answered, stress in her voice. "We have to wait twelve more hours before they'll treat it as a missing persons case."

"I'm so sorry to hear that, Lily. Is Ryan still there?"

"No. He and his girlfriend went back to Miami."

"You didn't speak to him after he left your house last night?"

"He texted me. Says he'll be in touch. We're more concerned about Adam at this point."

"I understand. Call me if there's anything I can do."

Josh phoned Fleiss and told him about his meeting with Hotchkiss.

"I haven't heard from him," Fleiss said. "Hang on. Marsha!"

Seconds later. "Nope, he hasn't called."

"Well he said he would, and we have a tentative date to go riding. It'll happen. What's the rush?"

"Zachariah is sponsoring the Abu Dhabi Grand Prix and wants to use the name."

"I'll see what I can do."

Josh spent an hour cruising the net, answering emails,

checking the biker blogs. He checked out the Janus, a brand-new motorcycle from Indiana that resembled a classic British Brough, but was simple and lightweight, with a two hundred and fifty cubic centimeter engine, a hard tail and a floater seat. Seven thou. Maybe this was what cycling needed, an approachable, lightweight bike built for fun. It had worked for Honda, Yamaha, Suzuki, and Bridgestone, back in the day. Before he was born. Serious bikers absorbed the history of motorcycles through osmosis.

Through the open window, Josh heard commuters coming home on Ptarmigan. He recognized the sounds of their vehicles. Norman in his giant Armada. Professor Emeritus Peterson in his Boxster. Phil Bass in his Lexus. Bass was president and founder of the Ptarmigan Home Owners' Association which had been seeking to buy Josh out for five years. They were up to seven hundred and fifty.

Josh didn't hear the electrics. He didn't trust any engine he couldn't hear or smell. There was probably a low fluorescent hum inside the cabin to remind them of their offices. And now Harley Davidson had invested in an electric motorcycle factory. It was like John Wayne announcing he was vegetarian.

At five, cars began arriving across the street. Josh and Fig went out on the front lawn and watched as a Rob's Ribs van pulled into their drive. Josh went inside, fed Fig some Purina beef in gravy, showered, and burrowed through his dresser, choosing a navy-blue West Coast Tee, a Bill Blass gray silk blazer that Fig Newton got him, fresh blue jeans and sockless moccasins. He headed across the street as a Tesla glided up the perfect black asphalt leading to the Lowrys'. He passed several cars parked along the drive, a Mercedes, two BMWs, a Lexus, and an Infiniti. As he reached the level at the top of the drive, a Leaf crept up on him.

Josh entered through the open front door where the party was in full swing, a mover and shaker party, with well-heeled genteel professors, realtors, developers, media magnates and their classy wives. They held stemmed glasses and chattered brightly. Josh wound through the crowd in the living room, decorated in Danish modern, past the fireplace above which hung a Jerry Bingham painting of Indians on horseback, out through the sliding glass doors where people sat around round wooden tables beneath umbrellas, and stood in clusters by the pool. Two hired teaching assistants in white jackets dispensed drinks from a portable bar. Josh spotted Dave and Louise talking to Mayor For Life Saul Brogden by the pool, George and Gracie chasing each other around their feet. Josh went over and handed the Scotch to Louise.

"Thanks for inviting me, you guys."

Dave turned toward him beaming, hugged him, which surprised Josh. Dave turned to the mayor. "Saul, this is our neighbor Josh Pratt, who saved our dogs."

Brogden, a short man with a big nose, big white mustache and close-cropped white hair, shook his hand. "Mister Pratt. Dave's told me a lot about you."

"Mister Mayor."

"Please call me Saul."

Louise took Josh by the arm. "There's someone I want you to meet."

Uh-oh. Here it comes.

She led him counter-clockwise to the far side of the pool, backing up against the woods, where four younger guests, possibly faculty or teaching assistants, stood in an intense huddle holding drinks. A thin young man with rimless glasses and a sprout of broccoli-like black hair gestured with his finger at a stout woman, half her skull shaved, the other side dyed purple, looking at him in defiance, hands on hips, while two others looked on. The other man appeared to be Indian. The woman was tall, statuesque, with tanned muscular arms and Frida Kalo brows. She wore creased slacks that cupped her ass like two aggies in a velvet bag, and a crisp white blouse with the sleeves rolled up past the elbows.

Purple top said, "That's bullshit, Roger, and you know it! It's just an excuse to perpetuate male hegemony."

"Excuse me!" Louis said brightly.

The conversation stopped as they all turned.

"Ray, may I borrow you?"

Bemused, the tall woman, who had full lips and great cheekbones, joined them as they walked a little way off. "Whatcha got?" Her voice was low and intimate, like a Howard Hawks woman.

"Ray, this is Josh Pratt, our neighbor who saved our dogs. Josh, this is Ray McRaney. She's head of the Rise Up Dance Studio."

She had a cool grip. "Louise has told me so much about you!"

"It's all lies."

Ray laughed with a little snort. "Where is the famous Fig? They told me you were bringing Fig."

"Fig spends enough time freeloading off the Lowrys."

Louise turned away. "Gotta go, kids! The Chancellor just arrived."

Ray turned back toward Josh with bright brown eyes. Those brows. "I met Fig! What a super dog! You should have brought her."

"She's across the street."

"Oh! Can I say hello?"

"Let's eat first!"

They stood in line at the buffet table, heaping their china plates with mixed greens and cornbread and barbecued ribs. Josh put two large linen napkins and silverware in his pants pocket, and they found a table on the far side of the pool. Josh took his jacket off and folded it over the back of a chair.

"Oh!" Ray exclaimed. "I love your tattoos!"

Josh's sleeves were a kaleidoscope of colors and images including roses, tribal bracelets, a sacred heart, and a mountain waterfall.

"I wonder how they'll look when I get old."

"I have a tattoo, but I can't show it to you right now."

Josh looked at his plate. "How will we eat this without looking like we survived a massacre?"

Ray tore off a rib. "You've got to use your hands."

She ate the rib like a cob of corn, unafraid to get barbecue sauce on her chin. As hubbub hovered and Chick Corea played over the sound system, they wiped themselves clean. The piped music stopped as Ben Sidran tickled ragtime from an upright close to the house.

"Can we see Fig now?" Ray said.

"She's just a dog."

"She knows things."

Josh rose. "Sure." He put his jacket on and they walked down the driveway and across the street. Cars were parked on Ptarmigan in both directions. They went in through Josh's open front door where Fig leaped up, licking Ray effusively.

Ray knelt to embrace her. "Oh, I love this dog so much!"

"Do you have a dog?"

"I have a cat. Louise tells me you're a kung fu expert."

Josh laughed. "I don't know where she gets that. I know a kung fu expert."

"Nelson Ferreira? I have two students who train with him."

She was easy to talk to. Josh showed her the house, the deck he'd built, the hot tub, and the garage. He wished he'd take down the framed black velvet of a scantily-clad model draped over a Harley chop in the living room. Ray gave it no notice.

"Would you like something to drink? I've got ginger ale and beer."

"I'll take a beer."

They sat side by side on the wooden bench on the deck watching the sun strike the tops of trees.

"The Lowrys are great. They always look after my dog."

"They told me how you rescued their schnauzers."

"I'm not picky. I'll take any dog that crosses my path."

They lapsed into an easy silence. Her hand crept over his.

"Would you like to see my tattoo?"

CHAPTER

39

BIKE TALK

She stood, turned, and lowered her pants revealing a blue, gold, and purple dragonfly on her rump, looking demurely over her shoulder, knowing the effect it would have.

Turning to him, she stood boldly with her legs apart. "What's under your shirt, I wonder."

Josh stood and peeled off the shirt, revealing the gold and green dragon winding around his torso. She touched the scales, traced its tail. They embraced with the ferocity of an airlock. He cupped her buttocks and they ground like mortar and pestle.

Fig watched them, tail thumping the leather sofa, as they passed through the living room hand in hand. Ray removed her pants and threw them on a chair, and when Josh had stripped down to his jockey shorts, she reached down, pulled his penis through the hole and went down on him, looking up with big brown eyes. Women had gone down on him before. But not a woman like Ray. Biker chicks. Her unibrow undulated like a break-dancing caterpillar.

He forced himself to think of the apocalypse, crawling on hands and knees through charred cinders, chewing broken glass to keep himself from coming. He raised her up at the waist and they fell into bed, her on top, hands on his chest, looking down, slowly grinding her hips until he couldn't stand it anymore and rolled her over.

Music and laughter from across the street entered through the open window.

"Wow," she said after. "Just wow."

"I haven't been with a woman for a while," he said.

"Well now you're with me."

He winced and sought a new position.

"What's wrong?"

"I got a few cracked ribs."

"Oh no! Seriously? Did I do that?"

Josh laughed. "No, a two hundred and fifty-pound wide receiver did."

"That's a big wide receiver."

"You're telling me."

The old lizard brain reared up and said, *hold on thar! Josh Pratt belongs to no woman!* But maybe she just meant it for tonight. He needed a woman in his life. He was all for getting to know her.

"What's with that brow?"

Ray laughed with that little snort, drawing a hand across her unibrow. "It's just there. Why? Too much?"

Josh traced the brow with his finger. "Just right."

Fig pushed the door open and pounced on the bed.

"Do you make a living teaching dance?"

Ray wrapped her arms around Fig and snuggled. "Sort of. I write a lot of grant proposals and that keeps me afloat. Dance is a way for troubled kids to find themselves, build self-confidence and character. National Endowment for the Arts, the Carnegie Institute, that sort of thing. Would you like to see one of our performances?"

"Maybe. I admire what dancers do."

"Maybe?"

"The last dance I saw was at The Playas Club."

The unibrow rippled. Josh swung out of bed. "Come on! The party's just getting started."

"I'll look like a tramp!"

"No, you don't, and no one will notice. Trust me. They may even have forgotten our names."

Josh downed a couple ibuprofen and they headed back across the street at dusk, with a cool wind blowing down the avenue bringing it with it the promise of fall. Wisconsin had three great seasons. Only winter was unbearable, unless you liked riding from tavern to tavern on a snowmobile. The town wagered on which giant pyramid of snow, deposited in parking lot corners when it was ten below zero, would last the longest. The winner, West Towne in 2011, was June 1.

The party roared with squeals of girlish delight, manly laughter, a donkey, the Bee Gees, schnauzers. They walked up past the Porsches and Teslas and let themselves in through the white picket gate to the back yard. A hundred people milled around the lighted swimming pool. Chinese lanterns adorned the trees, and strings of lights ran around the lawn. Fireflies twinkled in the trees.

Louise Lowry zeroed in like a remote-controlled drone. "Where have you been? I want to introduce you to some people!"

"Ray wanted to see Fig."

"Cole Duesing wants to meet you."

Josh let Louise lead him by the hand, while he held Ray's. "Who's Cole Duesing?"

"Hello! American Appliance? On the Beltline?"

"Oh sure. The big box guy."

"American Appliance!" Ray sang in a music hall baritone, doing a soft shuffle. "People you can reliance!"

They approached a tanned, wiry man with a full head of silver hair wearing a pale-yellow sports shirt, his crenelated arms fully tatted. He turned as Louise touched him on the shoulder. Big handlebar mustache, big nose, skin like old leather, deep set eyes peering from beneath an occipital brow. An old bad ass.

"Cole, this is Josh Pratt, the private investigator I was telling you about."

Duesing extended his big-knuckled hand. "So, this is the famous Josh Pratt."

Josh cringed. All he wanted was to be left alone. "Thank you, sir. It's mostly horse shit."

"Yeah, well ninety per cent of everything is mostly horse

shit. You're a biker?"

"Yes, sir."

"Me too. All my life. What do you ride?"

"Modified Road King. You?"

"I got a new Fat Bob and a '49 Knucklehead I'm restoring, one of those new Indian Chiefs, a BMW 1000S, a Diavel, and I have one of those new Duck vee-fours on order. I'll have the first one in the Midwest."

Louise, put her hand on Ray's arm. "And this is Ray McRaney."

Duesing took her hand bowed in a courtly manner. "A pleasure, Miss McRaney."

"Louise said you had a problem."

"Some son of a bitch stole my '66 Shelby Cobra."

"Did you report it to the police?"

"A week ago."

"Where'd they steal it?"

"Right out of my garage on East Johnson. You think you could find my Cobra? I put a lot of sweat into that baby."

Josh handed Duesing his card. "What about your employees?"

"I got a guy lives on site. Known him all my life. I'd trust him with my life. We had a fucking twenty-minute blackout last week. The whole near East Side."

"I'll come by next week."

"The sooner the better. Want to talk to you anyway. Bring your bike."

"I live right across the street."

Duesing headed for the house. "Let's go."

Josh and Ray followed through the chattering house, out the front door, down the drive past a silver Audi A8 convertible.

Duesing pointed. "That's mine."

Fig trumpeted from the fenced-in back yard. Josh entered his code and the garage door slid up revealing his grime-encrusted Road King, the Basket Case Harley, lacking only a seat, and the Hawk GT. Duane's Camaro was in the other spot.

Duesing walked around the bike. "Oh yeah. You ever put it on a dyno?"

"No."

"You ride 'er over, I got a dyno. Love that Hawk, too. Don't suppose you'd like to sell it?"

"No."

He squinted at the basket case. "Man, this is like something you'd see at Sturgis."

"I rode a hard tail to Sturgis three years in a row."

Duesing squinted. "Ouch."

Josh's phone rang. He didn't recognize the number.

"Josh Pratt."

"Mister Pratt, this is Chief Morris down in Creighton. There's been a fire."

CHAPTER
40

FIRE

Josh held up a finger and excused himself, walking out into the front yard. Fireflies danced in the shadows to a chorus of crickets. He smelled honeysuckle and pine, the aroma of the rich.

"What happened?"

"At five-thirty we responded to reports of a fire at the Gehrke residence. When we arrived, the entire house was ablaze, impossible to enter. It took three fire departments three hours to put it out. We can't get in there yet because it's still burning, so we don't know if anyone was inside."

An iron fist squeezed Josh's heart. He prayed silently for the Gehrkes. "What can I do?"

"Do you know the whereabouts of Professor and Missus Gehrke, their son Adam, Ryan Gehrke or Monique Vigil?"

"No, sir, I do not. The Gehrkes told me that Ryan and Monique were returning to Miami."

"Can you account for your whereabouts at that time?"

"Yes, sir, I can."

"We're looking for Ryan and Miz Vigil."

"Did you check the airlines?"

"Yes. We've issued an APB."

Josh thought about Vigil. Her murderous hatred. But it made no sense. If she were in love with Ryan, would she murder his parents? Was Vigil capable of love, or did rage govern her every move?

"Do you have any ideas?" Morris said.

"Vigil."

"Yes. We've thought of that. We've contacted the FBI. Will you let us know if you hear from any of them?"

"Of course. What about the kid? Adam?"

"No idea. Hopefully, he wasn't involved."

"Do you know how the fire started?"

"We're still investigating."

"Anything I can do."

"Sorry to upset your evening."

Josh returned to the garage. Ray saw his face.

"What's wrong?"

"I just got some bad news. Mister Duesing, please excuse me. I'll be in touch."

"Sure. And call me Cole."

Duesing turned, walked out of the garage and headed across the street where the party was in full swing, a carnival on a hill.

Ray took Josh's arm. He would have preferred to be

alone, but he couldn't give her the heave-ho. Not after making love to her. "Let's go in the house."

Josh went into the kitchen and poured a couple fingers of Jim Beam into two glasses. One glass featured the Avengers. The other, Quick-Draw McGraw. He went into the living room, handed one to Ray, sat on the sofa and turned on the television.

"The people I was visiting, their house burned down."

Ray sat next to him, thigh touching. "Oh no! Was anybody hurt?"

"I don't know." Josh thumbed through the channels. Of course, there was nothing. It was too insignificant for national news and had not yet filtered up through local. Josh didn't know what to do. Maybe he should go down there, see if he could help with the investigation. More likely the police would regard him as a fifth wheel. Maybe he should go to Miami. He thought about contacting Stoeckle, his national security handler. But the Creighton PD had already reached out to the FBI. If Ryan or Vigil used a credit card or booked a flight, they would find out.

If Vigil had done it, where would she go? Would she take Ryan? Did Ryan know? It didn't make sense. He got up, went into his office and sat at the computer. He was no Microchip, but he knew how to research people online. A minute later Ray appeared in the doorway.

"Maybe I should go."

Josh got up, squeezed her. "I just need a little time to sort through this. What's your phone number?"

She handed him a card. "Will you?"

"I always do what I say."

She leaned back. "Yes. Yes, I believe you do." She came into his arms and kissed him before turning and leaving without a backward glance. Josh used duckduckgo to search for Monique Vigil. The results filled three pages. He clicked on a link to an article she wrote for *Rise Up!*, "a journal of feminist anger and empowerment."

We are told to know our place, hold our tongue, keep our heads down and not to look massa in the eye. As a liberated slave and angry black woman, I celebrate my autoethnography to advocate for more black feminist autoethnography as a theoretical and methodological means for womyn academics of color to chronicle the pride and pain of Afro Womyns' Feminist Autoethnography (AWFA.) AWFA is a methodological and synergystic system for Afro Womyn Academics to deconstruct white male privilege, and to use anger as a cleansing force against the Racist Hierarchy.

AWFA is a system to problematize the omnipresence of racism and sexism in the everyday lives of Afro Womyn. Situating my anger as righteous and fully justified, I locate my voice directly in response to controlling imagery, such as the malicious ruby that denotes angry Afro Womyn as unruly, while simultaneously highlighting the need for "progressive Black sexual politics".

Josh wished Randall Kleiser hadn't left. Kleiser was one

of those guys who seemed plugged into the internet. He could breach any firewall, figure out any password. But Kleiser was in the wind, leaving Josh to his own poor devices, or relying on Dovetail, Aaron Kofsky's internet security company. Kofsky owed him. Owed him big time. Or maybe they owed each other.

"Whassup?" the programmer answered.

"Might need your help with a problem."

"Right now?"

Josh heard laughter, conversation, and Springsteen in the background. "Can I drop by tomorrow?"

"Just a sec."

Josh waited while Kofsky consulted his calendar. "I can fit you in at nine."

"I'll be there."

He went to the Miami-Dade Property Appraiser page.

- Search by Address, Name, Folio, and Subdivision name
- View key property characteristics, ownership, and sales information
- View assessment, exemption benefits, and taxable value information
- View current and prior year aerial imagery
- View building sketch (if available)
- Zoom in/out map features
- Apply layers to the map
- Detach the aerial map into its own window allowing

for a larger viewing window

- On the map, double click on a condominium complex to list the individual property owners
- Print the matching results of a partial search
- Copy matching results from the print page to a spreadsheet or other application
- Links to "Other Governmental Jurisdictions" such as cities, the School Board, the South Florida Water Management District (SFWMD), etc.
- Links to other Property Appraiser applications

He entered Monique Vigil in the search space. Within seconds, he found two properties in her name, a condo at The Helix on Arch Creek Road in North Miami, and a storage unit at STORE-IT out near the airport. He did the same for Ryan, whose house in Coconut Grove was owned by his LLC, RGInc.

Josh felt sick to his stomach. He felt responsible in some way. His gut told him it was no coincidence. But it wasn't he who'd chosen to share his life with an angry black feminist. It wasn't he who'd stolen Ryan's painting. Would he ever finish cursing his father? Would he ever be free of the anger?

It felt like something was about to happen. It felt like impending doom. What was the word? Josh rummaged through his memories, long night-time conversations with Chaplain Dorgan. The Sword of Damocles. That was it.

On the other hand, he'd just got laid.

CHAPTER

41

ADAM

Jermaine Carter shared a dilapidated farmhouse five miles east of Creighton with Walker Blum, an aspiring deejay and rapper who peddled marijuana to support himself. They'd met in the unemployment line when Jermaine was fired from Mickey D's for cursing out a customer who felt that his order was taking too long.

"Why don'tcha try the Chick Fil-A down the street, motherfucker! Maybe they'll throw in a blow job for your white ass!"

Carter and Blum hit it off immediately, recognizing in each other kindred souls, young men cut off from their families, no visible means of support, dreaming big of living large, with very fine opinions of themselves. Blum had the reefer connection. He got it from some Mexicans who lived in Chicago.

Carter had been up all night at a rave where he moved a

half pound and traded an ounce for a gram of primo flake. He was pulling his beige Corolla into the dirt driveway at seven with the radio on when he heard the news. He shut the engine off and sat there, gazing through the dirty windshield at the shabby front porch, the fading white paint, the green shutters, Adam's dirt bike leaning against the foundation. Well fuck. Somebody had to tell him.

Carter shook a line out on a CD case—classic NWA—and fortified himself. He took the three front steps with a leap. Before he'd dropped out, he'd been on the varsity basketball Terriers at MLK High School in Rockford. Then that stone racist Nielsen, the fucking music teacher for fuck's sake, a man who made typewriter paper look dark, found an ounce of meth in his locker. Carter knew who'd ratted him out, a jealous junior B-ball player named Sandford. So, Carter waited in an alley one day after school, crouching behind a dumpster with a baseball bat, and when Sandford took his usual short cut, up popped Carter.

"Surprise, motherfucker!"

Carter broke both Sandford's legs. Motherfucker never make the team now.

Carter entered the decrepit living room with its thread-bare carpet and ancient furniture, including two wooden kitchen chairs that had been pulled from a dumpster. The only new object in the living room was the forty-eight-inch flat screen Hi-Def Toshiba. The remote, two game consoles, empty beer cans, a smeared hand mirror, an overflowing ashtray, and several video game boxes crowded the makeshift plywood table, resting on four cinder blocks.

The old farmhouse had three bedrooms on the second floor. Carter ascended the Machu Picchu-like stairs holding on to the rope bannister and went to the front bedroom, which they'd used to stash stolen goods, and where Adam Gehrke slept on an air mattress. A fat fly buzzed against the closed front window through which the morning sun flowed in abundance. Carter had always liked Adam. Adam's brother was a stone revolutionary, an uppity nigger who threw off massa's chains, throwing away a lucrative NFL career to fight racism. Carter and Adam had talked enough to know they were on the same page.

He nudged the mattress with his steel-tipped red wing. Adam rolled over and mumbled something. Carter nudged it again.

"Adam. Get up."

Adam opened his eyes. "What?"

Carter sank to his haunches. "Listen, man. I just heard it on the news. Your house burned down."

Adam sat up blinking, not yet awake. "What? Huh?"

"Yeah. Your house burned down. The firemen have been out there all night battling the blaze."

"Fuck you. That's not funny."

"Dude. I ain't lyin'. Turn on the news and see for yourself."

Adam pulled out his smart phone and went to the home page of the *Creighton Picayune*. There it was at the top of the page.

FIRE CONSUMES HOME. A three-alarm fire broke out in the early hours of the morning at Three Six Six Plimsoul Street in Creighton, the residence of Creighton College professors Eric and Lily Gehrke. Authorities do not know if anyone was at home at the time of the blaze and have been unsuccessful at contacting either of the Gehrkes or their seventeen-year-old son, Adam.

Adam looked up, stricken. A hand squeezed his heart. He felt as if he couldn't get any breath and for an instant, his vision blurred. As Adam began to cry, Carter backed out of the room.

Adam loved them. They'd been good to him. But as Ryan had reminded him, there were not his people. Who were? Ever since he understood adoption, he'd dreamed of tracking down his birth parents. His mother was a famous singer, too young to raise a child. His father was a star quarterback. More likely, his mother was an under-aged crack whore and his father was one of her johns. He constantly searched within himself for signs that he was an addict, or otherwise flawed. They said LSD could fuck up your chromosomes big time. Maybe that was why he couldn't carry a tune.

It didn't matter. He still had family. He had Ryan. Ryan was rich and powerful, but he'd pissed off the Man and now they were afraid to hire him. Afraid of what the Man might do. All those brave NFL owners who talked constantly of their abhorrence of racism, while beating their black girlfriends and insisting they call them massa.

Ryan would rise again. He was merely in a state of transition, from athlete to leader. Over two million fans had signed a petition demanding that he be reinstated. Ryan was beyond that now, in the footsteps of Martin, Malcolm, and the Reverend Al. He was down with the struggle. How much was due to self-enlightenment and how much to Monique, Adam didn't know. He didn't want to know. Adam was deeply ambivalent about her. He admired her mad physical skills and the way she spoke the truth loudly, unapologetic, but she was angry all the time and had no sense of humor. The only time she looked like she was enjoying herself was when she was facing a camera or beating the shit out of someone.

Adam had met her in April when Eric and Louise had agreed to let him spend spring break with his brother. It was his brother, for Chrissake! Ryan's devotion to Adam was eternal. Ryan would never do anything to harm his brother, physically or mentally.

Ryan had set Adam up with one of his girlfriends. Tandy had been a cheerleader until the coach decided she weighed too much, which was ridiculous, because she was built like a brick and mortar store. There wasn't an ounce of fat on her. Over the weekend, she popped his cherry. They spent nights down at the beach listening to music and watching the bikes go by.

They smoked a little reefer too.

When he returned to the lily-white environs of Creighton, Adam felt out of place, syncopation in the land of the polka. Then he met Carter, and Carter showed him the hood in Rockford and Milwaukee, places he felt he belonged—or should have belonged—had not fate plucked him for adoption. He didn't belong anywhere. The Gehrkes had done their best. They were good people. He was an ungrateful little shit and even as he wept for his foster parents, he knew instinctively that they were dead, and he knew he'd get over it.

He knew he would never return. There was nothing for him left in the smoking ruins of Three Six Six Plimsoul street. He felt no sentimental attachment to its sports trophies, hip-hop records, or comics.

He picked up his backpack, feeling the weight of the slab sending an electric crackle through his veins. The weight of history, in his hands. It was a sign, an indication that God had great things in plan for him, for Adam now had within his possession a document that could change the course of history. What he did with it would determine the future.

CHAPTER

42

BI-AXIAL

Saturday morning, Josh kicked out in the Dovetail parking lot in a high-tech park in Middleton. The lot backed up to a wood whose mature elm and oak cast shade all the way to the building, an enigmatic black glass slab that would have given Buckminster Fuller an orgasm. There were eleven other vehicles in the lot including three Teslas, two Leafs, two Priuses, and a toad-like Volt. The remaining vehicles all burned death metal, poisoning the air, mutating mammals, rendering the earth unlivable for generations to come.

Like Josh's bike.

He buzzed the door while someone eyeballed him. The door buzzed back, and he entered the chill dry, hermetically sealed environs of the modern tech factory. The receptionist had him sign in and put on a lanyard before directing him to Kofsky's office, on the top floor.

The elevator opened onto the hushed corridor of the

fifth-floor leading straight back to Kofsky's office which occupied the length of the north side, tinted windows admitting a glory of light. From the elevator fifty feet away, it was like looking through a tunnel to the world.

Kofsky sat at his free-form walnut slab swiveling from monitor to monitor. Josh saw one screen on which numbers danced like a May Day Parade in Moscow's Red Square. Kofsky held up a finger while he entered something on the keyboard, turned to another screen, did the same. Josh sat in a fifties-modern chair with boomerang legs and armrests.

Kofsky looked up. "What do you need?"

"Can you use face recognition software to find a seventeen-year-old runaway?"

"That's a tall order. We can't access the national security grid, if that's what you mean. Who's the kid?"

Josh told Kofsky how Duane had arrived, and everything that had happened since.

"Now Adam's in the wind and I'm partially responsible. I don't think the Gehrkes' house burning down was an accident."

"Well that makes it murder. Who did it?"

"I don't know. I have some ideas."

"Josh, I'd love to help you but we're under the gun now and I can't spare any personnel. I'll take a look when I get home tonight. Send me any pictures you may have of this kid. I'm not promising anything. We have limited access to national networks, but I'll see what I can do."

Josh thanked him and rode to Hotchkiss' house on the

lake. Sheila answered the door looking realtor smart in a pleated skirt, V-necked sleeveless paisley purple silk blouse, Lolita glasses, and Brahma boots, clutching a portfolio.

"You just missed him. He's working with some back-woods barnyard mechanic."

"Who?"

"He won't tell me, like I'm some kind of industrial spy." She held her hand to her mouth and spoke in a plummy English accent. "Very hush-hush, sub-rosa, on the QT and the down low."

Josh laughed. "Is he on his bike?"

"Always."

Hanging in the entry alcove was a Roland Sands jacket. Josh had always wanted one. He picked it up. "Noice."

"I got him that for his birthday."

Josh stuck his hand in the inside pocket and pulled out a brochure for The House On the Rock.

"Ever been?"

"No. I hear it's insane. You?"

"No, but I've been meaning to go." Josh flipped through the brochure, stopped, flipped back at a picture of a podium housing an unfamiliar motorcycle. He could barely make out the sign. Bass Bi-Wheel, 1990. It rung a bell.

"May I take this?"

"Sure. I gotta go. I have to see a man about a house."

Josh rode home found several pictures of Adam from his Facebook page and forwarded them to Kofsky. He researched Bruce Bader Bass.

Bruce Bader Bass is an autodidact and polymath, the inventor of the Bruce Bader Bass Grand Symphony Sedan, the Bass Bi-Plane, the Bass Bi-Wheel, the deduction oven, the Bass Ornithopter, the Terra-Dactyl, the Instant Milkshake, and many others. Altogether, he holds one hundred and twelve patents. A restaurateur and hotel operator, Bass can often be found behind the chef's apron at Be Well, his restaurant in Lone Rock. During the week, he is usually at work on a new invention at his garage and museum in rural Wisconsin.

A longtime supplier of Hollywood props, Bass has worked with Stephen Spielberg. He helped locate islands in the Mississippi for the U.S. Corps of Engineers, pioneered the use of infra-red photography, built a thirty-one-foot scale model of the U.S. Constitution.

Bass is that rare individual, the American eccentric, a man who wakes up each day to a fresh slate. He has taught himself chemistry, mechanics, quantum physics, the violin, and fly fishing. Bass graduated magna cum laude with a degree in engineering from the University of Wisconsin in l971. He has a Masters degree in mathematics from Stanford.

His younger brother Phil is a developer.

Phil Bass! Josh's neighbor who kept trying to buy him out! Josh dug out is card and phoned him. A secretary answered.

"Mister Bass' line."

"Josh Pratt for Phil Bass."

"Just a minute, Mister Pratt."

Josh listened to Montovani.

"Josh Pratt! What can I do for you, buddy?"

"Hi, Phil. Is Bruce your brother?"

"Yes. What's up with Bruce?"

"Does he still have his garage out west of town?"

"I believe so. We don't talk much."

"Could you give me the address?"

"Just a sec."

Seconds later, Bass gave him the address.

"Thanks, Phil."

"Sure thing. Let me know if there's anything else I can do for you."

Bass didn't ask about the home owners' association, or their offer.

While he was on the phone, Fleiss called.

"Do something, willya? The Abu Dhabi Grand Prix is just around the corner."

"I'm on it, boss."

Josh searched for the Bass Bi-Wheel.

The Bass Bi-Wheel is an experimental motorcycle that uses a one thousand cubic centimeter five-cylinder bi-axial engine. Specifications: 67 x 56 Bore and Stroke (mm), 125 HP @ 7,500 RPM (max engine output speed) with 119 NM of torque. The engine weight is 86 pounds including ancillary parts- minus the starter-generator. The bare engine dimensions are a diminutive-16.69 L x 9.52 W x 9.52 H (inches).

The schematic showed five parallel cylinders circulating around a central axis. The cylinders moved forward and backward, delivering their power stroke on the forward motion. The surrounding bodywork was fifties streamlining with full-valanced fenders, a smooth tank, and a nacelle with a short windshield. Josh was intrigued. As a biker, he was interested in all the ways you could power two wheels, from one cylinder to six. Suzuki had fielded a wankel in the seventies. Electrics didn't do it for him. He needed the smell of gasoline, the sensual rise of RPMs sending a tingle through his whole body, the mechanical snap when he changed gears.

He did a map search and located the Bass Garage in Iowa County, in the driftless area. He phoned Ray.

"May I take you out to dinner?"

"What time?"

"Six?"

"Sure. Will you pick me up on your motorcycle?"

CHAPTER
43

BACK AT AUGIE'S

Josh wore a Hawaiian shirt decorated with surfers and the covers of Beach Boy albums, sharply-creased khakis, lace-up Skechers, and half a can of Axe Body Spray. Ray had a condo at Monona Shores, looking across the lake at the Capitol building. Josh rolled into the tree-shaded lot. Every spot was filled so he kicked out on the sidewalk. There was plenty of room. On the way to the door he counted three Chevy Volts. They were cheap because of the Electric Car Tax Credit, which rewarded buyers with substantial rebates. One had an I'M WITH HER bumper sticker. Josh entered the airy foyer, with its rust-colored tile floor, and phoned Ray.

"I'm here."

"I'm on my way."

Seconds later she appeared at the head of the stairs, kind of like the Black Widow, wearing black hip huggers and a sleeveless black T, with a red bandanna tied around her forehead.

"Let's go!"

Josh held the door. "What's with the bandanna?"

"I'm a pirate!"

Ray spotted the bike instantly waited for Josh to get on and hold it upright. They cruised counter-clockwise around the lake as the sun settled into Lake Monona. Josh rolled toward the capital, peeled off on Wisconsin Avenue, up Langdon to the Edgewater, where he kicked out on the apron.

"Won't they haul your bike away?"

Josh smiled.

"I guess not."

The maître d', a stunning blonde in a sapphire dress smiled. "So nice to see you again, Mister Pratt."

"Thank you, ma'am." He led Ray into Augie's Tavern overlooking Lake Mendota over which the sun lowered like a dowager settling into a hot tub. They took a booth in the dark lounge where they watched the sunset through tinted windows. A ramrod straight waiter snapped to attention and handed them each two hard rectangular menus.

"Good evening. I'm Lewis. I'll be your server tonight. Can I start you off with a drink?"

"I'll have whatever IPA on tap you recommend."

"I favor the Tyranena."

"Sounds good."

"Perfect. And you, ma'am?"

"I'd like a whiskey sour. Jim Beam is fine."

"Excellent."

Lewis withdrew. The piano player laid into Steve Wonder's "Superstition" with a boogie-woogie beat. Ray danced along with her fingers.

"You like jazz?"

"Well I don't know much about it, but I like what I hear."

"Anything you'd like to hear? The piano player takes requests."

"How about 'Tonight' from West Side Story."

Josh got up, walked around the bar to where Hines sat at the piano, head tilted back, eyes closed, fingers moving with a life of their own. Josh stuffed a twenty in the tip jar.

"Lady wants to hear 'Tonight' from West Side Story."

Without dropping a note, Hines opened his eyes. "What lady?"

"My date, Ray McRaney. She's a dancer. Come on by when you take a break."

Lewis was setting down drinks when Josh returned. "Have you decided or would you like a few more minutes?"

"A few minutes, please," Ray said.

Josh picked up the menu. "These fried clockshadow creamery cheese curds look good."

Ray perused. "Locally sourced artisan charcuterie."

"I think it's cheese and meat on a board."

Lewis returned. They ordered the cheese curds. Ray ordered the pan seared Great Lakes walleye.

"Perfect."

Josh ordered the seven-ounce certified angus filet.

"Awesome."

"So, what's up with you, Josh Pratt? Got any family?"

"No. What about you? Any siblings?"

"I'm the baby of five children. My folks live in a little town in Nebraska. All my siblings are doctors or scientists. I'm the black sheep of the family."

"Tonight" rippled through the room, both hands working.

Ray smiled, crossed her long elegant fingers and rested her chin. "Wow."

"He'll be over here in a minute."

"The piano player?"

"Yup."

Lewis arrived with their entries. Josh ate like a man with a job to do. Ray ate slowly, thoughtfully chewing each piece as if wondering what to say about it. Hines segued into "Debbie's Waltz".

As the waiter cleared the dishes, Hines ambled over, a big man wearing pleated trousers, suspenders, and a white shirt with diamond cufflinks. He stopped at the table.

"Good evening, ma'am. The management cautions you that this gentleman is a rogue and a ruffian."

"Ray, Bobby Hines. Pull up a chair, Bobby."

Hines hooked a hardwood chair and pulled it up, sat, shook hands.

"Nice to meet you."

"You are a fabulous piano player!"

"Thank you." He turned to Josh. "What happened?"

Josh told him everything that happened at the Gehrkes. Ray watched, an expression of horror creeping across her face.

"They burned the house down and the kid is in the wind?"

"Yeah."

Ray ordered another drink. "I thought you said your parents were dead."

Josh turned toward her. "My old man is evil. I hope to never hear from him again."

Ray looked like she was about to say something. Her eyes widened and she relaxed.

"You need any help, bro?" Hines said.

"Best you stay out of it. I don't know what's going on."

"What about the boy, Adam?" Ray asked.

"I'm doing what I can."

"Doing what?"

"Searching for him."

"At the Edgewater?"

Josh sighed. "What do you want me to do, Ray? It's a big country."

"I know. I'm sorry. It's just so...terrible."

"I know."

Hines stood. "Stay cool."

He rose, returned to the piano and began to play "Somewhere Over the Rainbow".

The waiter was about to intrude, but he noticed that Ray was weeping.

Josh scooted his chair around and put an arm around her shoulders. "What's wrong?"

"I'm sorry, I don't know why I get so emotional. That story you told. It's so awful. I guess we like to think we live in a nice, safe city surrounded by friends and family."

"There is no cure for the human condition."

Seeing his chance, Lewis swooped in. "Could I interest you in some dessert?"

Josh felt Ray's hand on his knee. "Just the check, please."

She clung to him fiercely on the ride back to Monona, where he kicked out in a visitor's space. They went up the stairs hand in hand.

"Don't touch the cat," Ray warned.

"Is he vicious?"

"His name is Sid Vicious."

"Seriously?"

"Seriously."

They could hear Sid wailing from behind the door. Once inside, Ray stooped to stroke the purring orange tabby's back, its tail arched in ecstasy. "Leave the man alone, Sid."

Careful to give Sid a wide berth, Josh followed Ray into the bedroom.

"Do you have some ibuprofen?" he asked.

"Do you have a headache?"

"My ribs."

She went into the bathroom and returned with a large

jar. The lid was loose. He poured a couple into his hand, tossed them back, refastened the lid, went into the bathroom, and filled the tiny plastic cup with water. He washed down the pills.

When he returned to the bedroom, Ray turned to face him wearing only her panties.

CHAPTER
44

SID VICIOUS

For a while the only sounds were panting, faint salsa through the open windows, and Sid Vicious scratching at the door. Afterwards she lay in his arms and traced the scar tissue across his abdomen. Most of the time you couldn't see it because of the dragon.

"How'd you get these?"

"Mountain lion."

"Come on."

"Freddie Krueger."

Ray rocked back on an elbow and regarded him coolly. "I can never tell if you're fibbing or not."

"I did tell you I had no parents. I never knew my mother. My father abandoned me at a truck stop when I was fifteen. I don't ever remember being held or him telling me that he loved me. Some of the women did that. I remember some of them. I remember them by the way they smelled, and their sad eyes. They were the type of women you found drinking and smoking alone in bars around ten o'clock.

I couldn't even say the word love until I was thirty."

Ray's arm snaked around him. "I feel so bad for you!"

"You needn't. I'm happy. I'm in a good place. I've got a dog and a woman."

Her grip tightened. "Are you going to spend the night?"

"Not tonight. But I will."

Ray swung her long legs out of bed. "You want coffee?"

"I'm fine. I'll call you tomorrow."

Ray got up, visited the head, then left the room. Sid Vicious sauntered in, unleashed a long string of feline epithets, and sauntered out, tail held high.

He liked her. But they'd only just met. Josh was grateful to have a girlfriend who wasn't in rehab or constantly threatening to kill herself. The Bedouins had never valued etiquette. They had their own form of chivalry, but it was only reserved for women who passed the test or were grandfathered in by belonging to a Bedouin.

Josh went to the bathroom. After he had washed his hands, he opened Ray's medicine cabinet. The usual collection of drugstore nostrums. Force of habit. He returned to the bed. The neat condo was finished in blond hardwood with a walk-out deck overlooking Lake Monona. Josh could see the gold capitol dome gleaming in its spotlights. Madison across the water, a shining city on an isthmus. Above the bed, a framed black and white photography of Mikhail Baryshnikov dancing Apollo. Baryshnikov was pictured arcing over the stage like a rainbow, arms outstretched, toe on point, freed from gravity. A framed poster advertised the Rise Up Production of *The Nutcracker* directed by Elizabeth Ray McRaney.

He pulled on his pants, looked around for his shirt before remembering he'd ripped it off in the living room.

His balls itched. Josh found the only way to both satisfy and forestall future itching was to use a stiff bristle hairbrush. He pulled down his shorts, stretched his balls and scratched them with Ray's hairbrush brush as Ray came through the door holding his shirt.

"What are you doing?"

"I'm scratching my balls."

"With my hairbrush?"

Josh set it down. "I'm sorry. I'll get you a new one."

She held up his shirt. "It's all right. Sid Vicious pissed on your shirt."

Josh took the shirt. "Do you have something I can borrow?"

Ray grabbed the shirt back. "Sure. Leave it. I'll wash it."

It was a long kiss and when Josh tore himself away it sounded like Velcro parting.

Josh headed home in a brilliant white, never-before-worn, Neko Case Tee-shirt. He circled the capital counter-clockwise, headed down West Washington to Fish Hatchery to the Beltline. Traffic was moderate even at this late hour. Peeling off at Mineral Point, he headed south and west. Leaving the city and entering the dark cool tunnel of Ptarmigan, he inhaled deeply of the night scent, pine, a whiff of manure, honeysuckle. He counted himself lucky.

Fig announced his arrival as he triggered the garage door, rolled in and kicked out. He looked over at Duane's Camaro. He'd donate it to Purple Heart Cars.

Josh lowered the garage door and went inside where Fig jumped him. Josh was almost too tired for his nightly prayer, but he got down on his knees, made Fig sit, and bowed his head. Fig bowered her head too.

"Dear Lord, please let Aaron Gehrke turn up in good health, grant the Gehrkes swift entry to heaven or wherever, and watch over my loved ones."

Josh crawled into bed. Fig leaped up.

He was too jacked-up to sleep, so he went into the office and searched for Adam online. There had been no new Facebook entries in three days, when Adam had joyfully announced that Ryan was visiting. Josh had three friend requests from young women with enormous cleavage. A biker friend had posted Ride For Realities on his page.

He checked his email.

Hello Dear, nice to meet you. My name is Cristy Kayembe, i am 26 years old, i am a orphan now leaving in the refuge camp in Dakar Senegal as s result of the killing of my parents by my wicked relatives who plan to take over my father's wealth.

Please i decided to contact you because i want to seek your assistance to stand as my foreign partner for the urgent claim of the money that my late father deposited in a bank in London before he died which he used my name as the next of kin,

As soon as i receive a reply from you, i will introduce myself to you better and send you more details about the fund. hoping for a reply from you soon. Cristy

Josh used to just delete and block, but now he forwarded them to Fleiss because he thought they were funny. Fleiss had run through dozens of fellow lawyers, legal secretaries, hookers and divorced women. "I'm where relationships come to die," he boasted. He'd been married three times. Josh never met any of them. Fleiss kept no pictures. Josh pitied his friend and had an urge to intervene, but then he'd be like Louise Lowry. No, the dude was on his own.

Josh went into the living room, flopped on the sofa and turned on the television. Fig came in with an accusatory look, crawled on the sofa and lay in his lap. Sheriff's deputies searching the remains of the Gehrke residence had found two bodies.

Josh felt sick to his stomach. Sensing his distress, Fig whined and licked his wrist. Finally, as the sun rose behind the trees across the street, Josh dragged his ass back to bed, followed by Fig, and this time he slept.

CHAPTER

45

BRAH

Adam rode south on remote county roads, hoping to reach Paducah by evening. Carter, who dabbled in racial politics, had friends who would put Adam up for the night. He headed toward Miami. He didn't know where else to go. He'd phoned Ryan a dozen times, but it always went straight to voice mail. Maybe Ryan had ditched that phone. Or maybe he was somewhere where he couldn't get a signal. If the phone rang while Ryan was riding, he'd never know it. Adam's little Yamaha howled like a banshee and vibrated like an electric toothbrush. Around two in the afternoon he stopped in a tiny town south of Decatur to fill the tank, take a break, and get something to eat. Ryan had slipped him five hundred bucks.

Adam pulled into a Seven/Eleven and got off the gangly machine, removing his helmet and balancing it delicately on the bike's handlebars. Two white boys with stubble, smoking cigarettes, wearing farm hats nudged one another.

"That's a pretty bad machine, you got there, brother," one of them said as Adam went inside, ignoring them.

He gave the cashier ten dollars. "Would you turn on pump four?"

"Sure enough."

Adam went back out to his bike. As he was topping off the tank, the two white boys wandered over.

"What is that? A Yamaha 250?"

Although Adam was several inches taller, he looked like a pipe cleaner and they looked like beer kegs. His father and Ryan had often warned him that there were crackers out there, but he hadn't really believed it. How could he explain to them that he was the adopted son of white liberal college professors, that his brother was a star football player and civil rights activist? That he knew math and they didn't? That he had a bright future while they were condemned to work as mechanics and field hands for the rest of their miserable existences?

Except now, with his parents dead, his future was in the air. What would happen? Maybe Ryan would seek guardianship. He could live in Miami. But with Ryan under a cloud, not just because of the kneeling thing, but because of possible ties to violent gangs, could that even happen? Who else was there? Adam thought of Eric and Lily's siblings. They made the Gehrkes look like Klan members. Adam didn't know if he could do that.

But right now, he had a problem.

"Yeah," he said.

The one with a beer gut, wearing his KIND DUB hat with a flat brim sideways, rocked back and hooked his belt. "That's a mighty big engine for a goony bird. You think you can handle it?"

Adam replaced the gas cap. "Why?" he said without looking up. "What do you ride?"

Kind Dub pointed at himself in mock disbelief. "What do I ride? What do I ride?" He turned toward his partner. "Did you hear that?"

"Tell him what you ride, Dale."

"I ride a fucking two hundred and fifty horsepower John Deere thresher. You don't look old enough to have a driver's license."

Now Adam looked them in the eye. "Why don't you call the cops?"

"Why don't we just fuck you up ourselves?" Dale said.

Adam pulled out his phone and held it sideways, activating the video recording. "Well let's get to it, you crackers. I got both your faces on film, *Dale*, and unless you kill me, I'll get your names from the cashier inside, or the cops when they come. So, what's it gonna be? Check it out. We got an audience."

The two turned to see a man and a woman, who'd pulled up, watching them from the sidewalk in front of the stair. The one with his hat centered put his hand on Dale's shoulder.

"Come on, Dale. Let's go."

Dale spat on the Yamaha's seat and walked away, muttering. Adam used a paper towel to clean it up, went inside, visited the john, bought a pack of Slim Jims and a Monster Energy Drink, paid the cashier, stuffed them in his backpack next to the slab, and went outside. It was only then that he saw someone had phoned him. He didn't recognize the number. He dialed it.

Ryan answered.

"Adam! How the hell are ya, bro? I've been worried sick about you!"

"I tried to call. You got a new phone. I guess you heard."

"I heard." Ryan's voice cracked. "Monique told me. We've been on the run ever since. Sure as shit the cops are gonna blame me and not that motherfucker Pratt!"

"Pratt? Come on, man."

"What, you think he's some kind of hero?"

"He's a bad dude!"

"He ain't shit. Where you headed?"

"I'm heading for Miami, man."

Ryan held the phone and had a whispered conversation with Vigil.

"Ah, listen, dude, you okay for now? 'Cuz we ain't gonna be back in Miami for a couple days, at least. You ain't thinkin' about talkin' to the police, are you?"

"I would never do that, man. I don't know what's going on. Once they get their hands on me, that's it. They'll put me in protective custody or farm me out to my Uncle Terry. I'd rather kill myself."

"Where are ya?"

Adam told him. "I got some people in Paducah."

"What people?"

Adam told him.

"And this dude, Carter. How do you know him?"

"We dealt a little weed together."

"Okay. Sounds like a gangster wannabe. He flash any guns?"

"Nope. Never saw a gun."

"Okay. That's cool. Listen, I got a new phone. You got the number?"

"I got it."

"I may have to ditch this one too. I think the fuckin' Feds are on my ass, but if I switch, I'll call you and leave you the new number."

"Ryan, why can't I come to where you are?"

"Ah, you can't do that, brah. I'm in the middle of something. I'll be done in a couple days. Say listen. I know some people who might be able to put you up for a while. Say, how you thinkin' of gettin' to Miami?"

"I was gonna ride my bike."

"Hells no! You can't ride that tiddler halfway across the country!"

"Well I can't rent a car, either."

"Okay. Okay. Let me look into it and I'll get back to you. We got friends all along the way who'll look out for you."

"Who's we? You and Monique?"

"Hey, I know she comes on a little strong but she's really a good person. You'll see when you get to know her. You got enough money?"

"I still got the five bills."

"Okay. Okay. Stay chill now, and I'll check in with you every twelve hours. Okay?"

"Yeah. Okay. I love you, Ryan."

"And I love you, bro."

Ryan had not told his brother about the slab. He was afraid someone might be listening. He strode quickly to his bike put on his helmet and rode off before the police arrived. Because sure as shit, someone had called them.

CHAPTER

46

DESERTED

Fig had had enough. It was past ten and she hadn't been fed. Fig knew her rights. She was entitled to at least two meals a day plus treats, and a five-mile run every morning. She stood on the bed and barked at the back of his head.

Josh groaned and turned over, only to have his face slathered. "All right. All right. What time is it?"

He looked at the clock. It was ten. He went to the bathroom, into the kitchen, nuked an Old Monterrey Cheese, Bacon and Egg Hot Pocket, and opened a fresh can of Purina for Fig. He put on a pair of baggy shorts and a Triumph Tee-shirt. As he laced up his Adidas, he looked at Fig who stood by the front door, grinning.

"Can you believe Sid Vicious pissed on my shirt?"

Fig barked. They ran toward the southwest, past White Oaks , Phil Bass' toney walled development, past unimproved land sprouting FOR SALE signs, until they came to the University Golf Course. It was two and a half miles around the course. Although dogs weren't allowed, they ran in the rough, usually over a well-worn trail, and nobody hassled them. Josh loved the smell of the woods, his feet pounding the ground, propelling him through the woods, Fig running at his side. Twice she veered off to take after squirrels, but each time she returned, the squirrels having ascended. The third side of the square was past another new development in progress, several sprawling estates with mature landscaping as well as a couple under construction, elaborate wooden frames slowly clad with *faux* brick or stone.

No cookie cutter houses out here.

They waited for traffic to break on County M, as trucks and cars rolled by.

"Let's go!" Josh said.

They ran across the highway and back to Ptarmigan where they headed toward the city facing traffic, running in the bike lane. As they neared the house, Phil Bass' wife Molly passed and waved in her Mercedes sports car. Josh waved back.

He got back at eleven-thirty, showered, went online. The Creighton PD hadn't finished with its autopsy, but everybody knew it was the Gehrkes, and speculation ran wild if it had anything to do with Ryan, who was in the wind.

A grim-faced reporter looked at the camera across the street from the smoldering ruins. "Police are trying to locate the professors' son, Ryan Gehrke, known for his game-winning runs for the Miami Dolphins, and most recently, for taking a knee to protest racial injustice during the playing of the National Anthem. Dolphins head management insists that their failure to renew his contract has nothing to do with his controversial position.

"Investigators have determined that an accelerant was used, which makes this a homicide.

"The search also continues for the Gehrkes' younger son, Adam." The TV flashed his image. "Adam was home the night the blaze broke out but left the house several hours prior to ride his dirt bike. If you see Adam, please notify the nearest authorities."

The image changed to a run-down motel. "In other news, the trail grows cold for whoever is responsible for gassing a family of four in their motel room..."

Josh switched it off.

Marking the Bass Garage location with a red dot, Josh slid the map into the clear plastic pocket atop his tank bag and took off, heading west on County Road J. Nearing Elvers Junction, he saw a single headlight approaching and automatically gave it the wave. Only when the full-face helmet wearing rider returned the wave did Josh realize it was a scooter. Dumkopf!

Fucking scooters, man. If they were under one hundred cubic centimeters, they didn't need licenses. Millenials parked them on the sidewalks, chained them to bike racks and fitted them with trunks so they could sport My Other Ride Is A Broom bumper stickers.

Josh wound through the rolling hills and cool valleys until he came to Brotherhood Lane, just past Mitt Creek. Bass Garage lay a hundred feet off the road behind a chained gate. Overgrowth on either side was too dense to admit his bike so Josh left it on a concrete apron servicing a sewer line and approached the garage on foot. A sign hanging from the chain said NO TRESPASSING. A firm believer in private property, Josh nevertheless eased around the concrete gate post. Looking for cameras or electric wires, he walked up the curving gravel drive until he saw the garage, a long, low, rust colored wooden building with a gently arcing roof. Four dark, dirty rectangular windows faced front. A pair of cameras hung discreetly from the eaves at either end of the building. Connected to the main building by an old Airstream turned lengthwise like a hall was a pole barn big enough to hold a yacht. Josh examined the facade carefully.

He cupped his hands. "HELLO! MISTER BASS!"

Robins and grackles burst from the trees scolding.

He repeated his greeting.

Save for the birds, silence loomed. Josh approached the front door and rapped on the square window. He rang the bell. The steel door was locked shut with a deadbolt.

Aware he was trespassing, Josh circumnavigated the building clockwise, walking past an occluded horizontal window to the big back yard, surrounded by an eight-foot hurricane fence. He spotted two cameras. Josh would have had some dogs. Josh continued to circle outside the fence, picking up brambles and worrying about ticks. The land cleared behind the pole building, trampled flat by vehicles. A collapsible steel garage door sealed the rear entrance. Josh went to the rear door, rubbed dirt on the window and peered inside, seeing an enormous vehicle that looked like a hyper-thyroid Jeep with a curving Mercedes greenhouse, but without complex curves. Massive, like a German Command vehicle designed for the Eastern Front. Other shapes loomed in the background, some covered with tarps. He saw what might have been a bi-plane, or some kind of harvester near the front of the big building.

When he got around front, he pulled up his pants. No ticks. He fished out his notepad, pen, and card and wrote, "Dear Mr. Bass: I am looking for Edwin Hotchkiss. Would you please ask him to give me a call? PS: I got your address from your brother Phil, who is my neighbor." He jammed the note and card in the edge of the front door and retraced his steps back to the lonely county road, got on his bike and headed for town.

CHAPTER
47

SHAUNDRA

As soon as Josh and Hines left the gate area, Duane pulled out his wallet and handed Merle a hundred-dollar bill.

"What's this for?"

"Get something to eat. I gotta go do something. If I'm not back by the time you start boarding, get on board. I'll be along in a few minutes."

"Oh, honey, are you sure?"

"Of course, I'm sure!"

She watched him go with a sinking feeling, knowing she would never see him again. At the same time, some little part of her inhabited by the Imp of the Perverse celebrated. Duane was bad news. She'd always known he was bad news, but that was her character flaw. She'd always had bad luck with men. Her first husband was a serial abuser and philanderer. Her second was a coke addict. After that, she gave up on husbands, drifting from relationship to relationship, falling for the bad boys, cocky overgrown adolescents with bandannas tied around their throats, neck tattoos and pinky rings. She'd dated her share of bikers.

Right up until they shut the door she half-expected him to appear. Silly girl! Her only child, Shauna, was the result of her first marriage. Ted stuck around a couple years, long enough to see Shauna enter the first grade, and then one morning Merle woke up and he was gone. He'd cleaned out their bank account. It was a good thing she had a job at Delton's Dental, which she clung to for years, long enough to see Shauna go to high school.

That's when the drifting began. Delton retired and she went to work for a man named Chuck Grandy, who'd become a dentist so he would have access to pharmaceutical grade cocaine. At least that's how it seemed to her. He was generous with the toot and it wasn't long before Merle woke up every morning with a line. Grandy, who'd always struck her as jumpy and paranoid, became more erratic, and had soon driven away most of his client base. One day he phoned her and said he had an emergency, he wouldn't be in that day, and would she please contact his appointments and set a new time.

She was in the office in a strip mall on Munger when four police arrived with a warrant for Grandy's arrest for mail fraud and money laundering. Word spread among dentists and Merle couldn't get a job in Dallas, so she moved to Miami where she hooked up with an old high school pal. The old high school pal introduced her to her second husband,

Wyatt, who gigged around as Wyatt and the Low Beams, playing C&W in honky-tonks on the west side, but his real gig was dealing blow.

Right back in it.

One morning, following a forty-eight-hour jag that left her exhausted, dried-out, hung-over, nauseated, her nose bleeding, Merle gathered the wherewithal to gather her meager belongings and get the hell out of Wyatt's baking crib in West Miami. Once again, Merle called her old friend, who had just lost her roommate.

"ICE raided the place and took her away along with five other people, so you can move right in."

Merle and Joan shared a baking third story apartment in Hialeah while Merle dried out and made the rounds. She answered an ad on Craig's List looking for a dental assistant and got the job. Sansun Mukerjee received his medical diploma from R. Ahmed Dental College in Kolkata, West Bengal, and had hung his shield at a strip mall on East Forty-Ninth Street, which he shared with Chung's Tae Kwon Do, Gator Liquor, E-Z Money, and Burt's Comics and Games. Soon Mukerjee had a growing clientele from Miami's burgeoning Indian community.

One night, Joan and Merle hit South Beach to see a KC and the Sunshine Band tribute band called Let In the Sun, at Bonnepetit's, one of those places who checked clients at the door for beauty and sophistication. In this case, the bouncer, a hulking Indian named Sammo, was one of Mukerjee's clients and waved them through.

She was sitting at the bar drinking a vodka gimlet when a gnarled bad boy in a Stetson, wearing a Western shirt with mother of pearl buttons, took the seat next to her.

"Buy you a drink, darlin'?"

Within five minutes, he'd told her he was good friends with some big shot football player, and would she like a line?

The flight attendant woke her. "Ma'am, we're landing. Please put your seat upright."

They landed. She thought about phoning Josh but that felt like betrayal. She got her bag, headed straight for the Skylight Lounge and ordered a vodka gimlet. She waited for an hour before phoning her daughter who worked at Home Depot to come get her.

"Ma, I don't get off until four."

"I ain't goin' anywhere. Phone me when you get near the airport."

At least she had her laptop. She got a coffee and cruller from a Dunkins, sat at a table in the food court surrounded by travelers and their luggage and booted up Maeve Binchy. Merle had always been a reader. Her favorite contemporary authors were Jude Devcreaux, Kathleen Woodiwiss, and Binchy.

Stoneybridge is a small town on the west coast of Ireland where all the families know one another. When Chicky Starr decides to take an old, decaying mansion set high on the cliffs overlooking the windswept Atlantic Ocean and turn it into a restful place for a holiday by the sea, everyone thinks she is crazy. Helped by Rigger (a bad boy turned good who is handy around the house) and Orla, her niece (a whiz at business), Chicky is finally ready to welcome the first guests to Stone House's big warm kitchen, log fires, and understated elegant bedrooms. John, the American movie star, thinks he has arrived incognito; Winnie and Lillian are forced into taking a holiday together; Nicola and Henry, husband and wife, have been shaken by seeing too much death practicing medicine; Anders hates his father's business, but has a real talent for music; Miss Nell Howe, a retired schoolteacher, criticizes everything and leaves a day early, much to everyone's relief; the Walls are disappointed to have won this second-prize holiday in a contest where first prize was Paris; and Freda, the librarian, is afraid of her own psychic visions. Sharing a week with this unlikely cast of characters is pure joy, full of Maeve's trademark warmth and humor. Once again, she embraces us with her grand storytelling.

Merle was deep into Binchy's warm, soft duvet of a novel when Shaundra called.

"Mom, I'll be at passenger pick-up in five minutes."

"Thanks, dear. I'm on my way."

Putting her laptop into her over-the-shoulder feedbag, Merle extended the handle on her little roll-along and joined the throngs heading for baggage claim and ground transportation. Signs everywhere welcomed visitors to Dallas, touting its many cultural achievements, the Arboretum, the Dealey Plaza Sixth Floor Museum, Dallas Museum of Art, the Perot Museum of Nature and Science, Dallas World

Aquarium, and of course the Cowboys.

Jockeying for position among the Yellow Cabs, Ubers, Lyfts, and Mercedes, Shaundra approached in her white 2008 Pontiac G8. Nobody told her that Pontiac was going belly up. Shaundra pulled adjacent to a BMW 740 and beeped. Merle went around the back of the Beemer as Shaundra got out. They embraced.

"Oh honey! It's so good to see you!"

"You all right, Mom?"

"I'm just fine."

"You alone?"

"Just me, sweetheart."

A traffic cop approached. "Ladies."

Shaundra tossed Merle's bag in the back seat, they got in and began their circuitous journey out of Dallas Fort Worth Airport.

"How's Bill? How're the boys?"

"They're fine. Byron's anxious to see his grandma. So, did you finally dump that shitbird?"

An overwhelming sense of grief and loss came over Merle. This was her life. She'd never had a successful relationship with a man.

"Mom, are you crying?"

Merle pulled a tissue from her purse and dabbed at her eyes. "In answer to your question, I'm through with him. He dumped me at the airport. Said he'd be right back. I waited an hour."

"Praise Jesus. You just missed Ian. He left yesterday for a

six-month deployment."

"Oh dear. I was hoping to see him! How old is he now?"

"He's nineteen. We're very proud of him. We heard about that shooting in Arizona. Did shit bird have anything to do with that?"

"Honey, it was a bad trip. I knew better, but I still agreed to meet him in Vegas. He was running some kind of scam on that football player who took a knee."

"Ryan Gehrke?"

"I went to Vegas to meet him, but before he arrived, Gehrke's men found me and used me to lure Duane to a bar. They held us prisoner at the South Point waiting for Duane's son to arrive with that stupid painting."

"What? They held you prisoner? Did you tell the police?"

"I couldn't. Duane has warrants. I've got a few unpaid traffic bills in Miami."

"Mom! Unpaid traffic bills are the least of your worries! That's kidnapping! You should report it."

"That's easy for you to say. Just let me decompress for a day, okay?"

"Okay, but there's no drinking in front of the kids and don't bring any drugs into the house."

"Can I have a fuckin' beer?"

"Yes, Mom, you can have a beer. Bill won't be home 'til nine. I'll pick something up on the way home. Will you eat Vietnamese?"

"I'll eat a Vietnamese, I'm so hungry."

It took an hour to reach Shaundra's modest ranch-style

on Grassmere near Love Field. The single garage was open and filled with bicycles, charcoal grills, inner tubes, a work bench, cans of paint, lawnmower, garment bags and boxes. The yard was hard-baked earth. Nobody had used the lawnmower in years. When it rained, it rained hard, and drummed off the flat earth into the street and the gutter. Sometimes the gutter couldn't handle it all and there was flooding.

A yellow bicycle lay on its side by the front door.

"Byron's home."

For a moment, Merle forgot about how to smuggle a bottle of Jim Beam into the house as Shaundra opened the door.

"Byron! Your grandma's here!"

"Just a second, Ma!"

A minute later, a gangly teenager with a flop of cowlick wearing ultra-baggy satin gym shorts, Adidas Harden shoes, whose colors reminded Merle of sorbet, and a LeBron Tee-shirt burst through the door and hugged her.

"Merle!"

"Byron! How the hell are ya, kid?"

"I'm averaging twelve points a game!"

"That's terrific, kid!"

"Byron, you're gonna have to sleep on the sofa for a couple days."

"No prob. I may go crash at Pablo's house."

"You check with Maria before you do that and let me know."

"I will, Ma."

Shaundra opened the door. "Well, come on in."

Merle wheeled her bag down the hall into the boy's room, decorated with posters of his favorite NBA and NFL players. Shaundra hovered, eager for gossip, but the phone rang. They still had a land line.

"Make yourself at home."

Alone in the room, Merle dropped to the bed and shuddered.

CHAPTER 48

ENTER THE NINJA

Still no word on Adam. Josh called Kofsky, but he was in a meeting. He called Chief Morris in Creighton, but he was busy at a crime scene. He called Agent Stoeckle at NSA, but he was unavailable. Josh went to his notebooks.

Before he vamoosed, Randall Kleiser had recommended a programmer named Ninja Preston from St. Louis. Josh had no way to contact Preston, and no way to contact Kleiser. He needed a dark web expert to find him a dark web expert.

Kofsky returned his call. "What?"

"If you can't be my tech guy, at least help me find a tech guy."

"You're a detective. Why can't you find one?"

Kofsky's words hurt. Josh knew he wasn't the sharpest knife in the drawer, and that he was tech challenged. He made up for it through dogged determination and solid basics. It was a miracle he could use a computer. But Kofsky was right. Josh went to the floor-to-ceiling bookshelf that covered one wall of the office and ran his finger down the jumble of titles stashed in no particular order. Dashiel Hammet's *Red Harvest*, *Zen and the Art of Motorcycle Maintenance*, Robert Clouse' biography of Bruce Lee, six inches of *The Horse*, a stack of *Backstreet Choppers*, a stack of *Easyriders*, until he found it. *You, Too, Can Find Anybody*, by Joseph J. Culligan. He'd picked it up at a garage sale. Culligan listed seventeen categories of searches starting with "Driving Records, Registrations & Titles". The chapters included births, deaths, marriages and divorces, social security, federal records, works' comp, abandoned property, bankruptcy, child support, boat and vessel registration, national archives, national cemetery system, bar associations, and foreign diplomatic representatives and foreign consular offices.

Josh started with an online search for Ninja Preston. Ninja. What kind of name was that? The Greater Saint Louis Phone Directory, including East Saint Louis, listed over a thousand Prestons. He used Wolfhound to search for Ninja Preston.

Bingo.

Ninja Preston had released a Youtube video called "Baskin' In The Heat". Josh brought it up. Shot outside on a sunny day at the beach, with dozens of beach goers lazing in the sun at the edge of a sky-blue lake, Josh could almost smell the sunscreen. Ninja Preston was a slim black man wearing baggy plaid shorts, a pink Lacoste shirt, Foster Grants and a pith helmet, shaking it to a sinister beat. His funky dance steps were one hundred and eighty degrees from his outfit.

Here we are all baskin', baskin' in the heat. Lookin' for that tan to show you got the meat. White folks all be baskin', just like baked Alaskan, baskin' in the heat. Looking to get neat.

He shimmied over to a spectacular blonde in cat's eye sunglasses and a blue bikini.

Take a look at Gloria. She's from Hyperboria. She chose not to froze when it got to her toes, and now she's baskin'. Baskin' in the heat.

Ninja extended his hand, pulled Gloria up and they jitterbugged, him wheeling her around in the air like a Hula Hoop. They stood back to back.

Here we all be baskin', baskin' at Lake Carlyle. Baskin and robbin' like Baskin and Robbins, and we're doing it in style…

Below the video Josh left a comment. *Dear Ninja. I would like to hire you. Josh Pratt.*

That was enough. If Ninja were so smart, he'd know how to find him. Josh headed for the Essen Haus. Maybe Hotchkiss would show up. The bike lot was jammed with BMWs, Triumphs, and home-made cafe racers but no Brough. Josh took the last spot and went inside, where he spotted the Bunkers seated at their round table.

Josh got a draft and joined them. "Got room for one more?"

Homer Anthony and Jeff Bohm slid sideways. Josh

hooked a chair from the next table and squeezed in. Six bikers sat around the table, their Joe Rocket, Icons, and Bilt jackets neatly folded over the backs of their chairs, their helmets pushed to the center stand on the floor.

"What happened to you last Saturday?" Anthony said. "One moment you were there, the next you were gone."

"I had to check something out. What did I miss?"

"Jeff nearly hit a deer on the ride home."

Jeff shook his hand out and whistled. "I had to stop and check my underpants. It stepped out of the woods about twenty feet in front of me. I was doing at least fifty."

"He rode around it in the ditch," Anthony said. "I don't know how you didn't lose it." He turned to Josh. "Did you find Hotchkiss?"

"Still looking. Have you seen him?"

Anthony shook his head. "Nope. That boy's paranoid. He thinks we want to steal his ideas."

Josh scratched his head. "What ideas?"

"Exactly."

A tatted dude with a beard nursing an Irish whiskey said, "Harley's introducing an electric bike."

"Bullshit," Bohm said.

"Inevitable," Anthony said.

"Fuck," Josh said.

"Have you ridden an electric bike? I have. They work fine, except there's no noise and no vibration."

"You know what?" Josh said. "All these electric vehicles run off coal-burning power plants. So, you don't see a cloud of smoke coming out the exhaust. You don't see the power plants. Out of sight, out of mind. I like to feel the vibration and hear the engine. I like the smell of gasoline and having to shift gears. I'm diggin' in my heels. Not only that, but I hate my fucking smart phone."

"Well, all right!" Anthony said.

"Tell us how you really feel," Bohm said.

The tatted dude said, "I'm with him. Just because it's new doesn't mean it's good. Progress. Fuck progress!"

Josh pumped a fist. "Yeah!"

"I will bet you a thousand dollars my Tesla can beat your Harley through the quarter mile."

"Let me think about that, counselor."

Anthony tapped his phone, which rested flat on the table before him, as did all the others. "Do you mean to say you don't find this an essential investigative tool?"

"No, I recognize what it means. You can't be a modern investigator without good computer and internet skills. Especially now, that everybody's got a camera. I know it's affected your business, counselor."

Anthony signaled for a waitress. Everybody re-upped.

"It sure has. The fact that there are a thousand independent videographers in any crowd these days has created an entirely new branch of litigation. Had a case last week. Nice house in Cherrywood. Someone keeps stealing their expensive potted plants right off the stoop. My client and his spouse both work during the day so nobody's home, and it's a fairly rural area with big lots. So my client installed a tiny camera under the eaves. Sure enough, next day the thief comes, they watch the video and Missus Client's jaw hits the floor. It's her old rival from high school. High school for chrissake! This is twenty years ago! This woman has been driving across town to steal my client's potted plants! She's still got the stupid breast tattoo of a unicorn she got in high school. So, we depose her, show her the tape and she says, 'That's not me. I don't know who it is.'

"So, we back up and freeze the video with a nice clear picture of her unicorn. The judge looks from the video to the woman and raises her eyebrows.

"'Everybody has a twin,' she says."

Josh's phone rang. He didn't know the number. He stood.

"'Scuse me, boys."

"Now don't go runnin' off without saying goodbye," Anthony said.

Josh went out on the back deck. "Josh Pratt."

"My man, my man, my man. This is Ninja Preston."

CHAPTER 49

BLOODY YANK

"Wow," Josh said. "That was fast."

"That's why they call me Ninja."

"You know who I am?"

"I know all about you, man. You are some kind of moth-erfuckin' bad ass. How'd you hear about me?"

"You were recommended to me by another IT specialist, Randall Kleiser."

"Whatchoo need?"

"I need you to help me find a runaway boy."

"Got any money?"

"Some."

"Well you in Madison and I'm in Saint Louis, but all things are possible over the internet. I'll send you a link you can use to send me the particulars."

"You have my email address?"

"I got your email address, your social security number,

your Visa and Mastercard numbers and the VIN on your Chrysler."

"Okay. I'll send you everything I have shortly. Is this a good number to reach you?"

"I change phones every other day. I'll reach you. You can use that link."

"Thanks, mon."

Josh went back inside. "Sorry, boys, gotta go. Tell Hotchkiss to call me."

Josh rode home. Ninja's link was in his inbox. Josh wrote a report detailing the case. It began, "My father abandoned me at a truck stop when I was fifteen." It included news reports covering the Ryan Gehrke story, the fire, and numerous pictures of Aaron culled from his website and the local newspaper, which had followed his budding athletic career. Josh pushed the send button.

His ribs ached. He downed a couple ibuprofen and searched the news. Ryan and Vigil were in the wind. Josh went into the garage with Fig and mounted the Mustang Solo Seat to the Basket Case Harley. It was ready to go. Josh had the tank painted at Tankwerx in Middleton, a deep blue with orange flames.

He ushered Fig back into the house, put on goggles, backed the bike up and rolled down the driveway to the curb. It had a V80 S&S engine cradled in a soft-tailed Red Barron frame. The only actual Harley part was the tank. Josh had added baffles in deference to his neighbors. The front fork had a slight extension and sported a disc brake.

He opened the petcock, primed the throttle and pushed the button. The bike emitted a thunderclap and roared to life, causing leaves to shiver. He snicked into gear and felt the grunt as the bike chirped with massive torque.

Josh headed southwest past Phil Bass' baronial estate, past Reg Norman's French Provincial plantation, past the upscale gated community sprawled beneath the leafy bower until he came to the University Golf Course. He cut down through Mount Horeb with its carved gnomes lining Main Street, toward Yellowstone Lake State Park in Lafayette County. South of town, he spotted two deer grazing in a clump of trees, including a six-point buck.

The road meant freedom. Freedom from worry. Freedom from other people. Ironic he had spent so many years riding in a pack. It wasn't the same thing. Considering the amount of booze and drugs they did, it was a miracle he was still alive. Others weren't so lucky. For years, Josh had ridden with a patch for Snake on his vest. The Bedouins were on a run up through the Upper Peninsula when Snake struck a deer in such a way that the antler pierced his forehead and protruded from the top of his skull. Grunt Cake got off, gripped the deer by its other antler and slit its throat. The rest of the gang hogpiled on the deer as it went through its death throes, then they cut off its head.

Some squids stopped and one of them tried to take a picture. Grunt Cake ripped the camera from his hands and threw it in the woods. When the ambulance arrived, they were stunned by the blood and gore. They transported

Snake to a hospital in Marquette, where he died.

Josh cut down through Lee Valley Road, a meandering, forested path of magic, which brought him to Moscow Road which cut over to Horseshoe Path, which brought him to Lake Yellowstone, a pristine blue eye rimmed with shaggy green. He rode around the lake, inhaling the evening air. The sun hung low in the sky, but it would still be light out by the time he got home.

On the way back, winding through Primrose Mewa Ridge, he saw a wolf standing stock still in the middle of the tunneled two-lane blacktop. Josh stopped, shut off the engine and watched the wolf, as it watched him. A minute later it sauntered into the woods. Josh started the bike and continued.

As Josh rode up Ptarmigan, Phil Bass was retrieving his mail from his brick-enclosed mailbox on the road. Josh stopped and shut off the engine.

"Josh! What can I do for you?"

"I went by Bruce's garage today. It was closed down. Is he around?"

"I think so. Want me to check?"

"If you don't mind."

"How 'bout I just give you his phone number? You can tell him where you got it."

"That would be great, Phil. Thanks."

Bass removed a business card and a pen from his breast pocket, wrote something down and handed it. Josh noticed the big knife riding in Bass' pocket on a clip. A gentleman always carried a knife. Even CEOs. Josh had one in his pocket.

Bass' card said "Bass Custom Homes, from the luxurious to the sublime."

Josh wheeled into his open garage and parked the Basket, going in through the kitchen door where Fig whooped and hollered, picking his phone up off the counter. They went out on the deck as the sun dipped its toe in the horizon and dusk rolled over the land bringing it with it the scent of lilacs.

Josh had three messages.

Fleiss: "Any progress? These guys are getting antsy."

Ray: "What are you doing, Big Boy? Want company?"

Hotchkiss: "What is it with you bloody Yanks? Hound a man to his grave, do you. Give me a call."

Josh called Hotchkiss. It went to voice mail. "Call me."

He called Ray. "Sure. I'll cook."

"Want me to bring anything?"

"Bring some beer. Something local."

Josh went into the kitchen, excavated a frozen pork loin, nuked it, put it in a bowl with a can of defrosted condensed orange juice, soy sauce, sesame oil, garlic and brown sugar, and set a box of Zahrain's Red Beans and Rice on the counter. He mowed the lawn, took a shower, and played catch with Fig in the back yard. When he returned, Hotchkiss had returned his call. Josh called him back.

"All right, listen, you bloody Yank. You're so damned pushy! Bruce says you stopped by the bloody shop. Why don't you come out here tomorrow afternoon and we'll talk."

"Edwin, you should be talking to Fleiss, not me. There's

a lot of money on the line. They want to secure the rights before the Abu Dhabi Grand Prix."

"Oh really? I was there in '09. Pater died before he could attend. What's this bloody shyster's number?"

Josh told him.

"I'll give him a call right now, and I'll see you tomorrow afternoon. You are coming, aren't you?"

"I wouldn't miss it."

Josh had traded his jeans in on cargo shorts, Crocs knock-offs, and a blinding white tank top next to his tanned and inked skin. He made a salad from red leaf lettuce, scallions, orange peppers, cucumber, broccoli, carrots, and red cabbage. He mixed olive oil, balsamic vinaigrette and pesto in a plastic container for the dressing.

NSA agent Stoeckle returned his call. "Sorry I didn't get back to you sooner. The feds want Ryan Gehrke on a tax beef."

"You know about his parents' home?"

"Yes. Do you know where he is?"

Josh dug out Franklin Munche's card. "No. But I was approached last week by a Franklin Munche, a Miami lawyer who claims to represent him. Munche is with Boyd, Askew and Evans." Josh gave Stoeckle the phone number and email.

"Do you know about the slab?"

"What slab?"

"The slab that says Africans discovered the New World hundreds of years before Columbus."

"No. Tell me about the slab."

CHAPTER 50

WHAT IS A MAN?

"Could you persuade your father to file charges?" Stoeckle said.

"I have no way of contacting him. What's wrong with the tax beef?"

"Prosecutorial leverage. Never mind. Do you have any pictures of this slab?"

"Yes. I'll send them to you. I also sent them to Professor Gehrke at his university address."

"Do you have his email?"

"Just a sec." Josh dug out Professor Gehrke's card and read Stoeckle the email. "Ryan's younger brother Adam is missing. He's probably frightened and alone. I'll send you pictures. Maybe you can use facial recognition software to find him. He could be a witness to your federal beef, so you have a reason."

"All right."

"You can do this?"

"Facebook has the best facial recognition software on the planet."

The doorbell rang, Fig woofed.

"Gotta go. I'll talk to you later. Thanks, Roland."

"Later."

Ray wore hot pants, Josh's shirt freshly laundered, a backpack, and carried a brown paper bag from Cookies Unlimited. "I brought dessert."

Josh waited until she set her stuff on the dining room table before kissing her. Dinner was delayed.

They drank beer on the deck while Josh grilled the pork loin. Fireflies appeared against the dark curtain of the woods separating Josh's house from the estate in back, which was part of White Oaks Estates, Phil Bass' deal.

"Oh, I just love them. When I was a little girl, we used to catch them tear off the luminous tails and wear them as jewelry."

"That's horrible."

"I know. I was a rotten child. What's happening with your case?"

"What case?"

"The house that burned down."

Josh told her about finding his father in his living room, Ryan Gehrke, the slab, all of it.

"So, you're telling me this boy Adam is missing?"

"I've got some people working on it."

"And this slab? What's that about?"

"Some people believe that once the slab establishes that African explorers discovered the Americas centuries before Columbus, it will lead to wide-spread civil unrest, whatever the fuck that means."

Ray stood, stripped off her clothes, lifted the lid to the hot tub and got in.

"It means there are unstable personalities eager to take advantage of the situation. I'm thinking of this woman Monique. She has her own Youtube show. I've seen it."

"Why?"

"I thought she had something to say. You can't deny that racism exists."

"I don't."

"As a white American, don't you feel just a little bit responsible?"

"Nope."

She splashed him. "You're such a troglodyte!"

Josh stood and took off his clothes. "That does it."

It was ten by the time they were dry.

"You're welcome to spend the night," Josh said. "Sid Vicious needs a break."

She wanted to watch Rachel Maddow. Josh read some comics he'd picked up at Westfield.

When it was time for bed, Josh knelt on the floor and folded his hands. "I'm going to pray for Adam, if you'd care to join me."

Ray stared open-mouthed. "Oh, what the hell. I'll pray for him too. Only I pray to Gaia."

Fig lay on the floor with her snout between her paws.

"Dear Lord, please look after Adam Gehrke and keep him safe from harm."

Josh turned on the ceiling fan which he'd installed and got in the king-sized bed. Ray lay down and Fig insinuated herself between them. The only sound was the whirring of the fan blade and the crickets through the open window.

Since prison, Josh understood that a man needed to believe in something bigger than himself if he was going to be happy. God filled some of that, but the rest was a gaping hole which others called family. He was a dubious candidate for patriarch. He wasn't sure he wanted children. But he understood the appeal, that man was an animal, and that it was only natural for animals to reproduce and to love their spawn. The family was the essential unit. You cared about your family, then your friends, then your neighborhood, then your state, then your country, then the whole wide world. In that order. That was only natural.

Ray was a living, breathing, beautiful woman, utterly desirable. But who was she on the inside? He saw the warning signs, yet he knew happily married couples who were polar opposites. She liked rap; he liked the blues. She liked sushi; he liked hamburgers. She was a lifelong Democrat; he was a libertarian with enough guns to take over Guatemala. But they agreed not to argue, not over diddly shit. The important thing was that they had each other's back, they were deeply committed to making one another happy. Wasn't that more important than for whom they voted?

He and Fig Newton had only been together a couple of months, but he had found her perfect in every way. They both loved the same music She never talked politics. They'd talked about moving in together. Then, POOF! Vanished, leaving a black hole in his heart. Yet she was with him every day. Not a day went by he didn't wonder what their life would have been like.

Duane had not been helpful. It wasn't until Josh was in his twenties, serving six years for atrocious assault, that Chaplain Dorgan explained to him what it meant to be a man. Got him reading the Bible. Josh liked *The Complete Illustrated Children's Bible*, *The Action Bible*, *The Illustrated Bible Story By Story*, R. Crumb's *Genesis Illustrated*, and Justin Green's *Binky Brown Meets The Holy Virgin Mary*. Josh wasn't book smart. He knew that. But he trusted his common sense and moral compass that had emerged during his years in prison.

Josh didn't delude himself that he would be a good father, but he knew he would be a better father than Duane. He didn't want to get ahead of himself. He'd always been careful. He'd left no children behind. He read somewhere that a woman retained DNA from every man with whom she'd slept. But what if they used condoms? Here was a woman. She was fun and exciting. But there were problems. There were always problems. It was too much to expect a man and a woman to be perfectly compatible in every way and never argue. Sure, he heard from couples who claimed they never argued. He didn't believe it. The arguments may be genteel, conducted in dulcet tones, but there were disagreements. There were always disagreements. No matter how hard man and woman tried to merge, they remained two separate entities with separate personalities. Relationships took work. Josh wasn't afraid of hard work. He could only play it forward and see where it went.

Ray snored softly. That could be a problem.

From the other room, Josh's phone chimed. It was eleven. Whatever it was, it could wait until morning.

CHAPTER
51

MY LIFE WITH A SERIAL KILLER

When she was twenty, Merle dated an abusive thug named Earl. Merle and Earl. Cute. Earl beat her, drank pathologically and had a murderous temper. He was a fun guy when he was sober. But get four boilermakers in him and he wanted to inflict pain. After he'd inflicted enough pain on her, Merle got a restraining order. Earl got drunk one night and got pulled over a half block from her house where the cops discovered six outstanding warrants. Exit Earl.

But word filtered back from the Farm. Earl had friends on the outside, blamed Merle for his problems, and had hired a hit man. Likely bullshit, but Merle was twenty, scared, no family. Her Baptist parents had given her the heave-ho when she'd become pregnant at seventeen. She'd been on her own ever since, in foster homes for a couple years, and then working odd jobs until she'd saved enough money to attend dental school.

Merle was eight months pregnant when she was in an auto-mobile accident. Casey at the wheel. Merle in shotgun. Headed toward The Branch for some country line dancing. Casey was soused, having prepped for the evening with some blow and Southern Comfort. Being the good mother that she was, Merle had turned down the blow. The hospital delivered a healthy, five-pound baby girl which Merle gave up for adoption.

Merle doubled down. She took a job as a wet nurse. She scrimped and saved and lived with unsavory roommates un-til she'd scraped together the tuition for Concorde Career College in South Miami. She still liked to party, but she held it together long enough to earn her degree in a year. She went to work for a big firm in South Miami.

Twenty years later, she had a coke habit and a condo. She was over at her friend Rachel's place one night sipping Chardonnay and doing lines with the television turned to mute in the background when a familiar face appeared, handcuffed, between two police officers being hustled from a courthouse in bright sunlight surrounded by reporters and police.

"Turn it up!" Merle howled.

Rachel stared at her in consternation with a grin. Merle pointed at the TV.

"Turn it up! I know that guy!"

Rachel picked up the remote.

"...suspected in as many as nine other murders in a four-state killing spree. The suspect, Earl Shumpeter, was dubbed as the Dumpster Killer for his propensity to leave bodies in dumpsters."

"Oh my God!" Merle howled. "That's Earl! I dated him

for a year!"

"No shit. I've heard of the Dumpster Killer. Seriously? You were in a relationship with him?"

"I lived with him!"

"No way."

"You should write a book. Your life with a serial killer."

"I can't write!"

"I know a guy, writes porn for money. Musta written a dozen books already. Tell him what happened, he'll write it, and you'll split the profits."

"I don't think he was a murderer, back then. But he was headed that way."

Rachel hit the mute. "Well fuck him. Let's go to Lopez. They have karaoke tonight."

A month later, on her thirty-seventh birthday, Shaundra appeared outside her door.

"Are you my mother?"

Merle was in rehab at the time and had her shit together. They embraced. Merle told her what had happened. Shaundra was just happy to have found her birth mother. From then on, they were family. Shaundra married Bill Blanchette, sales manager for a custom furniture manufacturer in Dallas. Merle was there for the birth of her grandchildren.

But mostly, she was in Miami, cleaning teeth. Then she met Duane.

Here she was, hiding in her grandson's room at her daughter's house in Dallas. Not even a half bottle of Southern Comfort could drown the dread lurking in her stomach like a psychopathic rat.

How could she be so stupid? What genetic flaw caused her to make choices that were not only bad, but catastrophic? Men. She was talking about men. She knew how to buy a car without getting screwed, and which olive oils were pure olive oil. It was only in relationships, the single most important aspect of her life, that she was perverse.

She should have taken one look at the ink running up and down Duane's corded arm, the cig dangling from his lip, the way he strutted when he walked, and his casual familiarity with any woman under fifty, and known.

She should have known.

He could not have been more apparent than if he wore a sandwich board that said, TROUBLE.

What was it about Merle that doomed her to a life of disappointment? Aside from the obvious? Why did she always choose the bad boy losers? She'd grown up on her own, even before being thrown out. Her parents were distant, incapable of showing affection. Her father would beat her with a switch if she transgressed. Neither parent cared how she did in school, not even when the counselor visited to tell them that Merle got in a lot of fights.

The only time they supported her was when the guidance counselor called them in to tell them they'd found marijuana in Merle's locker.

"What the hell you doing in Merle's locker?" her father roared. He was a libertarian. Every word out of his mouth was libertarian. His socks were libertarian. He always carried. He'd stopped a gas station robbery once. Government was Satan. He resented every dime he was forced to pay *at the point of a gun* in taxes. He drank Coca-cola out of a bowl. He supported legalization of all drugs and prostitution.

As a child, she fantasized that these weren't her real parents, but as she grew older, she sometimes wished she'd been adopted.

Too late for that. Water under the dam. She made her bed. Rachel's words came back to haunt her.

"You should write a book. Your life with a serial killer."

What were the odds she would survive a relationship with a serial killer? But it wasn't Earl about whom she was concerned. What were the odds she would survive relationships with two serial killers? The things Duane told her when he was drunk and high came back to haunt her.

"Nobody ever gets the best of me. I keep track. It may take days, it may take years. It may take the rest of my life, but I always get 'em back. Payback is a motherfucker." He cited several examples.

But it wasn't his words. It was when he abruptly bolted from the boarding gate in Denver. Where was he going? What was so vital he had to abandon her? It bothered her throughout the flight to Dallas, during which she drank three small bottles of vodka. It bothered her all the next day until she knew she would get no sleep. She pulled out Josh's card. She dialed his number. She heard it ring.

She canceled the call.

Payback is a motherfucker.

CHAPTER

52

BRUCE BASS

Josh rose to the smell of coffee. Fig hadn't wakened him because Fig was fascinated with Ray in the kitchen. Josh sat up, wiped his eyes, pulled on some pants, went into the kitchen where Ray, wearing hot pants and one of Josh's Triumph Tees, was making omelets from eggs, cheddar cheese, and ham. Josh kissed her on the neck and poured himself a cup of coffee.

"Fig and I go for a run every morning."

Ray plopped a plate before him. "Really? I'll join you."

"We usually do five miles."

"No prob."

After breakfast, Ray rinsed the dishes and put them in the washer, pulled sweats, a white headband and New Balance sneakers from her bag and stretched in the living room, giving Josh an excellent view of her butt.

"You lead," he said.

Ray's Prius was parked in the driveway. As they ran toward town, Phil Bass passed and honked in his Lexus SUV. Josh waved back.

"My neighbor," he explained.

Ray had no problem keeping up. When they got back, Josh let her have the shower first while he checked his phone. Fleiss called.

"Hotchkiss called," the message said. "Good job! Give me a call when you get a chance. I may get you a bonus."

Ray came out in cargo shorts and a fresh Hawaiian shirt imprinted with hibiscus, waves, and surfboards. Josh tried to grab her, but she stiff-armed him, pecked him on the cheek and headed for the door. "Call me later!"

Josh gathered his papers including title and headed for the DMV on his Road King to license the Basket Case. The DMV was housed in a weird new quasi-mall with a massive portico on Excelsior Drive. Josh parked in back with other supplicants, in a space reserved for motorcycles. Inside, he stood in line in the massive license renewal building and took a number. One thousand four hundred and fifty-seven. He took a seat near the back in one of the institutional plastic chairs and reached for the book in the pocket of his cargo pants, *A Splendid Savage*. It was about a dude named Fred Burnham who was a scout in the American West and in the Boer War. Josh loved that shit.

Josh heard snippets of Spanish and Chinese. The board above the desks said one thousand three hundred and ninety-nine. He joined Burnham sneaking between trenches during the Boer War until the woman next to him, who was nursing a baby, nudged him.

"Hey," she said. "Is that you?"

Josh looked up. His number was blinking.

"Yes, thank you!"

An hour and fifteen minutes had passed. He followed the signs to a gun metal gray desk behind which sat a weary civil servant with curly gray hair, a set of *pince nez* hanging from her neck. He gave her his papers.

"Hmmm," she said. "This sounds interesting. Do you have a picture?"

Josh dialed one up on his phone, showed it to her.

"Sweet. All right, there's a forty-five-dollar registration fee. How would you like to pay?"

It was noon by the time Josh walked out of the DMV clutching his new plate, which he slipped into the tank bag on his Road King. He headed west on tertiary roads winding through forested hills toward the Bass Garage. He stopped in the middle of the road beneath a canopy of trees a quarter mile down Brotherhood Lane to watch a juvenile black bear amble across the blacktop. Josh kept his distance, knowing its mother would not be far. Sure enough, a few minutes later mom broke cover and dashed across the street, urging her spawn into deeper woods. It was one-fifteen when he pulled into the open gate of the garage, and kicked out next to a tricked-out Dodge Magnum.

Josh pressed the buzzer next to the front door, glancing at the camera hanging from the eaves. A minute later the door opened in the hand of a man built like a bulldozer with a gray beard wearing denim coveralls. A slide rule poked from a pocket. He looked like a Mt. Horeb troll. He peered up with twinkling blue eyes.

"Are you Pratt?" he growled. "Edwin isn't here yet. Come in."

Josh entered an office with a wooden counter and a checkerboard tile floor with mismatched chairs and a cheap table on which rested various technical journals including *Popular Science*, *Popular Mechanics*, *The Engineer*, *Model Engineering*, and the latest *Cycle World*. Behind the desk, shelves were crammed with car, motorcycle, and airplane models, along with framed photos of Bass in younger days posing at the wheel of the Grand Symphony Sedan, astride the World's Longest Motorscooter, in the cockpit of his bi-plane, with Governor Tommy Thompson, Richard Nixon, Buzz Aldrin, Bill Clinton, Charlie Daniels, Dan Gurney, and many others.

"You want the tour?"

"Sure."

Bass motioned him around the counter through a door into a garage crammed with vehicles and equipment. He stopped next to an old-fashioned red and white Coca-Cola dispenser with a vertical door through which you pulled bottles, opened it and pulled out a Coke.

"You want something to drink?"

"I'll take a Coke, thanks."

Bass handed him one. "So, you're my brother's neighbor, the one who won't sell."

"I was there first."

Bass laughed. "Phil and I don't talk much. He thinks I disapprove of his bourgeoisie lifestyle."

"Do you?"

"To a certain extent. I've always been a nuts and bolts kinda guy. Phil was always management. I worked for General Motors for nine years as a designer. I was in the union." Bass held his bottle with pinkie extended. "He's always been like this."

"He thinks I'm an eyesore."

Bass laughed. "Good on ya! I love Phil, but I rib him relentlessly. I'm the black sheep of the family. Never mind I'm a Pierce Engineering Genius Award recipient, and graduated *magna cum laude* with a Master's Degree in Engineering from Stanford. I don't live in a fancy house and hobnob with the mayor."

"Looks like you've done plenty of hobnobbing," Josh said.

"I was trying to promote my business. I hold over one hundred and twenty-seven patents. My inventions are used by several Fortune five hundred companies, including Westinghouse and Ford."

Bass paused before an eight-foot object shrouded by a dust-covered canvas. He whipped off the canvas, raising a cloud of dust that danced and glittered in beams of light shining through industrial skylights. Josh blinked.

A male department store mannequin was mounted on a broad base wearing a combination vest/harness made of black nylon strapping, with hard nylon clamps and many pockets. The figure leaned forward to offset the weight of an electric motor connected to a shaft from which hung three carbon fiber propeller blades. Extending downward and back from the engine like a dragon's tail was a light metal framework ending in a combination fin and stabilizer.

"This is a personal helicopter for commuting. It hasn't been tested."

Josh reached toward the joystick in the dummy's hand. It had a red button on the top.

Bass swatted Josh's hand away. "Don't touch that! You have to be inside the blades, or it will chop your head off. I've got a remote starter. Step back."

Bass pulled out his smart phone, poked and slid. With a whoosh and a whine, the personal helicopter shuddered, its blades whirling and rising like a flushed pheasant. The black blades blurred, the chopper straining at its base. Bass pushed a button and the thing settled down.

Bass showed Josh the world's longest motor scooter, by-passing other covered objects until he came to a glass door. They passed through the Airstream, maybe ten feet, with windows looking out both sides, to the front where Josh's bike was parked, and to the rear, the fenced-in area Josh had observed previously. Opening the door at the far end, Bass led him into the pole barn, a relatively new addition.

Bass flipped some switches and ceiling-mounted spot-lights highlighted a massive vehicle with two sets of front wheels.

"The Grand Symphony Sedan."

CHAPTER
53

AXIAL ROSE

It was huge. It looked like something out of *League of Extraordinary Gentleman*, with its massive fenders, elongated hood, and landau roof. The running boards could accommodate two men on each side. The front bumper looked like a cow catcher.

"Holy shit," Josh said. "What's under the hood?"

Bass had to reach to get to the old-fashioned leather straps holding down the hinged hood, which sprang up at his touch revealing an enormous V-12.

"It's a smaller version of the Rolls Royce V-12 used to power the Spitfire during WWII. My version uses an aluminum block and only displaces six liters. It'll only do about a hundred and seventy due to streamlining issues."

Josh stared at the elongated cylinder head embossed with the Bass logo and six custom exhaust pipes angling down and to the rear. "You made that engine?"

"Oh yes. The machining still exists at a plant in Indiana. It also features independent suspension on each wheel. Let me show you the interior."

Josh followed Bass to the rear, which rode high like a monster truck. Bass unhinged the rear hatch and as it rose with a faint hiss on pneumatic valves, an aluminum stairway unfolded to the ground. The roof was six feet off the ground. Bass led the way into the aircraft-like interior, with seats on either side of a narrow corridor which rose into a console between the front seats.

"The engine develops seven hundred horsepower and six hundred and eighty four pounds of torque. I've had it up to one fifty, but that was on state roads."

"Is it running?"

"Oh yes. Fully operational. I've loaned it out for certain events. Phil used it once at the opening of one of his developments. It gets about six miles to the gallon and has a range of one hundred and fifty miles."

Bass walked around the vehicle to a large, skeletal installation resembling a giant bird fossil. "This is my ornithopter. Unfortunately, the ride is too rough for any serious application." He continued to what looked like another personal helicopter, only this one had a fuselage and a tiny cockpit. "My gyrocopter. I envisioned this as another form of personal transportation. It uses a variation of my co-axial engine. I sold a few."

"Anybody crash?"

Bass ignored him, as he walked over to an elaborate recliner with an arm-mounted dash and a joystick protruding from the bass. "I have back issues. This is my massage chair, powered by a Yamaha five hundred cubic centimeter single cylinder engine."

"No shit. I remember that bike. But why use a gas engine for a massage chair? Why not electric?"

"An excellent question. The proof is in the pudding. The chair uses a series of automotive-like pistons that can pummel your back five hundred times a minute. You can adjust contact depth to the millimeter. Would you like to try it?"

Josh lived with pain. "Sure." He settled into the massive chair, tilting back.

"I retrained the Yamaha electrics. This model had a kick-starter. I'll start it for you."

Josh felt Bass adjusting things in back and smelled gasoline. Seconds later the engine roared into life and a velvet fist began pummeling his back up and down on both sides of his spine. The pleasure was so intense he forgot everything else and just lay there, listening to the engine wail, smelling gasoline, and letting the chair work.

He pushed the stop button. "Can I get one of these?"

"Unfortunately, it's a one-off. I sold seven patents in connection with this chair, but there's not much demand."

"Can I buy this one?"

"That's part of my permanent collection. Let me show you my book."

Bass dug around in some boxes and handed Josh a heavy coffee table book in portrait format with a wrap-around dust jacket depicting Bass standing in front of the garage surrounded by his inventions: the Symphony Sedan, the ornithopter, the gyrocopter, a Stearman Bi-Plane, the World's Longest Motor Scooter, and some kind of speedboat on a trailer. The title in circus like lettering was *The Many Worlds of Bruce Bader Bass* by Rhonda Stevenson. Josh set it on a table and thumbed through.

"How much?"

"I'm selling them for sixty. They retailed for one twenty-five."

Josh dug out his wallet and handed Bass three twenties. "Will you sign it?"

Bass opened the book to the title page and wrote, "To Josh, Your Friend Bruce Bader Bass."

"I saw you had some kind of installation at the House on the Rock, a motorcycle or something. Is that around?"

"Ah. You're referring to my axial five-cylinder. No, I withdrew that exhibit some years ago when Hotchkiss approached me about reviving the Hotchkiss Brand."

"So, where's the engine?"

"It's in the new Hotchkiss."

"Where's the new Hotchkiss?"

"Hotchkiss has it."

"How does it work?"

Bass led the way to the other building, to the office where he sat down in front of a computer and brought a schematic of the engine, five cylinders arranged around a center axle. "It has no valves. Each cylinder is two hundred cubic centimeters. The pistons drive a star-shaped element called a reciprocator as they rotate slowly around the axle, allowing the elements to move in a wave-like motion. Three spark plugs, it has the same number of power strokes per revolution as a six-cylinder engine, but of course it's much simpler and lighter."

Josh watched the computer animation. "Holy shit. Why isn't someone building this?"

Bass looked up from beneath hedgerow brows. "We are. That's why I've entered into a strategic partnership with Hotchkiss."

"What about electricity?"

"That's just a fantasy. From where do they think the electricity comes? Unicorn farts?"

A faint buzzing permeated the office and grew louder, like the approach of some insect. A helmeted rider entered the compound on a sleek bike, the engine concealed with art deco bodywork. From the Union Jack on the helmet, Josh knew it was Hotchkiss.

Hotchkiss kicked out next to the Road King as Josh and Bass exited the building. Josh walked all around the sleek bike which looked production ready. There were no logos.

"So, this is the bike of the future."

Hotchkiss unstrapped his helmet and set it on the bike's flat seat. He wore a Roland Sands jacket and boots decorated with orange flames. "The Sheiks can have the bloody company if they back the Snark."

"The Snark?"

"The Snark. Big Lewis Carroll fan. My great, great grandfather knew him, you see."

He struck a dramatic pose. "Just the place for a Snark!" Hotchkiss declaimed in a stentorian voice. "I have said it twice: That alone should encourage the crew. Just the place for a Snark! I have said it thrice: What I tell you three times is true.

"The crew was complete: it included a Boots—A maker of Bonnets and Hoods—A Barrister, brought to arrange their disputes—And a Broker, to value their goods."

Josh clapped.

"Done a bit of theater, at Cambridge, you know. *Taming of the Shrew*, that sort of thing. Every proper English chappie must play his Shakespeare."

The Snark looked like many motorcycles blended into one, an amalgam of every non-cruiser ever built. Josh set a hand on the UJM handlebars. "I don't suppose I could take it for a ride."

Hotchkiss grinned. "We would welcome your impressions. However, if you wreck it, that will be a million dollars."

"Do I have to wear a helmet?"

CHAPTER
54

THE SNARK

Josh emptied his pockets of everything but his wallet, plac-
ing his cellphone, knife and pocket change in the tank bag
of his Road King. He didn't want to feel anything jabbing
him while he rode. He swung a leg over, his feet easily reaching the ground.

Hotchkiss offered him the helmet, but Josh declined.

"I can't afford to crash. Don't worry. I'll be careful."

He pushed the starter button and the engine buzzed to
life with a weird, whirring sound, half turbo, half gerbils in
a wheel. Turning the bike toward the gate, Josh snicked into
first and released the clutch, feeling the torque propel him
like the Bay of Fundy going out, he eased onto the crumbled
blacktop and headed southwest on Myhr Trail, one of those
winding, plunging roads created by glacial run-off. The
glaciers had stopped midway down Wisconsin, and their
melt had carved the southwest section into a wonderland of

wooded valleys and spectacular views. Josh fixed his eyes on the road ahead, feeding the surge but not pushing the bike any faster than he would ride the Hawk GT.

He felt the beast buzzing between his feet, heard the unearthly wail of its three-into-one pipe. No more syncopated beat. Cruisers played the blues. Crotch rockets rocked bop. The Snark channeled Don Ellis. Five cylinders, three exhausts made for a weird time signature. The Snark rolled easily into corners, its trad front fork handling the potholes with ease, the single rear shock smooth and accommodating. Josh rose up out of a gully and found himself on top of a denuded broad hill with a string of giant wind turbines waiting for the wind. Bird choppers. The road stretched before him ruler straight for about a mile and he let it out, snicking through the gears to sixth. The Snark leaped forward with turbine-like power, the wind tearing at Josh's goggles. It had no speedometer, just a digital readout of revolutions, temperatures, and sine waves beyond Josh's understanding, but it felt like well over a hundred.

Josh rolled back the throttle and used the enormous disc brakes to haul the Snark down. He turned around in a field entry and headed back toward the garage. From atop the hill, he could see all the way to Baraboo's Blue Hills rising over a sea of green. Wisconsin was so green. He couldn't imagine living anywhere else. A hawk gyred over the valley.

As Josh descended into the cool valley, he found the exhaust note exciting, but muted. Hotchkiss didn't want to attract attention to himself. Josh wondered if Hotchkiss had been riding the Snark the first time he saw him. Josh wanted one. He wondered when it would go into production. He wondered whether they'd build him one. He wondered if he could afford it.

Josh had no money problems thanks to the deal he'd worked out with the National Security Agency which put him on the roster as a consultant, ever since his encounter with the spook killer known as the Jesuit. The Jesuit had killed Fig. Josh had killed the Jesuit.

Since then, Josh had justified his retainer by alerting the NSA about industrial spying and foiled a robbery of an Army arsenal, both in connection with his undercover work with The Jugan. Josh could easily afford to purchase one of Phil Bass' mini mansions, several of which were for sale just down the street from where he lived. But the ranch house suited him. He was a meat and potatoes kind of guy.

As he approached the Bass Garage, he saw a silver SUV parked by the front door. Hotchkiss and Bass stood next to each other with their arms crossed. It wasn't until he got in the gate that Josh saw the visitors, three men and a woman holding pistols on the inventors. Ryan Gehrke, Monique Vigil, Baby Face and Malcolm.

For an instant it occurred to Josh to lay a doughnut and hightail it. He rolled the bike to a stop next to his Road King, shut it off, and got off.

"Wellll," Vigil purred. "Billy Jack is back."

Josh pushed up his goggles and got off the bike. "What's up?"

"Come on, Pratt!" Gehrke said. "We want the slab."

"We don't have it. Adam has it."

"Bullshit! If Adam had it, he'd have told me."

Josh looked at Vigil. "Did you set that fire?"

Vigil's face twisted in hate. "Fuck you, cracker!"

Gehrke looked like he was about to make another run. Josh let his hands go loose at his sides.

"You think I'd kill my own family?"

"I didn't ask you."

"She was with me the whole time, you sorry-ass excuse for a human being. I guess the acorn doesn't fall too far from the tree."

Josh felt fury brewing in his gut. He bit his lip. Words seldom solved anything. He motioned Gehrke toward him. "Come at me, bro."

Vigil put a hand on Gehrke's arm. "Let me. I'd love to teach this cracker a lesson."

Bruce Bass raised his hands like an old-time prophet. "Neither Hotchkiss nor I have the slightest idea what you're talking about. Who are you? What are you even doing here?"

"Yeah," Josh said. "How'd you find me? What makes you think I have your slab?"

Malcolm reached in his pocket and pulled out Josh's cell phone. "We been trackin' you since Vegas."

A bolus of self-recrimination grew in Josh's gut. He wasn't the sharpest knife in the drawer.

"What about Adam, Ryan? Aren't you concerned about him?"

"Of course I am! We've been in touch. Don't worry about Adam."

"Shouldn't you be directing your efforts toward finding him? Is this slab more important than his life?"

"Don't lecture me."

"The slab proves that black people discovered the new world a century before Columbus," Vigil said in a steely monotone. "Do you have any idea what that's going to do to the world order when word gets out? Do you think that black people will continue to suffer institutional racism and harassment once it becomes known? I'll tell you what will happen. Righteous indignation will sweep through every dispossessed and underrepresented community. The people will rise up and smash the white power structure. It will change the course of civilization. It will right historical wrongs and put us on a path toward real social justice."

"Then you should be looking for Adam."

"I don't believe that," Gehrke said. "I think you and your old man are both too damn clever for your own good. I think you got it, and one way or another, we're gonna get it."

Bass waved his arms. "Listen. I'm an old man. If I don't go to the bathroom in the next sixty seconds, I'm going to piss my pants. I have nothing to do with this. Neither does Hotchkiss. Why don't you take your dispute elsewhere?"

"No way," Vigil said, each word cut with steel. "Malcolm, take this hairy cracker to the bathroom and bring him back."

Malcolm gestured toward the door. "After you."

CHAPTER

55

THE GRAND SYMPHONY

An uneasy silence prevailed. Babyface pulled out a cigarette and lit it, tossing the match to the ground.

"Why come here?" Josh demanded. "If you think I have the slab, why not come to my place? Why drag these people into it? They have nothing to do with it. They don't even know what you're talking about."

"Yeah," Hotchkiss said. "What's this slab?"

Ryan held his gun at his side. "You ain't about to make the same mistake twice. Oh yeah, your old man told me how he stashed the painting in your basement. See how well that worked out. No, you're too smart to keep it at your place."

Vigil gestured at the garage. "We may have to search this place."

"Suppose you find it? Then what? If it's real, it's a national historic artifact. It doesn't belong to you anymore than

Plymouth Rock or the Liberty Bell. The feds'll step in."

Vigil sneered with her whole body. "We have our own experts. We've got top universities lined up, offering us accreditation and resources. No way are we letting the corrupt federal government take this, to cover up this country's vicious legacy of racism and oppression. If necessary, we will call on hundreds of thousands of brothers and sistas and allies in the media and woke students to march with us. Maybe millions. How do you like them beans, cracker? How'd you like to see a million fists raised on the National Mall?"

Josh mimed eating popcorn.

"Look here," Hotchkiss said. "I've always supported you chaps. Bass and I have nothing to do with this. We hardly know this man. Why don't you take your business elsewhere and leave us out of it."

Gehrke showed his choppers. "Pip pip, old chap!"

A dull thunk issued from in the garage. Josh looked around. He was the only one who heard it.

Gehrke stuffed his pistol in the small of his back and threw a leg over the Axial. "So, what's so special about this?"

"It's got a five-cylinder axial engine," Josh said. "Goes like hot stink."

Gehrke hit the starter button and the engine whirred. Hotchkiss flinched and put out his hands.

"Relax, your lordship. I'm just gonna run it around the yard."

Gehrke snicked into gear, popped the clutch, and dragged

the bike around in an insane oval, the rear tire spinning out of control sending up a plume of smoke.

"Stop that!" Hotchkiss said.

Gehrke rolled back, put it in neutral and pulled it upright. "Or what? How much does this cost? Could you build one for me?"

"It's priceless. That's the only prototype. It took ten years and over a million dollars."

"Well are you gonna make 'em or not?"

"Now that we have a viable prototype, I will try to attract a coterie of interested investors. If all goes well, we will purchase and refurbish a machine shop in Indiana and begin production, but I don't foresee that happening for at least three years."

"How much?"

Hotchkiss threw his hands in the air. "Impossible to say, but it won't be cheap. We're looking at thirty to fifty thousand pounds."

"How much is that in dollars?"

"About sixty-six thousand dollars."

"I hope you give it a better kickstand and a loud horn," Josh said.

Hotchkiss raised his sunglasses. "What's wrong with the kickstand?"

"Look at it."

Gehrke set the sidestand and got off. He shoved the bike and it started to fall over.

"No!" Hotchkiss yelled.

Gehrke's hand lashed out and seized the bike by the seat strap, pulling it back upright. He pointed a finger at Hotchkiss. "Gotcha."

"This bike this needs a center stand," Josh said.

"We will offer a full line of accessories including a center stand, windshield, and outer wear."

Vigil vogued forth. "Well you're just a regular capitalist powerhouse. What is this lord shit? Are you some kind of English royalty or landed gentry?"

"My Great Grandfather Geoffrey was Earl of Berkfordshire, and my uncle Roderick served in the House of Lords. But I don't profess any titles myself."

"Y'know," Vigil said, "this is the kind of shit we been talkin' about, this classist, racist, sexist shit wherein a handful of entitled pigs who inherited their wealth perpetuate an unjust system designed to exploit the working man."

Hotchkiss gaped. "I beg your pardon?"

"'I beg your pardon?'" Vigil aped, enjoying herself. "Bloody hard cheese, isn't it?"

"Have you ever studied history?"

"Don't lay that condescending bullshit on me. Have you read Franz Fanon, Karl Marx, Howard Zinn, Noam Chomsky? Of course not. All you know is what they teach you in some British boarding school filled with white supremacists."

"You don't know what you're bloody talking about! Hotchkiss Arms has raised more people out of poverty then every bloody rapper in history!"

Vigil pounced. "Hotchkiss Arms? As in weapons?"

Leaning back against the SUV with his arms crossed, Gehrke grinned. "Preach it, Sistah!"

"Oh, for bloody sake...of course arms! How else are people supposed to defend themselves? We didn't really get going until the Boer War, and then came World War One, which was hardly Britain's idea. Do you even study history?"

"I study the history you don't, the history of white oppression, colonialism and racism! Let's talk about India, Afghanistan, and Rhodesia!"

"Ancient history."

Vigil started hopping around, like a guy working himself up. "I know you. I know your type. Afraid to get your hands dirty. Always hire someone else to do your dirty work. I could lay you out in ten seconds."

"Don't be absurd," Hotchkiss sniffed.

Vigil put up her fists like a nineteenth century boxer. "Come on, hot shot, Mister Imperial Colonial, let's you and me go at it. You're a big bad Brit, you've got me by sixty pounds."

"I won't stoop to fighting a woman."

Vigil danced forward.

"I'll have you know I was captain of the boxing team at Eaton."

Vigil barked. Gehrke laughed.

"A hundred bucks on Monique!" he sang.

Josh turned to Hotchkiss. "Don't do it."

Vigil walked up to the Brit and slapped him across the

face. Hotchkiss stepped back, shocked.

"No more, I'm warning you!"

"Or what? Come on! I'm just itching to kick your butt!"

Gehrke pulled out his phone and started filming. "Do it!"

Behind him, the segmented metal garage door in the pole barn rolled into the ceiling with a rumble. Everyone turned to look. The snout of the Grand Symphony Sedan emerged, the car rolled into sunlight, turned toward the main entrance and took off, rear wheels throwing a rooster tail of dust and gravel.

Gehrke stepped away from the SUV and the Grand Symphony Sedan caught him on its cowcatcher bumper, hurling him through the air like a broken doll.

CHAPTER 56

SHOWDOWN AT THE BASS GARAGE

Babyface turned and sprinted. The car swerved and ran him over, leaving a flopping pile of laundry. Vigil pulled her gun, took a stance and squeezed off five shots at the sedan, which went into a NASCAR spin, turning one hundred and eighty degrees to point at her.

Vigil sprinted out of its path, tore open the door to the SUV and peeled out, smashing into the chain link fence at the side of the gate and tearing it down. The massive vehicle fishtailed onto the crumbling county road, nearly ending in the ditch, recovered, and burning rubber. They listened in shocked silence as its noise retreated.

The Grand Symphony Sedan came to a stop. The rear gate lifted, and Bass crawled out like a troll emerging from his hole. He walked from Gehrke's body to Babyface's.

"I'll call the sheriff."

Iowa County Sheriff Art Stone arrived in a Dodge Charger with a deputy twenty minutes later to find Hotchkiss, Bass and Josh seated at a picnic table beneath a towering oak, drinking bottled water. They all stood as the sheriff approached, his deputy heading for the bodies.

"What happened, Bruce?"

"The four of 'em showed up, pulled guns, and demanded some kind of slab. I didn't know what the hell they were talking about. Then the woman started making all sorts of threats. When I went to the bathroom, they sent one of 'em with me with a gun. I thought he was going to kill me. I warned him about the one-man helicopter, but he had to push the button anyway. You'll find him inside the second building with his head attached to his body by a thread."

The deputy looked up from Gehrke's corpse, where he crouched. "This one's got a gun, Art. So does the other one."

The distant wail of sirens grew louder until an ambulance and another sheriff's department vehicle pulled into the lot, disgorging two more deputies and two EMTs. Stone sat at the picnic table to take their statements, starting with Bass. Deputy Arnstein questioned the three survivors inside the air- conditioned office, while deputies photographed the scene, bagged the guns, and gathered up the bodies. Josh watched as they removed Malcolm's body on a collapsible gurney. Two more ambulances arrived. Then it was Josh's turn.

He sat across from the sheriff on the rough, one-piece picnic table that looked as if it had been sitting in the yard forever.

"Let's have your version, Mister Pratt."

"This all started when my father showed up at my place last week." Josh told him about the confrontation in Vegas and the slab. Stone used a digital recorder and took notes in an old-fashioned spiral notepad. Josh talked for twenty minutes, pausing from time to time to sip water. Stone took it all down. When Josh finished, Stone poked at his personal device and showed it to Josh. The Righteous Hour's home page showed Vigil in full harangue, fist clenched, spit flying, head framed by that improbably black Brillo.

"Is this the woman to whom you're referring?"

"Yes, sir."

"Wait here just one minute." Stone rose, went to his vehicle and sat inside with the engine running and the air conditioning on. He returned ten minutes later and eased himself onto the bench. He was a squat fiftyish, preceded by a gut.

"You have to come into Dodgeville and give a statement."

"Can't I give it out here?"

Stone stared at him with a mixture of patience and pity.

Josh was going to be tied up for hours. Fig had plenty of water and would just have to wait on dinner. "All right."

It was four-thirty when they pulled into the Iowa County Sheriff's Department, a long, low brick building with shallow slanting roofs surmounted by huge radio towers. They parked in the fenced-in lot in back and entered the refrigerated building where Stone deposited Josh in an interview room with a tile floor and Formica table.

"You want something to drink?"

"I'll take a Coke if you got it."

Stone returned with a chilled can and a slight man in heavy glasses and a suit.

"This is assistant attorney Norman Hodge."

"What's he doing here?"

Hodge sat down. "I need to hear your story to know what charges to file."

Josh folded his hands. "Come on, Hodge."

Stone sat. "He's here to see I don't step in shit. Relax. You'll be out of here in an hour. This is going to be a Category Five shit storm, trust me. You got your dead ex-quarterback, the shoot-out at Hoover, and a known trouble-maker; that would be you."

"All right. Let's get on with it. What do you need?"

Josh talked while Hodge took notes. He knew they were filming him through the one-way window. He didn't care. He had nothing to hide.

A woman stuck her head in the room. "Sheriff, WISN Milwaukee is here, and someone from Fox News."

"Can I get a ride back to my bike?" Josh said.

Stone stood. "Come on. Let's both get out of here."

Stone cued the rear gate from his car, shutting it behind him.

"You're a trouble magnet."

Josh shrugged. "I don't look for it."

They rode the rest of the way in silence save for radio outbursts and a couple of exchanges with deputies.

"Sheriff, TV news people are here, from Madison."

"Set up a perimeter, no one inside that gate. What are they doing?"

"They're filming from outside. There's some news babe with 'em, long black hair. She's talking, dude's filming."

"Leave 'em be. There's nothing to see. We'll be there in ten minutes."

"Katy Varner," Josh said.

"Who?"

"The news babe. I know her."

"Great."

By the time they arrived, the remote patch of county road fronting the garage was parked up with news vans. Stone hit the lights and whooper to get through, where a deputy rolled the gate open, closing it behind them. The ambulances were gone, four county vehicles remained.

Josh got out of the vehicle.

"Josh!" Katy yelled from her side of the fence. Josh didn't look. He fired up the bike, headed for the gate, and rode east, choosing roads randomly, leaving it all behind. Gehrke dead, Vigil and Adam in the wind. He hoped the boy was all right. As for Vigil, he tried not to wish her ill.

Dear Lord, please grant me the strength not to wish that bitch ill.

It was past seven and still in the eighties when he wheeled into his driveway. Fig was delirious until she had her bowl of food. Josh pulled out his phone and saw three unanswered calls. You couldn't hear or feel the phone while

riding. One was Ray, asking him to call her, the second was
from Fleiss, and the third was the same unknown number
he'd discovered that morning.

He dialed back.

"Thank you for returning my call, Josh," said a barely
audible Merle. "I have to tell you something."

CHAPTER 57

BAD THOUGHTS

A bolus of dread blossomed in Josh's gut. He pulled Fig to him.

"Go ahead."

"Duane didn't get on the plane with me in Denver. He went somewhere else."

"Did he know where the Gehrkes lived?"

"Yes. He bragged to me that he had plenty of opportunity to go through Ryan's computer and papers when he was partying."

"You think he set fire to their house."

He could hear Merle crying. Something covered the phone and she honked. "I'm sorry. I'm a wreck. I haven't been able to stop thinking about this. He told me things when we were together, terrible things..."

"Like what?"

Sobbing. "I'm sorry. He has a thing about payback."

"I know. Have you told the police about this?"

"No. I don't know what to do. I can barely admit it to myself. I can't tell the police. He'd kill me."

"Do you think Duane's a murderer?"

Her silence was eloquent.

"Have you heard from him since? Do you know where he is?"

"No."

"All right, listen. You at your daughter's place? Are you all right there?"

"I'm okay."

"Does Duane know where she lives?"

"No. All he knew, she lives in Dallas."

"All right. I'll do it. I'll tell the police. It's not like the thought hadn't crossed my mind, but he's my father, y'know?"

"I know."

"Listen to me, Merle. God loves you and wants you to be happy. Are you religious?"

"I try to be."

"Well a little prayer never hurt. I'll pray for you too. If you have to talk to somebody, see if you can find an honest pastor. Ask your daughter. Is she religious?"

"Yes. Both Shaundra and Bill attend Sunday services at Christ Lutheran."

"Well ask Shaundra, but don't tell her. She doesn't need to know. This is just between you, me, and a professional, if you need one."

"I understand. Thank you, Josh."

"Call me if anything happens."

"I will."

Josh felt sick to his stomach. With the exquisite sensitivity of her breed, Fig looked up and whined. Josh drew Fig close.

"He's no damn good, Fig. Never was."

Fig leaped off the sofa and ran to the door tail wagging. There was a knock. Josh opened the door on Ray, ravishing, laden with gifts. Her smile morphed to alarm.

"What's wrong?"

Josh held the door, waited for her to set down her bag and took her in his arms, crushing her.

"Have you been crying?"

Josh let her go. "No. Thought about it."

"What's wrong? What happened?"

"Do me a favor. Pour me a drink. There's some Buffalo Trace on the counter."

Ray took her bag into the kitchen, returning a minute later with two tumblers, neat. She handed one to Josh and sat next to him on the sofa, thighs touching.

"So?"

"I think my old man burned down the Gehrkes' house."

She grabbed his hand. "My god. Oh my god. Have you told the police?"

"I just found out. I don't know what to do. I have no proof."

"I think you should at least tell them," Ray said.

Josh wrung his hands and sighed. Ray was right. He dialed the Creighton Police Department and left a message for Chief Morris.

"Sir, I think you have to consider my father Duane as a suspect."

He clenched and gyrated until Ray climbed on top of him and forcefully moved the epicenter of his thoughts. He lay on the sofa with his pants around his knees. Duane was right. Sex superseded all else. Duane was wrong! God knew Josh had abused enough women, but that was before he knew any better. That was before he understood that in order for a man to be happy, he had to believe in something larger than himself. That's why people invented God. Not that God didn't exist, but if your own instant gratification was the meaning of life, shoot yourself now. Thus, God in his wisdom designed nature so that the end result of sex was children. Children transformed a man.

Or so Josh heard. It hadn't transformed Duane, who still didn't believe in anything greater than himself.

"Earth to Josh," Ray murmured in a calm low voice.

"Was I drifting?"

"Yeah, you were out there."

"Sorry."

"You've got to stop thinking about him."

"That's hard," Josh said. "Not a day goes by I don't think about him, and what he did to me. I suppose it could have been worse."

"You turned out okay."

Josh traced her unibrow with his finger. "All praise goes to Jesus and chaplain Dorgan."

"This chaplain must be quite a guy."

"Oh yeah."

Guilt elbowed out dread. He was a private detective. He should be able to track down Chaplain Frank Dorgan. The state would have his records.

Ray got up and slipped her Tee-shirt over her head. "I'm starving. I'm going to make dinner. Feed that dog."

Josh was starving too. After he fed Fig, he went online and looked for Adam. The news reports had tapered off, replaced by the *horror du jour*. Nothing. The boy had disappeared. He phoned Chief Morris again and this time got through. Morris sounded rushed.

"Listen, I don't have time to talk now. Still no sign of the kid, but the feds are talking to Franklin Munche."

"The feds?"

"Yeah. Interior has asserted authority over the slab. It has national historic significance. Can I call you back?"

"I think my old man Duane set the fire."

Beat.

"Huh?"

"Yeah. He's a vindictive son of a bitch, and he didn't fly to Dallas as planned. He jumped ship. Listen. Look at his rap sheet. I'm afraid to. Duane Elmore Pratt. That's all I know. I don't know his birthday, I don't know his social security number. And I don't want to know."

"Okay. We'll look into it."

"Thank you, sir."

Josh took a shower, put on crisp khakis and a Hawaiian shirt featuring portraits of the Beach Boys, hot rods, surfer girls, and waves. Ray had set the deck table with candles and tulips in a beer bottle. Something smelled delicious.

"Where'd you get those tulips?"

"I borrowed them from across the street."

It was past nine by the time they finished dinner and at long last Josh stopped thinking about Duane and his spiderweb of deceit. Josh was too exhausted to make love. They slept in his bedroom with Fig between them. In the middle of the night, he heard Fig whimpering, some puppy nightmare, and gently nudged her awake.

CHAPTER 58

ON THE TERRACE

As the days dragged on and Adam Gehrke failed to surface, the cloud over Josh's head grew dense. He tried to ignore it, but in the back of his mind was the thought that if he'd stayed out of it, if he'd never visited the Gehrkes and given them the slab, none of this would have happened. He told himself it was irrational. If Duane had done it, there was nothing Josh could have done. Duane was like Eugene Moon, the insane killer who'd turned Ginger Munz' son into an animal, killed Josh's girlfriend Cass, and worshiped at the Church of Payback.

Duane worshiped at the Church of Payback. Nothing larger than the self. Nothing larger than getting even. His life was simple and empty. He felt no connection to other people.

Ray began rehearsals for "Crumbling Infrastructure", an elaborate dance involving poles and trapezes to a jazz score by Bob Corbett.

Friday morning, Detective Calloway phoned.

"Let's meet at the Terrace. I'll buy you lunch."

"Okay."

At eleven, Josh rode to Cole Duesing's garage on East Johnson, a four-story red brick sculpture that had once housed a Sinclair service station, and was now devoted to Duesing's collection of rare cars. Josh wheeled his bike into the open garage door where Duesing met him wearing greasy gray cargo pants and a Victory tank top, wiping his hands on a blue cloth. Josh kicked out.

He shook Duesing's calloused hand with grease under the nails, noted Duesing's flat stomach and bulging biceps, the Marine tat on the left.

"Come on. I'll give you the tour."

The four floors were connected by concrete ramps. The first floor held mostly hot rods, including a chopped Model A with a 389 Pontiac engine, and a perfectly preserved red Yenko Corvair with the flat six-boxer, supercharged to two hundred and fifty horsepower.

"It's a bitch on the track," Duesing said.

They walked up the corrugated concrete ramp to the second floor, which featured classic muscle cars including every GTO ever built including the orange Judge, The SS396, Plymouth Road Runner, the rare Daytona Charger, and a stable of Mustangs, with a big gap in the middle.

"I don't collect any shit from seventy-six to ninety-three," Duesing declared. "Those aren't Mustangs."

He pointed to a pink AMX. "Bought that off a Mary Kay dealer."

Josh looked up and around. Cameras concealed in translucent hemispheres bulged from the ceiling. "Where was the Cobra?"

Duesing stopped, a crevice expanding from the bridge of his nose. He headed down the ramp.

"Come on."

They walked across the main floor to the other side of the building which opened onto Gorham Street. They came to a steel rail and three concrete steps down into what had been the Sinclair's service area, with two hydraulic lifts, one occupied by a blue '66 Nova. The corrugated steel door onto Gorham was closed.

"We were detailing it in here. The car disappeared on the twenty-fifth, sometime at night. I wasn't here. We have a night watchman, his name is Walker Cochran, had him for ten years. Known him all my life. We have an ALM security system which will instantly note a break-in and notify the police. Walker was on the fourth floor when it happened. You can't hear shit from the fourth floor."

Josh pointed to the camera.

"Yeah. At nine forty-five we had a power blackout. Hit the whole east side."

"Well somebody must have known that. How much is that Cobra worth?"

"A hundred grand."

"That's not worth causing a major power outage. Did

you contact the power company? What did they say?"

"They said they had a computer glitch."

"I'd look at the power company."

"What do you charge?"

"Five hundred a day plus expenses."

"Okay," Duesing said. "Come back to the office and I'll give you an advance."

Alliant was headquartered near East Towne Mall, but Josh had no intention of visiting. He needed a roster of personnel on duty that night to sift and winnow. Who were the single men? Who had a thing about sports cars? Who was on duty that night? Who knew about Duesing's collection? Josh had lived in Madison for years and had never heard of it until that night at the Lowry's.

Damn, I need a tech guy. Where's Ninja Preston?

Josh rode down Langdon. The tree huggers had succeeded in removing the cycle parking spots across the street, so Josh parked in the Lake street lot and walked to the Union. He was early. He copped one of the few remaining red round tables on the patio, and spread out, boots on one seat, backpack on another, as he walked to the outdoor beer bar and copped a ginger ale.

He sat at the table, put his feet up and gazed out at the sky blue of Lake Mendota, little white triangles darting like butterflies. Across the lake toward Governor's Island, a big motorboat pulled two skiers.

Josh phoned Preston. "Any luck with the kid?"

Preston sounded harried. "Hang on. I'm dealing with all

sorts of shit. I'll check. Can I call you back?"

"Sure."

Calloway headed toward him through the lunch crowd, scholars, students, hippies automatically giving him space. A tall black man with a lazy eye that stared at the sky, he radiated authority. He pulled out a chair, took off his blue sports jacket revealing a snub-nosed .38 in a shoulder holster and a gold detective's shield on his belt. He loosened his tie.

"Whaddaya want? Brat and a beer?"

"Just the brat, chief."

Calloway stood in line. Josh looked around. Over half the people there, sitting in a beautiful place on a glorious summer day, were immersed in their hand-held devices. Even couples sitting at the same table. Josh spotted a few familiar faces, students from the sixties who'd fallen in love with the place and never left. Some were still students.

Calloway returned with a plastic tray containing two brats with kraut, each in a cardboard schooner, and a pint of beer.

Calloway squeezed yellow mustard on his brat. "What would the summer be without a Josh Pratt shoot-out?"

"I'm just trying to raise awareness," Josh said.

"How'd they find you?"

"They bugged my phone."

Calloway bit off a third of the brat, chewed thoroughly, swallowed, and drained half the beer. "I heard your father may be involved in the Gehrke fire."

"Yeah."

"I'm sorry."

Josh shrugged.

Calloway wiped his mouth. "I think Ashley's in a relationship with some character named Scipio."

"A Roman general."

Calloway grunted. "I looked at her phone. Maybe I shouldn't have, I don't know. Raising a teen daughter ain't all chitlins and gravy."

"Do you know who he is?"

"No. That's where you come in."

CHAPTER 59

DUNN TOOK THE COBRA

"I'll pay you," Calloway said.

Josh waved a hand. "Forget it. What have you got?"

Calloway reached into his jacket's inside pocket and withdrew an envelope. Inside was a copy of Ashley's phone records going back two weeks, her email, Twitter, Instagram, and Facebook addresses and a printout of text messages."

"What's Ashley doing now?"

"She got a job at the Nike Store at West Towne, she bikes and runs, and goes out on weekends with pals to hear music. Last week I got called into the principal's office. They found reefer in her backpack. They were kind enough to let me handle it, and she seemed repentant when I explained it to her. I'm a cop. I can't have my daughter having anything to do with reefer."

"Reefer's like chewing gum, these days," Josh said. "They're probably going to legalize it."

"Well that's another discussion and it isn't legal yet. The thing is, I can't tell when she's telling the truth. I thought I could. But I can't. Whatever it is, some combination of father/daughter miscommunication, pathology and good acting, I just don't know. I remember when I was a kid. If my father caught me lying, he'd backhand me across the face.

"We don't do that these days. Doreen and I have done the best we could. She's got good grades, she's got a full scholarship to Northwestern for track and field, she wants to study law, but I don't know. I just don't know. She's a teenage girl. Who knows what she's really thinking?"

"I'll look into it."

"Thank you. This is confidential."

"I may have to cue my IT guy."

"Do you trust him?"

Josh didn't know the IT guy. "If I don't, I won't."

Calloway offered his hand. "Thanks, brother."

Josh watched the big man go. Students and hangers-on hungrily eyed his table. He went home and phoned Ninja Preston.

Preston texted: *Turn on Skype.*

Josh moved into his office, Fig watching curiously. Josh brought up the Skype app and it began to ring, listing the caller as Sergeant Preston. Josh took the call.

A slim black man with a mustache appeared wearing a Sonic Youth T-shirt and fingerless black gloves, and several rings.

"You look at that shit I sent?" Josh said.

"Yeah. Your boy ain't surfaced. Bro, you need to drop that phone you're using. You bein' swacked."

"I know. That's why I need an IT guy. I know investigators who never leave the house. They do it all over the computer. I ain't that guy."

"Yeah, I know you ain't that guy. I looked you up. Didn't find much, but what I found was heinous. Listen. You axin' about Adam Gehrke. What's funny, I know all about Creighton, Illinois. Oh yeah. I got busted in Creighton a couple years back and spent a couple days in jail."

"Busted for what?"

"Spook shit. It's gone now. I ain't surprised the university is mixed up with this shit. You recall a couple years ago when that student died from a scorpion sting, and they fired the professor?"

"No."

Preston made a poof gesture. "Ain't nothin'. Your boy ain't showed up on Facebook. He may have gone off-grid."

"He's only fifteen."

"I built my first computer when I was thirteen. By the time I was fifteen, I'd stolen twelve thousand identities from the Bank of America and sold 'em. I ain't that guy no more. Ain't saying I'm on the up and up. Always gonna be a macka and a playa. But now I'm more selective of what I do and who I do it for."

"So why trust me?"

Preston beamed. "You got good history. I like it. Plus,

you got that federal angle."

Josh was shocked. "What federal angle?"

"You on their payroll. Consider that my bonafides."

"What do I owe you?"

Preston passed his hand palm down. "Just wait. I ain't done nothin'. I get results, you get an invoice."

"You know who Monique Vigil is?"

"I seen her fight! She was at that house in Creighton. Adam's house. You want me to find her?"

"Yeah. I'll send you everything I have on her."

"You don't need to send me nothin'. I got it."

"Okay, got another job." Josh told Preston about Duesing's missing Cobra. "We're working for someone who works at Alliant HQ, who maybe has some connection to Duesing, or collects cars, or whatever. I'll send you pictures of the car and its particulars."

"Give me twenty-four hours. Listen. Ahmina send you some burners. You need to ditch that phone you got."

"But all my numbers and pictures are on it!"

"I got all your numbers and pictures. Ahmina overnight some shit. What's your address?"

An irritating shriek permeated the house. Josh looked outside. It was the leaf blowers. The neighborhood association had hired a lawn service to walk up and down Ptarmigan blowing leaves into the gutter, where the wind would redistribute them. Josh shut the window and went out on the back deck, followed by Fig through the doggie door. Josh was exempt from the neighborhood association because he predated them. He'd been grandfathered in. Phil Bass' offer for his property was now three quarters of a million dollars.

In deference to his neighbors, Josh had cleaned up his yard and hired a lawn service. The leaf blower grew fainter as it moved down the street. The stupidest invention ever. What was the point? Leaves fell in the street, so what? Who objected to the leaves? There was no trash to speak of on Ptarmigan Road.

His phone dinged. Unknown sender: Go back on Skype.

Josh went back inside. Maybe it was time to turn on the air conditioning. He pushed the office window all the way open and turned on the ceiling fan. He went on Skype. Preston grinned at him like Eriq LaSalle in *Crazy As Hell*.

"Henry Dunn took the Cobra."

"What?" Josh said.

"Henry Dunn, zone supervisor at Alliant Energy, was on duty that afternoon, an avid hot rod aficionado, belongs to several Facebook groups including Model Car Builders and Enthusiasts where he regularly posts pictures. He is a very fine modeler. Nine years ago, he bought a home theater from American TV. Said it quit working. They said he shoulda bought the extended warranty. He sued, and it dragged on for three years before he ran out of money."

"Dunn had a grudge against Duesing?"

"You got it! Dig it—they were in the same fraternity at the UW, Alpha Sigma!"

"Where's the car?"

"It's in his brother-in-law's barn near Barneveld."

Josh could not stop grinning. "Is this for real?"

Preston held out his hand. "That'll be five thou."

"Send me an invoice."

CHAPTER

60

HOME AGAIN

Josh studied the aerial view of the brother-in-law's farm near Barneveld. The brother-in-law, Jake Nustrum, rented the land to his neighbor who grew corn, and ran a roofing business from Barneveld, a town of less than two thousand on Highway Fifty-One. Preston learned about Nustrum from studying Dunn's Facebook page before uncovering their correspondence, in which Nustrum agreed to hide the Cobra.

Dunn had no plans to profit off the Cobra. He couldn't sell it. It was famous, its VIN registered with the Shelby Society. It was pure payback. Nustrum's wife Eleanor worked at a store in Mount Horeb. Their adult children lived in Madison and Illinois.

Josh phoned Ray. "Could you give me a ride tomorrow morning?"

"Sure. Where are we going?"

"Out by Barneveld."

"What's out there?"

"I'll tell you when you pick me up."

Ray picked Josh up at nine a.m. in her Prius. With a map open on his lap, Josh directed her to Nustrum's farm, located southwest of town. As Josh explained, they carved their way through glacial drift past harvesters working their fields, trailing clouds of dust.

"Just like that, huh?" Ray said.

Josh snapped his fingers.

"This Ninja must be some kind of genius."

"No shit. Now I need another genius to look into him."

"How come?"

They pulled around a corner and stopped to allow a pickup truck to back onto a dirt road. "I don't know. Just a feeling."

A little after ten, Josh told Ray to pull over. They were on Adrienne Road, which ran along a ridge top with expansive views of farms, hills, and valleys, Nustrum's faded red barn a quarter mile distant on the other side of the corn. Josh hoisted his backpack and got out.

"Thanks, Ray. See you tonight?"

"If you want to come by. We're holding rehearsals until nine."

Josh leaned across the console and kissed her, gave her the thumbs up, turned, trotted across the road, down into the weed-filled ditch, up the other side, where he put on leather gloves to ease himself through the barbed wire fence.

It was already in the eighties. Josh put on a beige Not Lame cap and sunglasses as he zig-zagged through the corn, sipping occasionally from a Yeti water bottle. The corn came to within a hundred feet of the barn. Josh paused within the corn, pulled out some small binocs, surveyed the yard. The broad, windowless side of the barn faced him, decorated by a Norwegian hex sign. The two-story wood-frame farmhouse sat at an angle, a clothes tree in the back flying pillowcases, shirts, and underwear.

The rear deck held a gas barbecue, a picnic table, and several potted plants, an old black dog snoozing in the sun next to a bowl. Josh hoped it wouldn't be a problem, but really, who paid attention to a barking farm dog? Josh watched for fifteen minutes, then walked toward the barn. When the old dog raised its head, Josh made smooching noises.

"Who's a good boy?"

The dog got up wagging its tail, came down the wooden steps up to Josh where it plopped and rolled over on its back.

Josh knelt and rubbed its belly. "Who wants a belly rub? Who's a good dog?"

Josh rose. The barn door was open. The interior smelled of hay, fuel and diesel, a row of stalls used to house roofing equipment. The Cobra was in the back, sitting on the wood floor, covered with a green tarp. Josh ripped the tarp off with a crackling sound and inspected the silver/gray vehicle. It was a beauty, with the 427 badge on the front fender. Josh raised the hood, checked the engine, closed it, got in the driver's seat and opened his backpack. He'd learned to hot wire cars when he was sixteen. Noticing a lump beneath the rubber floor mat, he pulled up the corner and there were the keys. He started the engine with a roar that shook the dust on the floor before easing it into first and leaving the barn, driving around an old pick-up truck. He drove around the house, down the dirt drive to County Highway CK, where an iron gate was locked shut. Josh took the bolt cutters from his backpack, snapped the lock, paused on the other side to close the gate, and took off down the weathered blacktop toward Highway Fifty-One.

On the road toward Madison, bikers and little kids gave him the thumbs up. A Corvette tried to goad him into a race, but Josh had no interest in being pulled over. He arrived at Duesing's garage at eleven, pulled around the block to Gorham, pulled into the driveway and honked at the corrugated steel door. He looked up at the camera above the door and waved. Seconds later, the door retracted into the ceiling and Josh pulled into the garage, where a man wearing mechanics coveralls gaped in astonishment.

The man closed the door. He was a lean, knobby guy with greasy hair and an Adam's apple. "Holy shit! That's it! Wait'll I tell the boss!"

Josh got out of the vehicle.

"Josh Pratt."

"Walker Cochran," the mechanic said, shaking hands.

Josh pulled out his cell phone and dialed Duesing.

"What?" the retailer barked.

"Your car's back. I'll send you an invoice."

"What? How?"

"Science, bitches!" Josh replied. "I had some help. I'll tell you later."

"Holy shit, that was fast! What do I owe you?"

Josh tallied up his fee and Preston's. "Five and a half gees."

"Send me an invoice."

"May I borrow one of your bikes?"

"Sure. Which one? What for?"

"To get home. Anything that runs."

"Take that Honda 1100. It's good to go."

"Thanks, Mister Duesing."

"Cole."

"Thanks, Cole."

Josh rode the Honda and by the time he got home he wondered where he could fit one into the garage. Duane's Camaro still occupied half the space. Josh planned to sell it for junk. He'd searched the glove compartment for registration or proof of insurance, knowing he would find neither.

There was still no word on Adam, Vigil or the slab.

Josh fed Fig, had three Slim Jims and an apple for dinner, showered, and headed for Ray's dance studio on the near east side, between East Wilson and Williamson. This was a light industrial area spotted with nightclubs like the Crystal. Josh rolled up to the loading dock and went in through the back entrance. The loading dock was two feet above the main floor which had been replaced with cedar. A barre ran the length of the left wall, which was mirrored. A lean young man and woman exchanged dance steps, while two women in dance leotards sat on a thrift store sofa sipping tea. Ray, wearing glasses, sat at an upright piano looking at a clipboard.

She looked up. "Hi, Josh. Take a seat."

Josh took a seat in one of several dozen folding chairs set up for the audience and checked his phone. Stoeckle had left a message.

"Adam Gehrke has surfaced. Turn on the news."

CHAPTER 61

PRINCE ABUBAKARI DAY

Josh and Ray watched the news conference at her condo later that evening. Franklin Munche of Boyd, Askew and Evans appeared with his client Monique Vigil, and Adam Gehrke to announce that he was representing Vigil against charges of theft brought by the Justin Crossley Estate. Munche wore a gray suit, white shirt, and red tie. Vigil wore a black, brown, and turquoise dashiki, her hair a wild black dandelion, her mouth a slit. Adam looked ill-at-ease in a blue suit with matching tie.

"Miz Vigil had no part in the theft of the Jesus Helguera painting, and no knowledge of its hidden contents when it came into Mister Gehrke's possession. Mister Gehrke died two days ago under mysterious circumstances in Wisconsin. The painting was stolen from Mister Gherke by an acquaintance, who hid it in his son's house. The son, Wisconsin private investigator Josh Pratt, subsequently delivered the historical slab hidden inside the painting to Ryan Gehrke's parents, Professors Eric and Lily Gehrke, of Creighton, Illinois. As you know, the Gehrkes died in a house fire five days ago. The police are still investigating. My client is not a suspect. She came into possession of the historic slab when Adam Gehrke, the Gehrkes' youngest son, delivered it to her at her home in Miami."

The screen jumped to an image of the slab.

"We asked Professor Wandre DeSchmidt, of the University of Miami History Department, to tell us what the slab says."

Video of the professor, wearing bifocals and a Nehru jacket. "In the name of the most holy," said a fruity voice, "the most exalted, most compassionate and wisest, his excellency, Prince Abubakari II, we claim this land for the Mali Empire."

Back to Munche. "Many questions remain unanswered, foremost of which, how did the Justin Crossley Estate come into possession of this historic monument? Who concealed it in the frame of a painting by famous Mexican illustrator Jesus Helguera? Was the estate aware of the slab? We have contacted Bullard and Bullard, executors of the Crossley Estate, but as yet, have received no answers.

"Mlz Vigil recognizes that the slab is of great historic significance and believes it is part of our national heritage. She wishes to donate the slab to the people of the United States. We are waiting to hear from the White House, the Smithsonian Institute, and the National Historical Publication and Records Commission on their proposals.

"It is my clients' wishes that the slab be available to the public, that its significance be reflected in school curricula and that the history of the United States clearly says that the New World was discovered by Prince Abubakari II and not Christopher Columbus. My clients would like the President to use his executive authority to change Columbus Day to Prince Abubakari II Day."

The camera pulled back showing Vigil holding a white cardboard on which was written, "WWW.PRINCEABU-BAKARIIDAY.ORG."

"Please register at our website and sign our petition asking the President to rename Columbus Day Prince Abubakarii Day." She gave the black power salute.

Ray hit the mute.

"What the fuck," Josh said. He pulled out his smart phone and used duckduckgo to search for the Justin Crossley estate.

Justin Crossley, November 6, 1858 – July 21, 1950, was an entrepreneur and turpentine baron who established the town of Crossley in Orange County, Florida, in 1890, and employed convicts and the destitute to extract the hard, sticky resin, which is used in boat construction, from pine forests. Crossley was one of the co-founders of the Okeechobee Railroad which brought turpentine and lumber to market.

Crossley's detractors have accused him of racism, rape, unlawful imprisonment, and incest.

Crossley's eighteen room mansion outside Clermont, Florida, is built entirely of native materials including cypress, pine and oak. A generous art patron, Crossley's collection included several by Picasso, Freda Kahlo, and Brancusi. He was a keen student of local history, and housed many historical documents in his home museum, which his heirs later bequeathed to the Florida State Historical Society.

Several organizations, including the Seminole Tribe of Florida, accused Crossley of stealing priceless artifacts from Native American land, and sued, unsuccessfully, in 1960 to have them returned. Since then, the State of Florida has ordered those artifacts returned to tribal lands.

Crossley's collection became a cause célèbre among intellectuals in the seventies who urged the family to donate it to the state. In 1979, the Crossleys closed their museum to the public. No one lives in the Crossley Estate these days. The four-acre estate is surrounded by a seven foot wrought iron fence and maintained by caretakers who live on the property.

It didn't really matter who stole the painting or how it came into Ryan Gehrke's possession. Done deal. Josh knew that in the days to come, law enforcement would ask these questions and initiate investigations. Groups girded their loins in anticipation of the shitstorm that would break out over ownership of the slab, which raised an interesting question. Where did Crossley get it? Had he come across it in Central Florida? That would put the kibosh on any claims that Columbus had discovered the new world.

Ray scooted next to him. "What is it?"

"The slab came from the Crossley Estate. He was some kind of turpentine baron. They're gonna be fighting about it for the next seventy-five years."

Ray took the remote from his hands, straddled him, and held his head. "Look me in the eyes."

Josh looked. She was beautiful.

"Now kiss me."

They lay sprawled on the sectional. Ray got up.

"Sid Vicious, you rotten little shit!"

Josh looked up. "What?"

"He pissed on your shirt again. I'll wash it. You should keep some shirts here."

"Why? So Sid can piss on them?"

Ray put her hands on her hips. "What? Is that too much of a commitment for you? What if I buy you some shirts?"

"I'll leave some shirts."

"But you're trepidatious. I can tell."

Josh waved his arms. "No, I'm all in!"

"I might be a serial killer."

"Perfect."

Josh stayed the night, got up early, kissed sleeping Ray, rode home, fed Fig, went for a five-mile run, showered, and checked his messages.

Fleiss said, "We signed the deal. Abu Dhabi invited everyone to the grand prix, including you. We leave on the twelfth. Let me know."

Hotchkiss said, "Well that was a bit of all right, thank

you very much. Not only did we sign a mutually beneficial agreement, but Abu Dhabi has agreed to purchase forty per cent of Hotchkiss Motorcycles with an eye toward producing the new model. We'll be out at the garage later this afternoon if you'd care to drop by. This calls for a bottle of the good stuff."

CHAPTER
62

DUANE REDUX

Josh submitted his invoice to Cole Duesing. Fig launched a fusillade. FedEx had a box for him. The box contained six black phones that looked exactly like the latest models, but with no discernible markings. They'd been 3D printed and put together by hand. Josh phoned Preston on Skype.

"The phones arrived. Now what?"

"There's a code on a piece of tape on each one. Take the one with the lowest number, go online and enter the code to activate the phone. Go here."

Preston held up a piece of cardboard with an internet address, which Josh copied into a pad.

"When can we get together?"

Preston displayed his choppers. "Well I got my thing in Saint Louis, and you got your thing up there in cheese country. We don't really need to meet face to face to get things done."

"Yeah, but I'd like to meet you."

"Well come on down."

Josh thanked him and signed off. He thought about it. Ninja had proven himself a valuable asset. Josh needed someone since Randall Kleiser took off, and Dovetail was too busy to serve as his personal IT. Josh had the goods on Aaron Kofsky, Dovetail's founder and CEO. He had extensive child porno downloaded from Kofsky's account. But as far as Josh could tell, Kofsky had been on the straight and narrow for at least three years, ever since Josh waved the sword.

Josh was always up for a ride. He could take the Great River Road down the Mississippi. He had some brothers in the St. Louis area. At two, Josh rolled west toward the Bass Garage. Ray. The woman thing was problematic. Always had been. He'd only had one serious relationship in his life, and it had only lasted a month. Perhaps if he and Fig Newton had hooked up and stayed together, they would have grown tired of one another. Josh had seen it happen. Perhaps it had been his one true shot at happiness.

He knew man wasn't meant to live alone, or at least, Man in the abstract. There were a lot of sorry sons of bitches out there who were incapable of relationships, or happiness itself. Josh had a dog who loved him. But it wasn't enough.

Ray was beautiful, smart, funny. If he had to have a girl-friend, let it be her.

The gate was open, the garage door was open, the Grand Symphony Wagon sat in the yard where Bass had left it. Yellow police tape still clung to the fence. Josh walked through the open garage door to the back, where Bass and Hotchkiss had the Axial on a dynamometer revving to ear-crackling thunder as they pored over a graph on a laptop. Josh stood a few feet behind them as they clucked and pointed, then shut off the engine. The sudden silence was unnerving.

"What's up, boys?" Josh said.

Hotchkiss jumped and squeaked. Bass turned toward him with equanimity.

"One hundred and twelve horsepower at six thousand rpm. Seems to be enough to propel one man down the road on two wheels."

"Is this the only working bike?" Josh asked.

Hotchkiss pointed to a bike covered with a tarp. "This is the second model. Old number one's under that tarp. This one is much closer to production."

"I'd love one," Josh said. "Where do I sign up?"

Hotchkiss laughed. "We're looking for investors."

"Seriously? Do you have a prospectus and shit?"

"We're drawing one up. You want a soda?"

They went out back to the deck extending into the yard. Bass upended a small charcoal grill into a trash container, loaded it with fresh charcoal and lit it. Hotchkiss went into the garage and returned with defrosted Sam's Club hamburgers, buns, and a bowl of ketchup packets. Josh had a beer.

Bass turned the burgers.

"Did the police charge you?" Josh said.

"No. They deemed the act self-defense. Now my name is shit all over the east side."

Many Madisonians expressed outrage that a privileged white male would be given a pass on mowing down a traditionally under-represented minority. Progressives seized on Bass as the new face of racism and excoriated him in print and online. Since Bass was not on social media, he didn't notice. His garage was not easily accessible by public transit so there were no demonstrations. Phil Bass was one of *Isthmus'* major advertisers. There was no mention of the bizarre killing. The *Wisconsin State Journal* and *Capital Times* relegated the story below the front fold. Everyone wished it would just go away.

Iowa County sent an extradition request to Dade County for Monique Vigil, whom they charged with trespassing, illegal possession of a firearm and kidnapping, since she had held Josh, Bass and Hotchkiss against their will. It was doubtful Dade County would act.

Since the slab, the media flocked to Vigil as if she were a rock star. Producers approached her about her life story or starring in a big budget biopic of Harriet Tubman. Marvel wanted to cast her as Storm. She was booked on three Sunday news shows. She was writing an autobiography. Dana White offered a flat mil to fight the woman's bantamweight championship. She was holding daily press conferences.

They shot the shit and traded stories. Bass fondly remembered his original Honda 450. "It was as big as a whale! We couldn't conceive of so monstrous a machine!"

It was dark by the time Josh got home. He opened the door from garage to kitchen. Fig sat holding her bowl, tail wagging.

"I know. I know."

Josh fed her, checked his messages. Katy Varner was all sweetness and cream. "Josh, call me. I would love to hear your thoughts on Ryan Gehrke. This is your chance to tell your side of the story."

Fleiss needed him to deliver a summons.

Hines left a message. "Dude, call me. This is insane."

Josh stripped to his skivvies and knelt by his bed, head bowed. Fig lay on the floor next to him, snout between her paws. "Dear Lord, thanks for watching over Adam, and please continue to watch over him and guide him so that he becomes a good man. And Lord, if it's not too much trouble, would you grant Harley-Davidson's product development a clue? It's not for myself that I ask. Amen."

He crawled into bed with the window open to admit a cool night breeze. Fig jumped up and lay down next to him.

"Good night, Fig."

He dreamed Ray had moved in with him. All the jars in the refrigerator had loose lids. He pulled them out: the pickles, mayonnaise, banana peppers, maraschino cherries, methodically tightening the lids and putting them back in the refrigerator.

Ray came into the kitchen and turned on the lights, blinding him. "What are you doing?"

"Nothing."

Fig's barking woke him. She stood on the bed, snout to the door, growling. Josh quickly got out of bed, pulled on jeans and moccasins and grabbed Sting, Frodo's officially sanctioned sword from Lord of the Rings. People had tried to kill him and would probably try again.

He crept through the house to the kitchen, where he heard some faint scratching from the garage. Josh went back through the darkened house, let himself out the front door silently, and saw that his garage door was open. He'd slept through it.

He stood in the open garage door and saw someone rummage around the trunk.

"Hey," he said softly.

Duane stood and turned with a big smile.

"Hey, I just came back for the car."

CHAPTER 63

THE PRODIGAL FATHER

Josh held the sword at his side. "I told you to never come back here."

"And I told you I'd be back for my car. What's the problem?"

"You set that fire. You killed the Gehrkes."

Duane's expression of surprise was manufactured, like Steve McQueen trying to act. The mouth too wide, the eyes too forcibly surprised.

"Where the fuck do you get that?"

Josh realized he'd left his cell phone in the house. "Wait here. I'm calling the police."

"What?"

"I'm turning you in."

"Bullshit!" Duane raged. "My own son? That's my fuckin' car! I told you I'd be back! Just let me take the car and you'll never hear from me again. I promise you."

"I can't do that, Duane."

Duane turned backed to the open trunk, grabbed something and whirled. "You missed this."

A small black automatic nestled in his hand like a viper.

Josh scoffed. "Whaddaya gonna do, shoot me? Then you'll have every cop in the country on your ass. Anything happens, Merle will phone the cops and tell them what she knows."

"She doesn't know shit."

"Why'd you leave her in Denver?"

"I had things to do."

"I know you, Duane. Payback is your religion. I know your type."

"Your type? You don't know me."

"Sure, I do. Just look up sociopath. Use Google."

"You don't know shit. How'd I raise such a dumb ass?"

"How'd you get in my garage?"

"You dumb shit. You told me the code! April one. April Fool's Day. Pretty goddamn appropriate, don't you think?"

Fig barked from inside the house.

"Go ahead. Take the car. How far do you think you'll get?"

"Maybe I'll take your car. Where are the keys?"

"In the house."

Duane gestured toward the door. "Let's go."

"Or what? You gonna shoot me?"

Duane showed nicotine-stained teeth. "Why not? Little

gun like this only makes a pop. Who's gonna hear it? Who's gonna report it? All your neighbors live so far away. You're a big shot now, livin' out here with the swells." He lowered the muzzle. "How bout we try one in the knee for starters?"

"I prayed for you, Duane."

"Thanks."

"Let me put Fig out back."

Duane waved the gun. "After you. I'll watch. That mutt ain't gonna do shit. All she wants to do is lie on the sofa and eat. Toss the sword."

Josh tossed the sword onto the lawn and walked back through the garage, thinking he'd kick the door back in Duane's face. But as soon as he opened the door, Fig's snout was in the gap pressing against him. He grabbed her by the collar. Duane pressed the automatic's muzzle against the small of his back. Josh walked Fig back through the kitchen and let her out onto the deck.

"Stay."

Duane opened the refrigerator, pulled out a beer and twisted off the cap with his teeth. "Now I want my other gun back and whatever else you took out of the trunk."

Josh picked the Chrysler fob up off the counter and tossed it to Duane who jerked sideways, let it sail past his head and fall to the floor. "Now son, you'd teach your grandmother to suck eggs. I taught you that one, don't you remember?"

Josh vaguely recalled Duane schooling him in self-defense which was mostly strike first with overwhelming force whenever you perceived subterfuge or disrespect. Throwing sand in peoples' faces. Kicking them in the nuts. Waiting for them around a corner with a baseball bat to the knees. He'd seen Duane in action a couple times in bars, the kind of bars that didn't care if you got shit-faced at three in the afternoon with your five-year-old son sitting on the next stool.

Big Hispanic dude. Took exception to something Duane said. Probably spic. Duane grabbing his bottle of Hamm's, smashing it down against the brass rail, and shoving the broken end into the startled man's gut. Duane grabbing Josh under the pits and hauling ass like Walter Payton smelling daylight.

Maybe he should have left Josh in the bar. Maybe he would have been better off.

"How far do you think you'll get?"

Duane stooped to retrieve the keys. "Who the fuck knows and so what? Nobody can prove I had anything to do with that fire. There are no witnesses. There's no evidence."

"How about that family you gassed in Rockford? Remember that?"

Duane's face darkened like tornado sky. "The fuck you talkin' about?"

"The Hardison Motel. What happened? They keep you up at night? You ask them to turn it down? Is that what happened? A family with two young children? And then you ran a hose from your exhaust pipe into their room?"

Duane's face seemed to contract within itself, the eyes sinking, growing dense, tendons running down his neck and an unconscious rictus, like a wolf backed into a corner.

"Where's the hose?" he said softly.

"The cops got it. And the duct tape. Did you forget to use gloves?"

Duane juked forward, fast for drunk in his forties, and smashed Josh in the temple with the flat of the gun. Josh grunted and went down. Fig stuck her snout through the doggie door and for an instant time stood still, Josh looking up at Fig through pain-hazed eyes, Duane looking toward the door, Fig looking at him.

Fig snarled. Fig attacked.

"NOOOOOO!" Josh yowled, kicking out at Duane's legs.

The gun exploded. Fig yelped and fell on her side. Josh crawled on top his father, wrenched the pistol from his grasp, and smashed it into his face again and again. He clubbed Duane into unconsciousness, then turned to Fig who lay on her side whimpering, blood running down her flank. Josh ripped his cell phone off the counter and dialed nine one one.

He lay with Fig in his lap, cradling the dog, pushing down on the wound, which ran along her left flank, with a fresh washcloth.

"It's okay, Fig. I'm here. I love you, Fig. It's going to be all right."

He heard the sirens approaching. He imagined the neighbors waking, sitting up, peeking out the window. Not him again. We really need to do something about that guy before he gets us all killed.

The EMTs arrived. He recognized a man named Steve Hernandez, a slim man with a black mustache. Steve looked from the moaning Duane to the bleeding hound.

"What happened?"

Josh looked up with flashing eyes. "Take Fig to the animal hospital! My father can wait."

IF YOU LIKED THE BIKER SERIES YOU MIGHT LIKE "RETRIBUTION: A TEAM REAPER THRILLER"

After he is betrayed and shoots the two most powerful men in the Irish Mob, John "Reaper" Kane is forced into hiding. He thinks Retribution, Arizona, is the perfect hiding place, but he is wrong. Underneath the old, crusty surface of the dying town, hides the Montoya Cartel, for they use it as a funnel to ship their drugs across the border.

Trying to lay low in a town gripped with lawlessness is impossible for the ex-recon marine, especially after the local sheriff is brutally murdered by the Montoya Cartel's sicario, leaving an old friend, Deputy Sheriff Cara Billings, the only person standing between them and the town.

Things go from bad to worse when Kane is arrested by Cleaver, the deputy in the cartel's pocket, for shooting a local gang member.

Enter DEA Agent Luis Ferrero who has expressed to his bosses for a long time the need for a task force to fight the cartels on their own ground. He's about to get his wish, and to head up his team, he wants the Reaper.

A thrill ride that doesn't let you go – Retribution is the first novel in the action-packed Reaper Series.

AVAILABLE NOW ON AMAZON

ABOUT THE AUTHOR

Mike Baron is the creator of Nexus (with artist Steve Rude) and Badger two of the longest lasting independent superhero comics. Nexus is about a cosmic avenger 500 years in the future. Badger, about a multiple personality one of whom is a costumed crime fighter. First/Devils Due is publishing all new Badger stories. Baron has won two Eisners and an Inkpot award and written The Punisher, Flash, Deadman and Star Wars among many other titles.

Baron has published ten novels that span a variety of topics. They have satanic rock bands, biker zombies, spontaneous human combustion, ghosts, and overall hard-boiled crimes.

Mike Baron has written for The Boston Phoenix, Boston Globe, Oui, Fusion, Creem, Isthmus, Front Page Mag, and Ellery Queen's Mystery Magazine.

* 9 7 8 1 6 4 1 1 9 9 8 6 5 *